All Saints

K T BOWES

Acknowledgement

To the hardworking volunteers who turn out every Saturday
and keep the beautiful game safe.
Businessmen, grandfathers, fathers and sons, uncles, cousins
and brothers don soccer strips and run out onto the pitch.
When they cross the white line, they turn into savage beasts
in the pursuit of the size 5 ball and a harmless game becomes
less about camaraderie and all about life and death.

You, the referee, are the enemy of their peace; abused,
challenged, and ridiculed.
Yet without your whistle, the game could not begin.

Chapter 1

My jaw ached like someone slammed me in the chin with a sledgehammer, the false joviality wearing thin. The bride glided across the dance floor, her body pressed close to her handsome groom and the silky white cloth streaming after her. My jaded mind worked overtime, drawing an analogy of spilled milk. She would wake up alone one morning and face the fact she'd turned her serial-cheat-boyfriend into a serial-cheat-husband.

"Ursula?" The use of my name drew me back to reality; a football club room in the ass end of New Zealand and I fixed the wavering smile back into place.

"Sorry, what?"

The bride's mother faced me, flaccid cheeks and an eyebrow raised in challenge. "I said, doesn't she look beautiful?"

My eyes strayed to the whiteness of the wedding dress and the lie of the fabric stretched taut against the swelling mound between pelvis and navel, straining to escape with every lurch on the dance floor. "Yep," I answered. "She looks amazing."

The officious woman nodded with satisfaction and asked the same question of the person seated to my left. Their gushing reply held more genuine enthusiasm, and I turned my face away to hide my smile, knowing she'd sit there for ages just to hear further sycophantic praise until the speaker ran out of platitudes.

The man to my right leaned closer and lowered his voice to a hushed whisper. "Does she realise her precious little girl's carrying a passenger?"

I glanced back at the mother and shrugged. "No idea. She will soon."

He chuckled and nodded in agreement, pulling a packet of cigarettes from his top pocket. As though drawn to the rustle of the box, the woman whirled round and fixed a beady eye on the guest. "You can't smoke in here, Mark Lambie. Go outside the back door!"

He rolled his eyes and nudged me on the arm. "Want some fresh air?"

I blew out a breath and nodded, scraping my chair back. "I'm not sure how fresh it'll be with you polluting it," I grumbled and Lambie grinned over his shoulder. He downed a tumbler of brown fluid and shoved the guest nearest the door, leaning down to growl in his ear.

"Give us a shout when the food comes out."

"The rabbit food or the proper stuff?" the man replied and Lambie roared with laughter.

"Screw the lettuce leaves, man! I want the real stuff."

The man in his early twenties grinned and then noticed me following, his facial expression assuming a more sombre look. "Hi Ursula," he said, sympathy etched into the lines on his forehead.

"Hey Craig," I replied and forced back the false smile, fixing it into place and pushing through the fire exit after Lambie.

I let it close behind me with more of a slam than I intended and chewed my lower lip to stem the pain of the niceties. Lambie seemed drunker out in the sunlight and lurched around like a skittle, trying to light his cigarette, finally inhaling a massive drag as the end flared orange. In his late fifties, overweight and unfit, he resembled a tramp in his oversized suit, and I felt a flash of compassion push through my own depression. I steadied his uncoordinated list with a hand on his arm.

"You're a bloody good girl," he slurred, drawing on the ciggie as though it held oxygen and not cancer. "I didn't think you'd come today. I told yer dad yer probably wouldn't."

"Why's that?" I stared up at the huge New Zealand sky and wished myself anywhere else but Auckland on a Friday night. Rush hour boomed in the distance as the city emptied like a sink hole, ready to fill back up first thing Monday morning. Lambie put his arm over my shoulder, as much for his benefit as mine.

"It's too soon," he said, his words slurring. I smelled the whiskey on his breath and the scent of bitterness rotting him from the inside out. "Your Pete's not been dead a few months. It's too soon to be at some crappy wedding with a knocked up bride." His voice caught, and I swallowed and pushed him upright.

"Get it together, Mark," I said, my voice stern. "Pete died at the end of last season. It was September, bro. We're in April and the start of a new season. It's a fresh start for all of us." I gritted my jaw and inhaled a deep breath, smelling the sea air and craving a walk on the beach. My toes peeked from my strappy sandals, begging to be released into the surf instead of cooped up in shoes at a wedding I hadn't wanted to attend. "But you're right," I conceded. "I didn't want to come."

"First premiership game tomorrow," he said, huffing on the cigarette again. "And we're gonna lose. Without Pete, we can't stay up in this league; we can't do it."

"Rubbish!" I gave Mark a shove and then let go, deciding he'd either sprawl longwise on the cracked car park or rally. He rallied. "I don't need this!" I said, my voice rising. "Just get it together, bro."

His eyes looked glassy as they stared at me, his lips pulsing around the pink tongue which peeked out. The man was a heart attack waiting to happen, sweat beading on his forehead and his greying hair slicked back like ploughed furrows. "Sorry," he gushed. "Pete was the love of your life."

My snort sounded cruel, and I regretted it as the sound reached my ears. "But I wasn't his!" I retorted. "Did I ever mention all the Saturday nights when he didn't come home after a game? Or the messages on his phone from the strays he met at the clubs while he celebrated a win? Probably not. Yeah, I miss him, Mark. I miss being married and hanging onto the hope that my husband might change and settle down. But I don't miss being second best. I don't miss lying awake wondering why I'm not good enough to come home to when he's forcing himself onto someone else in the back of his car or behind the bins outside a nightclub. What's to miss, Mark?"

Understanding dawned in Mark Lambie's eyes and they widened to double the size. "You knew?" He sounded surprised, and I wanted to laugh, holding onto the awful urge lest he dial for an ambulance to take me to the psych ward of Auckland General. "He used to get so drunk. We always tried to make him come home with us but him and Pike couldn't seem to stop."

I nodded, familiar with the after-match revelry, which left the soccer team hung over and uncommunicative most Sundays during the season. In the summer, most of them were nice guys, husbands, fathers, boyfriends and sons. During winter, they turned into monsters, screaming and swearing during games fuelled by testosterone and topped off with a trip into town, win or lose. Peter Saint acted that way all year round, his behaviour never altering through the changes of the season. I suspected Mark Lambie knew only half the story and as my stomach roiled in complaint, I knew I wouldn't be the one to enlighten him.

"Shit!" Spit exploded from Mark's mouth as he slumped against the brick wall of the club house. His breath caught in hitches and his chest heaved. "I wanted to tell you so many times." His voice emerged as a wail and I glanced towards the exit, hoping nobody came to investigate. I'd suffered enough humiliation for one lifetime.

"Mark!" My voice sounded commanding, forced from my chest cavity as though calling my thirty-one class members back to order after a windy playtime. "Get it together, dude!" I snapped. "I don't need this today."

"Sorry, I'm sorry!" Mark groaned, wiping snot and tears on the sleeve of his jacket. He lurched upright with effort and dropped the cigarette on the ground. "Does your dad know?"

The sneer fixed itself on my face before I could stop it. "What do you think?"

Mark touched me on the shoulder. "Yeah, we pretty much all guessed you didn't wanna marry Pete. It's hard to resist the pressure they put on ya. I should know what they're like. I dropped out of coaching this year, but when Terry and yer dad get involved, my word counts for nothin'." He dragged on the cigarette again. "They came to me during the break and said I had to; promised it would all be different if I came back."

I laughed, and the sound carried across to the building, drawing the attention of the table members nearest the door. "I can't believe you fell for it. There's no way they'll back off and let you coach. They'll have something to say about every single decision you make. Just like always." That went for my life, too.

Mark's face puckered in distress and he pushed the cigarette into his mouth, puffing as he struggled to light its successor. "You're so beautiful, though," he murmured. "I dunno why he'd go into town when he had you at home. You look like a model with your dark hair and gorgeous face." He glanced down at my dress, his eyes widening. "And the rest of ya is perfect. All the lads think so." He lurched again, and I winced at the backhanded compliment. Lambie shook his head and his eyes tracked back to the door. "I need another drink," he stated, an addict in the making. "It's the only way I'm gonna get through this season."

The smile disappeared from my lips, replaced by regret. "Mark! If it's making you so upset, then tell them no." I snatched the ciggie from his fingers and he ignored the interruption, reaching for another. His body swayed in the process, his knees threatening to buckle.

"Can't," he replied, dragging on one while lighting the other with his eyes closed. The raucous cough wasn't unexpected.

"I'll talk to Dad," I offered. "This is ridiculous."

"No, please don't!" Mark swallowed and his eyes filled with tears. "You can't. Bloody promise me, Ursula!"

He yanked the tie away from his neck and cast his eyes around the car park as though searching for something. I followed his gaze and saw a tall man around my age leaning his bum against a white car. He looked familiar, and I wracked my brain for his identity. Fine boned and muscular, his trousers sat nicely on a neat bottom and he crossed his feet at the ankles and stared at the floor as he spoke into a cell phone. Mark fixed his eyes on the smartly dressed male and then gripped my upper arm, his fingers digging into the flesh. "Promise?" he begged, and I nodded. I watched the man's lips moving as I propped Mark up one handed, guiding him backwards to lean against the rough brick.

"Who's that?" I asked, masking my interest in a bored tone.

"Foxy," Mark replied, hawking up a ball of phlegm and spitting it into the gravel. Disgusted, I let go of his arm and he tottered on unsteady feet as the fresh air exacerbated his drunkenness.

"Yeah, really helpful," I muttered. "Tells me everything I wanna know."

Mark lurched and the back of his head hit the wooden windowsill behind him. I looked around for help and weighed up the consequences of summoning aid from inside the hall. As I turned towards the doors, Mark snatched at the bottom of my dress, hissing, "Please, no," as he splattered onto the gravel.

"Don't be ridiculous," I said, nudging him with the toe of my sandal. "Get up or I'll call for help."

"What's going on?" The stranger appeared next to me, eyeing Mark from an elevated position. "Too much of the pop, Lambie?" he asked.

"I wanna go home," Mark replied, grovelling with his face in the sharp stones.

"I'll get Uncle Terry," I said, smiling in apology at the handsome male whose elbow brushed my upper arm.

"No!" Mark wailed, tugging on the bottom of my dress. A seam gave way at the back and my spaghetti strap dug into my shoulder, causing me to let out a hiss of annoyance and embarrassment. I felt pleased with my new lace bra, but wasn't thrilled at the thought of it being on show.

"Hey, dude, let go." The stranger squatted and gripped Mark's fingers in his, prising them away from my hem. He grabbed Mark by the shoulders and sat him up against the side of the club house. "Sit there a minute, man." Standing up, he turned his attention to me. "What's the story?" he asked.

I took a step back, sensing blame in his soft brown eyes. "Don't hold me responsible! He's drunk too much, and I followed him outside because he asked me to."

The man gave an upward nod. "What will you do with him?"

I gaped in surprise as the stranger placed the physical and emotional weight of Mark Lambie's plight on my slender shoulders. Indignation filled my expression, and I tossed my trademark dark curls and glared at him through determined blue eyes. "Nothing!" I said, surprised at the hardness in my voice. "What's it got to do with you, anyway?"

He raised his hands in defence and held them inches away from my shoulders. "Nothing at all. I'm just passing through." He glanced down at Mark as the drunk slithered onto his stomach and exercised his limbs in a peculiar lizard movement. "But we can't just leave him here."

"I can!" I snorted. "I'll send some of the boys out if you wanna stand there and watch him do a skink impression a while longer."

"No, please, not the boys?" Mark sobbed, rolling onto his back. "Foxy, take me home, man. Ursula will help you. I'm sorry. So sorry."

I winced and wrinkled my nose at the plea and heaved out a sigh. Foxy's olive-skinned face leaned into mine so he could whisper in my ear. "Is this about his wife?"

I glanced down at Mark rolling around in the gravel wearing his best suit, the belt holding up trousers three sizes too small and his stomach billowing over the waistband like a pillow. "Yeah," I relented. "Probably."

With a nod of acknowledgement, Foxy leaned down and hauled Mark up by his arm. While the man still tottered, he dipped his body and flipped the huge male over his shoulder, carrying him in a flawless fireman's lift. I watched, impressed, as he strode over to the white car, Mark's limp hand slapping his butt with the rhythm of his stride. My lips quirked, and I dashed back into the clubhouse to snag my handbag, following after the strange duo.

Chapter 2

"**I**f he pukes in my car, you're cleaning it!" Foxy jibed as we pulled up at the traffic lights. Mark Lambie lurched in the back seat and I struggled to prop him up with my body weight.

"He's heavy," I grumbled. "I'm happy to swap places."

Foxy glared at me through the rear-view mirror and I felt the intensity of his brown eyes weighing me up. I saw the questions in his eyes and felt relieved when he left them unasked. Being Peter Saint's widow hung like a millstone around my neck, bowing my head with the pressure and responsibility. My husband carried his secrets to the grave in Devonport overlooking the sea, but I lived with them daily.

"Why were you at the wedding?" I asked, making conversation. I watched Foxy's capable hands on the steering wheel as he made the turn into Lambie's road and then stopped for more lights. Lambie's face smacked against the side window.

"My sister's a bridesmaid," he answered, his tone dull. "She couldn't find a date at such short notice."

My brow furrowed as I pictured the bridesmaids; four lumps of women in too-tight dresses and stilettos. The fifth looked lean and out of place, a twig between voluptuous blooms in the hideous wedding photos. "The skinny one?" I asked, remembering the tanned skin and attractive Samoan features. Foxy said nothing, his eyes still on my face. "You're a good brother," I sighed. "Maybe that's what I need; a decent brother."

"You don't have one?" His question surprised me, and I shook my head.

"No. My life might've been different if I had."

The lights changed, and I expected the conversation to finish, but Foxy pressed on the accelerator and fished for more information. "What makes you say that?"

I shook my head and watched the suburb swim by in a blur, happy families in happy houses and me outside, as always. "My father wanted a son. He could've passed on the Saint legacy to him and I'd be elsewhere by now, doing amazing things with my freedom." I sighed, picturing blue oceans and endless beaches. Probably Spain. Maybe Italy.

"You could do that, anyway." His voice cut through my fantasy, dispelling it in the first drops of rain against the windscreen. A flash of anger clashed with the overriding sense of injustice.

"Really?" I bit, the sarcasm ugly on my tongue. "The only way to leave All Saints is in a coffin."

At the sound of retching I gave a hiss of annoyance and Foxy abandoned the car by the curb at a jaunty angle, wrenching open the rear door and jumping backwards as Mark projectile hurled onto his own grass verge.

I patted Mark's back and forced his face clear of the car's pristine interior, grinning at Foxy. "Nice reflexes there," I joked. "Dad needs a new striker."

Foxy pulled a face and shook his head. "He really wouldn't want me."

I gave Mark's back a shove and Foxy pulled as I pushed, sweating in the humidity until the large man stood with his bum balanced against the wing of the car. My exit was through my own side, eager to avoid the puke, and I waited until Foxy traipsed Mark right through it and up to his front gate. "You'd give Foxy a job as a striker, wouldn't you, Uncle Mark?" I asked with a smile, dodging the stinking wet hand the drunk held out towards me.

He shook his head, his eyes wide like saucers. "Bloody hell, no!" he exclaimed. "I'm surprised they let him in for the fat chick's wedding!"

I bit my lip and winced, mouthing an apology to Foxy. "Don't be rude!" I snapped. "He gave you a lift home, you ungrateful old man. Wait until Jackie's mother hears you calling her precious daughter a fat chick."

"She is," he growled. "And her mother." With a lurch, he made it through the front gate and negotiated the steps onto his porch. Instead of sobering up, he seemed to get drunker by the second.

"I don't get this." I put my hands on my hips and stared as Mark slumped onto the doormat, his back against the peeling paint of his front door. I waved my arm at him, confusion on my face. "You weren't like this when we left the clubhouse. Was there something in that cigarette?"

"Where are they?" Foxy asked, interest burgeoning in his expression.

"Front left pocket," I said, watching as he frisked Mark with capable hands. "No, inside top. Watch the sick on his shirt, though."

Foxy pulled out the packet and inspected it, poking his finger into the cardboard folds. "Na, this is shop bought. Just tobacco."

"So why's he getting worse?" I demanded. Staring at the unkempt bushes in Mark's garden, I cast my mind back to the scene in the clubhouse as Mark stood to go outside, inviting me to accompany him. He chucked back a tot of whiskey in one mouthful, but he'd done that twice before with little effect. "Maybe he just reached his limit," I conceded with a shrug. "Hey, lightweight." I shoved Mark's leg with the toe of my sandal. "Where's your door key?"

"In-shide," he slurred, and I rolled my eyes.

Leaning over his head, I pushed my knee against his cheek to stop him looking up my dress. Then I rang the doorbell and stood back. Fingers threaded their way round my hem again, and I wasn't quick enough. "No! Get off, Uncle Mark. You've got puke hands!" I dashed backwards, almost pitching off the porch. Only Foxy's quick reactions stopped me meeting a crispy looking rhododendron bush bum first. His right hand gripped my wrist and his left snaked around my back. Once I'd righted myself, a quick glare ensured he released me.

"I'm not doing that again," I insisted, jerking my head towards the bell. "You press it."

Foxy obliged, jamming his finger over the doorbell and holding it down. The noise of a police car two streets over obliterated the sound of ringing inside.

"Don't tell them!" Mark begged, tears welling in his eyes. I looked at Foxy in confusion.

"Tell who? Tell them what?"

"Good girl," Mark sniffed. "You always were a good girl."

I pulled a face of annoyance and turned, heading down the rickety steps to street level. "See you, Uncle Mark." I waved over my shoulder and strode towards Foxy's car, noticing the sheen of the paintwork in the confusing autumn weather. Sunshine beat down on the specks of rain from the momentary shower a few seconds ago, not a guilty cloud in the sky.

"Hey, we can't leave him there!" Foxy caught my arm and turned me so my breasts touched his shirt front. "What if he pukes and suffocates himself?"

"Then sit down next to him and make yourself comfy. Give me your car keys so I can go back to the farcical wedding."

"I'm not giving you my keys!" A dimple showed in Foxy's right cheek and I focussed on it to help me ignore his full, kissable lips and the angular cheekbones calling to the palms of my hands. I balled my fists to stop me thinking about how his rough shave might feel on the sensitive skin of my fingers.

"Then drive me back!" I snapped, turning and yanking on the passenger door handle.

"We can't just leave him!" he insisted. "It's not right!"

"His wife's there," I said. "We rang the bell, remember? It might just take her a while to get to the door."

"She's got cancer!" Foxy said, lowering his voice. "How's she gonna carry him inside?"

I snorted with laughter. "She won't need to. With a voice like nails on a blackboard, she only needs to shout at him and he'll crawl inside."

"What made you so hard?" His hand looped around the back of my neck, his dark eyes searching my face for clues. The invasion into my personal space made me tense in fear, and he saw the mist descend over my eyes. He still didn't move fast enough to avoid the swift kick I administered to his shin.

"Touch me again and I'll kill you," I , and he stepped back, circling me like a wary cat. Nodding once with slow precision, he deactivated the central locking and hauled open the passenger door.

"We shouldn't leave him."

"He'll be fine!"

The argument continued right up to the gates to the football club and Foxy drove past the sign marking the start of All Saints territory. I felt the involuntary shudder snake down my body from neck to ankles and gripped Foxy's wrist as it rested on the gear stick. "Please, could you give me a ride home?" I swallowed and worked on controlling the overwhelming sense of panic stomping through my chest.

"Why?" He brought the car to a halt and peered at me, his face filled with concern.

"I need to go home." I took slow breaths and fought the flapping fish in my heart as it slapped and leapt, threatening to pitch me over the edge. "Actually, don't worry." I gripped the door handle and gave a shove, confused when it wouldn't move.

"Hang on, hang on." Foxy pressed a button on the dashboard and I heard a comforting click. "It locks itself."

I nodded and swung my legs out sideways, still belted in as I pushed at the door. "Thanks."

"Look, stop!" Foxy grabbed my wrist and pulled, frowning as the contents of my handbag spewed into the foot well. "I'll take you home. Just close the door." The authority in his voice forced obedience, and I closed the door, feeling lipstick and a mascara under my shoe as I put my feet back on the mat. I chewed my lip and wouldn't look at him.

The car swung around in the car park like shears through silk and I heaved a sigh of relief as the All Saints sign asked us to 'Please drive home safely.' At the main road, Foxy straddled the lane and fixed his perceptive brown eyes on my flushed face.

"What's your address?" he asked, his hand on the indicator, ready to send the lights flashing left or right.

I swallowed and then gave the complete stranger my home address, wondering as he flicked the indicator right, if I'd made yet another monumentally terrible life choice.

Chapter 3

I poured wine with shaking hands and lifted the glass to sniff the contents. The merlot smelled okay although it'd been open for a while; probably a month or more. Marking school work filled my evenings nowadays and living alone offered no sober driver if I needed to dash out in an emergency. My father's health declined in fits and starts, and I wouldn't want to miss the end. I pursed my lips and forced the thoughts away. The smile fixed itself like a wooden mask as I turned and approached the small sitting area, handing a glass to Foxy.

"Thanks." He lifted it to his full lips and drew a healthy sip. He put the glass on the table and got comfy, bending one long leg beneath him on the two-seater sofa. His dark eyes followed me as I moved to the opposite side of the room and sat on the other one.

"Sorry, Mark was rude about your soccer skills?" I said. "I can't imagine why he'd be so nasty."

He raised his eyebrows and gave me a knowing look. "You can't?" Full lips quirked upward in a smirk and I laughed, despite myself. The sound seemed distant, as though it belonged to someone else. I'd forgotten what it felt like to find something genuinely funny without the jaded pinch which seemed to accompany my humour nowadays. The stranger studied me with calm assurance. "My sister just texted. She doesn't need a ride home."

"How come?" I asked, concerned for the pretty dark-haired girl in the long, silver gown.

He shrugged and looked unruffled. "Last time I saw her, she had her tongue pushed down the throat of a Devonport defender. I think she'll be fine."

I smiled and tried to remember the thrill of the chase, coming up against a bone jarring brick wall. My teenage crush married someone else and his donning of a police uniform meant he was dead to the Saints. There were few rules, but all three of them were written in family blood. *Thou shalt not marry a cop, a convict or a referee; of either sex.*

Foxy swigged his wine as an awkward silence descended and I dragged my rebellious brain back to the moment. "Why do they call you Foxy?" I asked, making an effort with the conversation as curiosity budded in my chest. The man intrigued me. He looked like any of the other soccer players in the club house; athletic, muscular and capable of running eight kilometres in a game without breaking a sweat.

"Teina Fox," he replied. "It's my name."

"You look familiar," I said. "Who do you play for?"

An expression of confusion moved across his face and he downed the last of his wine. "Why aren't you in the line-up this season?"

The strategic change stumped me for a second, and I swallowed and lowered my eyes. "I don't want to." I clenched my jaw. Teina watched me and sized up my reply, finding it wanting.

"That's crap."

My brown eyes flashed, and I felt an angry pulse begin in the side of my neck. "It's my choice!" I snapped.

He shrugged and still those dark eyes bored into my face. "You were the best defender they had. I've seen what's on offer and they'll struggle without you."

Misplaced vanity gave my ego a moment in which to stroke itself before I regained control. "It's nice of you to say that," I conceded. "But they'll be fine. They're a great bunch; they'll work for it."

"Na." Teina leaned forward and placed his glass on the table with exaggerated care. "You put those girls into that league; you should help keep them there."

I knew my smile appeared ragged as I seethed inside. "You know nothing about it."

He pinched his top lip between thumb and finger and sat as though ready to leave. My head screamed a warning at him to go, but my heart appealed to the inner loneliness I saw in his eyes and he gave a quizzical smile. "You're right; it's none of my business. Play, don't play. It's up to you."

"Thank you!" I snapped. "What I choose to do with my weekends will be my choice from now on."

"And what's that?" His tone seemed placid and so non-confrontational; a casual enquiry from a stranger. He didn't know me, my family or my circumstances.

"Pole dancing," I said, keeping a straight face. "I figure it'll be fun."

Teina's eyes crinkled at the sides and his lips spread in an attractive grin. "For who?"

"Whomever I choose to dance for," I replied and then bit my lip. Who was I kidding? I tutted and closed my eyes, pinching my exposed thigh hard enough to stem the unexpected flash of emotion.

I heard the sofa creak and tensed, waiting for the tap of Teina's shoes on the wooden floor as he left. His footsteps sounded light, and I jumped as the sofa cushion next to me dipped. He slipped an arm around me and kissed the side of my head and the fraternalism of the action stabbed at the root of my misery. "Sorry," he whispered. "My sister says I shouldn't bait people but I can't help it. Besides," he squeezed my shoulder, "your eyes flash when you're mad."

"And that's a good thing?" I asked, sounding sore.

"Yeah," he replied and kissed the side of my head again. "You know why."

But I didn't and the courage I needed to ask for clarification evaded me. I smelled pleasant aftershave and comforting maleness and in a fit of false modesty, shrugged myself free of Teina's arm and snatched up his glass. "I'll get you another." My legs felt shaky on the way to the kitchen and nervousness made me slop wine over the side of the glass. I put it into his hand and crossed to the other sofa, leaving the coffee table between us like a boundary marker.

"Who do you play for?" I repeated the question, watching his discomfort in the long blink of the enviable dark eyelashes.

"Nobody," he said, and I narrowed my eyes and let them rove across the muscular chest and athletic build. His gym training showed in the definition beneath the fabric of his shirt and he'd seemed at ease around the club house and Mark Lambie. Why would he lie?

"You're a referee." The realisation came to me as his identity fitted into place. In my mind's eye I saw the black shirt and shorts on the lithe body and marvelled he'd been allowed to attend the wedding. My family hated any brand of soccer authority, especially those in possession of whistles, cards and the ability to turn the game against All Saints. "You red carded my husband once," I said, a smile playing on my lips.

Foxy winced. "Yeah. Sorry."

"He deserved it." I shrugged. My mind wandered, remembering that one game when Pete didn't go out with the team to drown his sorrows. He came home to me that night instead, robbing my peace with his whining about the card and making me wish he'd gone on a bender that would last through Sunday when he rolled home stinking of beer, other people's scent and sex. Something happened that night; something I'd rather forget.

Foxy sipped the wine, silence growing between us. If I kept this up, he'd leave and I'd be alone again. The walls threatened to close in on me, squeezing so hard I couldn't breathe. I didn't want that; I needed his company, and I rallied, trying not to drive him away. "What do you do when you're not blowing your whistle?" I asked, wincing at my social ineptitude.

Foxy's dark eyes settled on me, his black fringe flipping into his face as he blinked. "Law," he replied after a moment's hesitation. "In town."

I nodded, sensing the thread of connection as he held my gaze and my stomach flipped. "From one sort of refereeing to another," I replied sagely, thinking of cops and hardened criminals and he laughed. His teeth looked straight and white against his olive skin, a small chip in the side of one of his front teeth marring the perfection, but making him seem less perfect. He leaned forward and sat his glass on the coffee table, stretching his arms backwards so that his hands touched the wall behind. Defined chest muscles and washboard abdominals pressed against his shirt and I caught the outline of a tattoo through his white sleeve. He studied me, his eyes calm and steady as he tried to read my thoughts. I held my breath and craved the feeling of his arms around me, crushing me to his chest and telling me everything would be ok. I wanted arms which weren't my dad's spindly, decaying muscle tone and empty platitudes. I ached to be held and cosseted, made to feel special and needed. I wanted it. I didn't want what went with it.

"I should go," he said and something clicked in my chest. His company provided a temporary balm for my unease. I'd lived in the apartment for six months and in that time had two unwanted visitors. I owned little worth taking, but they tossed the place both times. The second time they'd done everyone on my floor. Druggies, the cops reckoned. Loneliness snaked a cold hand around my heart and terrified me with the thought of the long, empty nights ahead. My singleness spread before me like an endless road of torment and rejection, resounding with the last words my husband spoke to me. '*Geez, Ursula. The only great thing about you is your Saint name. I don't know why I thought we could pull this off.*' His body lay in the cemetery as beetles and earthworms sucked the skin from his bones; more use in death than he ever proved to be in life. Yet still he retained the power to hurt me. An overwhelming need to overwrite the entirety of our marriage with something else drove me to my feet, desperate for the attractive male to stay. I owned nothing worth giving away and as I offered the final, most precious thing, my conscience screamed at me to stop.

Chapter 4

"I'm sorry. I don't mean to be so…" I scratched around for the word but only *hostile* presented itself. Teina Fox watched as I rose, picking my way around the coffee table until I stood before him, my face blank and expressionless as I worked to keep the empty need at bay. My eyes betrayed me and he read it there instead. "Will you hold me again?" I asked, desperate to touch the rippling muscle and feel his strength wrap around my body. He moved, and I inhaled a heady breath of his masculine scent. My calves pressed against the coffee table as he stood, occupying the remaining floor space between me and the sofa. I swallowed, waiting for rejection.

It didn't come. Teina said nothing, drawing me into his chest and enfolding me in his arms. He squeezed, and the breath went out of me in a whoosh. I snaked my arms around his waist and held on, desperate for it not to end. Safety enveloped me and I wished I could stay there suffocating in the clean smell of his shirt, my cheek pressed against the soft, expensive fabric. "Are you married? Or with someone?" I whispered, sparing a thought for the woman he belonged to, being thrust into my position of jilted wife and knowing I wouldn't be able to follow through and seat her on my victim's throne.

"No." His voice sounded muffled as my ear nestled against his chest, my makeup transferring itself to the white cloth with abandon. I pulled his left hand towards me, searching for the gold evidence and saw nothing as I slipped my fingers through his, mine tiny in comparison. When I tipped my head up and let his lips find mine, I tasted the merlot on his tongue and he explored my mouth with tenderness. He teased my senses, touching my tongue with his and then withdrawing it, kissing as though we were teenagers who hadn't worked out the mechanics of it yet. I bit his lower lip, and he groaned and released his tongue into my mouth again, letting me connect with him and taste his essence. My common sense screamed out a warning but for once, I ignored it, wanting to expunge my former life with an illusion of how it could have been; one-night stands, beer fuelled holidays. And babies.

The first time was a frenzied, mechanical union of lustful bodies and we undressed only the necessary parts of each other. My sofa creaked and groaned under our activity and

I blocked out the distracting noises as I satiated myself in the intimate live connection with another human being. We each took what we wanted from the other and lay exhausted in the afterglow, neither one of us wanting to break the atmosphere with futile platitudes as we waited for our heartbeats to return to normal.

"You ok?" Teina whispered eventually, surprising me with his caring. My foot rested against his calf and I felt the dark hair tickling my toes. He stroked my cheek and fixed a gentle kiss over my lips, his own trembling with the adrenaline withdrawal. The pressure of his body over mine pinned me to the sofa cushions and the uncomfortable gap between them, but it didn't matter and I dreaded him starting to move away in the ultimate rejection. I wound my arms around his neck like a baby monkey and tried to make the moment last, my face pushed against his shoulder. To my surprise he stroked my curls and kissed my neck and the underside of my jaw. He'd leave soon; walking out of my life as though I didn't matter. Because I didn't, not to him. Not to many people really.

"I've never done this before," I whispered and he smiled with his eyes.

"Never?"

I buried my face in his shirt to hide my embarrassment and shook my head. "Not like this. I don't know you."

Teina ran his thumb down my jaw line and his expression looked kind. He leaned up on one elbow and nodded, the movement slow and calculating. "Would you like to know me?" he asked, the crinkles in the outer corners of his eyes softening his angular face.

"You're a referee," I said, chewing my bottom lip in mischief. "I just broke a Saint rule."

"A cardinal rule too," Teina said with a low snort. He kissed my cheek, the end of my nose and then my lips as his eyelashes fluttered against my skin like falling rose petals. When he moved, I felt the hardness of his interest against my inner thigh and saw a vision of myself; falling like a loose stone into the swirling lava of volcanic lust. It served as a warning and I should have heeded it. I shouldn't have led the dark stranger through the apartment to my sterile bedroom and I certainly shouldn't have slipped out of my summer dress with such a frisson of excitement mixed with fear. I shouldn't have delighted in the way he undid the buttons of his shirt or the sound of it fluttering to the floor. From the first moment I invited him into my tiny flat, I suspected I was in trouble. I shouldn't have been surprised by its outworking.

Chapter 5

I woke with the taste of wine in my mouth, mingled with the masculine tang of Teina. I lay for a while listening to him breathe and feeling his arms tighten when I tried to shift. He'd moved his leg over me in the night and he lay awkwardly, his arms sheltering me. In the semi-darkness I examined his tattoo, watching the black lines morph into patterns and words across his skin. The sheet cut across his midsection and I watched him for signs of waking as I pushed it away with care, needing to see the man who gave me so much pleasure a few hours ago.

He disturbed, and I felt myself tense, afraid of his reaction when he woke in my bed. Me; a stranger.

"About last night," he began. I scooted up the bed and covered his lips with mine. His hands clasped my waist, and he kissed me back, inducing a sense of relief. The last thing

I needed was rejection and the slamming of Pandora's Box lid on my fingers. "I don't want to talk about last night," I breathed. "I just want to do it again, without talking."

"Fine. Because I'm not sorry." He bent his head and kissed me. I groaned and ran my hand across his torso, surprised when he froze under me. "What's the time," he asked, and I heard the panic in his voice. "I've got a game."

I glanced at the bedside table and saw the digital numbers flash to 5.35, relaying the time back to him. "We've got ages. Where do you have to go?"

Guilt slid across Teina's expression and he pursed his lips. "I'm reffing your guys at 3 o'clock." He frowned. "I should cry off the game and ask them to get someone else."

"I'm not affiliated to the club anymore," I breathed, sliding down his body to take one of the delectable nipples in my mouth. Teina groaned. I released the raised bulb and watched it lose some of the erectness as the pressure ended. "I'm the widow of last year's captain, that's all."

My words stung him and Teina tutted, strengthening his resolve. His determination to leave frightened me and I held him in place, needing to explore his body more. He'd given me a glimpse at a gripping book and threatened to steal it before I'd read the final page. "Stay?" I said, hating the edge of begging in my voice. "Just a little while longer." I sat up and settled my knees either side of his waist, nestling them into his soft skin. His hip bones dug into my calves and the discomfort excited me. When he flipped me over, the deep kiss frigged the electrical components in my brain, shorting out all good sense as his tongue caressed my lips and probed the depths of my mouth. Our teeth banged together and woke me from the stupor. "Not like this!" I gasped, fighting to remove the memory of Pete's missionary fumble and afraid of ever reading duty and disinterest in another lover's eyes.

Teina's eyes weren't indifferent. He kept me pinned in position, his body over mine as his finger traced the outline of my face. He kissed the end of my nose and walked his lips up to my forehead and over my right eye. "You're so perfect," he whispered, and I opened my mouth to contradict him. "He never deserved you." Teina's allusion to my husband caused a stiffening to begin in my spine and I raked his eyes with mine, searching for the knowledge I feared he had.

Compassion and need channelled into me from the deep brown eyes and I panicked. Raising a hand to push him away, I found my ready fist gripped in a strong vice and Teina drew my arm above my head. He nuzzled my neck and fixed my free wrist in his other hand raising it to join the other. "Sshhh," he commanded, authority in his tone. I pushed my fretting to one side for later and leaned into the sensations he drew from my inexperienced body.

"You won't hurt me?" My voice wavered in the half-light and Teina's eyes widened.

"No! Hell, no!" His body covered mine, and he pulled my arms down, wrapping them around his neck as he smothered my lips with his. "I promise," he whispered, and I believed him.

I trusted him enough to relax and an hour later he pushed me, giggling into the shower. "I have to go to church tomorrow," I said, running my hands through the dark curls. "But I'll be struck by lightning." My laughter sounded as fake as it was. I believed I'd be crimped the second I walked through the doors.

"A good Christian girl, hey?" he asked, rubbing shower gel onto my back.

"I thought I was." My voice sounded sad, even to me and I felt a sickness in my gut, as though I'd crossed a line and couldn't retrace my steps. My brain latched onto a vision of the vicar's face as he stood in front of the altar and smiled at me, genuine concern in his upturned lips and twinkling green eyes. Maybe I wouldn't go tomorrow after all. He wouldn't know what I'd done but God did. I chewed my lip and grew quiet.

"Are you okay?" Teina wrapped his arms around me from behind and his hairy chest felt safe against my back. I nodded and forced a smile onto my lips.

"This is new to me," I stammered. "I don't know what happens next."

"What do you want to happen?" he asked, his lips quirking at the edges as he turned me and pressed me into his body.

"I don't know." The fear returned, and a tremor began in my fingers, working its way up my arms and into my spine.

"What are you scared of?" he asked, his voice a whisper as he pressed a soft kiss to my damp forehead.

"Them," I breathed. "They won't allow it."

A moment of confusion crossed Teina's face as he held me at arm's length and studied me. "Who?"

I pushed past him and left the shower, almost breaking my neck on the slippery tiles. Teina rinsed soap from his chest and shoved his head under the water while I snagged a towel from the rail and covered my nakedness in a heightened flush of embarrassment. The muscles covering his buttocks attracted my gaze as I dried my face, using the towel to hide behind while I regained control. Teina stepped from the shower onto the mat, naked and unashamed. He tugged at my towel, making me giggle as he wiped his wet face on a corner of it and attacked me with tickles and kisses.

We shared the towel although he got the raw end of the deal after I'd dried myself on it. I relented and fetched a clean one from the airing cupboard in the hall, watching as he smoothed the fabric down his body. "I've never met anyone like you," he said, following me to the bedroom to dress. The rumpled bedding scratched bloody wounds in my conscience and I cringed and sat down on the mattress to avoid seeing it.

Teina's trousers slipped over his hips and he squinted to fasten the zipper. I swallowed and dreaded his answer to my question. "What does that mean?"

He sat on the bed next to me and pulled on his socks. "Everything about you is a paradox," he said. "You're funny and crazy at the same time." He pulled my face towards his and kissed me. "You love with fearlessness and then get so terrified. I can't work you out."

"Best not to try." I chewed my lip and reached for my discarded clothing, eying it before throwing it at the laundry basket in the corner. Teina shrugged into his shirt and I used his distraction with the buttons to dive into clean underwear and cover up in jeans and a sweatshirt.

"Can I see you again?" he asked, his tone light as he stroked a gentle finger along my nose and over the swell of my lips.

I nodded, an unconvincing action which made his brow furrow and his lips twitch. "You don't want to." He sounded cut, and I closed my eyes against his misery.

"It's not that. They won't let me."

His lips quirked. "If I want to see you, I'll see you," he countered, his expression serious.

I felt my temperature hike and an ugly flush creep up my chest and encroach on my neck. "You're not getting it," I said, my teeth gritted. "I do as I'm told. If they find out about this; I'll be in massive trouble."

Teina tutted and drew my face into his chest. "Geez Ursula. Massive trouble with who?"

"Uncle Terry and Dad." My voice sounded muffled, and he released the pressure on the back of my head.

"Seriously? How old are you?" I heard the scorn in his voice and knew my heart mirrored it. Anger flowered, and I gave his chest a shove, feeling the muscle tense beneath my palm.

"Mind your own business!" I snapped.

He nodded and took a step backwards. "If you don't want to see me again, you only have to say."

"I do," I groaned, hiding my face behind shaking hands. "But you'll never understand."

Teina looked at his watch and frustration burgeoned on his handsome, angular face. "I have to leave, but I intend to keep seeing you. You said you weren't affiliated to the club anymore."

I nodded, at the same time grateful and terrified. "I lied. My father owns a half share of the club."

"Shit!" he exclaimed and ran a hand through the dark wavy fringe. Then he laughed. "Ursula Saint. Of course he does."

I writhed my hands in my lap and watched him finish dressing. "Uncle Terry acted as chairman last year, but he doesn't want to after..." I couldn't say the words, *after his son died and he blamed me*. "Dad's chairman this season; while he still can. The brothers all used to have a quarter each but Terry and Dad bought out the others."

Teina wrestled with some inner demon and came to his own place of reckoning. "I don't care," he said. His lips brushed mine before he laced up his shoes and afterwards too, lingering as he tasted me and drew me in for more. I tried to read his face and discovered I couldn't; sensing something unpredictable and dangerous behind the piercing brown eyes. "See you at All Saints later," he whispered. My eyes grew wide, and I inhaled, but Teina placed a finger over my pursed lips. "I know, I know. I'll pretend I didn't just spend the night in your bed, or that I want to stay there for the rest of the weekend." His smile looked sad as the mask of bravado slipped and I read his face like an open book in the millisecond of grace it afforded me. "I'll talk to the convener and I won't ref All Saints' games again. Then there's no conflict."

I closed the door behind Teina Fox with a frown and leaned against it, knowing I'd seen something genuine in his eyes. It terrified me, promising hope while threatening heart ache. "You should know better," I told myself, tying my long curls back into a ponytail. "People like you don't end up with guys like him."

Chapter 6

"I hate that twat!" Paulie Saint spat, watching Teina stride across the pitch. I followed his gaze and ogled the neat buttocks encased in tight black skins beneath the referee shorts and remembered the sight of him naked, each muscle defined with hard lines.

"Don't you start!" I warned the man next to me in the wheelchair. "If you're gonna carry on the whole time, I'll stand somewhere else."

"Please yourself," Dad said, catching Paulie's eye, and they both chuckled. "He doesn't normally do our games. He's a national referee, not premier."

"They must be short this week," I mused.

"You'll be bloody short if you dump me again like you did last night," Dad grunted. "Making me beg for a ride home."

"You would've been doing that, anyway!" I snapped. "We got a ride there with Mark, remember?"

"Yeah, well, what the hell was he playing at, going off with you?" The bushy eyebrows narrowed in suspicion and I snorted with disgust and walked away. I didn't want to follow my father's dirty implication but used his filthy comment to avoid admitting we weren't alone.

Dad watched me leave but the irresistible pull of the black strip claimed his attention as he launched into a tirade of abuse towards Teina, who thankfully didn't hear. His lack of parentage would make little difference to his ability to control twenty-two tantruming, bratty adults as they brawled over a round sack of air in a muddy field. Bagging the referee took on a whole new meaning as Teina finished conferring with his assistant referees and strode back to collect the players waiting with impatience on the side line. My father's volley of abuse almost tipped him out of his wheelchair in the passionate delivery. Teina eyeballed him and lifted his index finger in warning, drawing a number one in the air. Dad got the message and whispered his bile to Paulie instead.

"Captains!" Teina's voice carried on the wind and I turned to watch as he beckoned to the team captains and gathered them for the coin toss. The object looked invisible from the technical area as all eyes followed something into the air and back to earth. The All Saints captain nodded and pointed away from the club house. I shielded my eyes and worked out the sun's position, knowing the home team wanted to run with the sun behind them for the first half, giving them an advantage in the second. At half time the sun would pitch behind the buildings opposite. Crafty. I eyed the opposition and hoped they prepared to spend forty-five minutes blind. My eyes strayed to Teina, realising they'd condemned him as well.

Teina's eyes flicked to me for a fraction of a second and I watched as his lips raised in a smile. Misinterpreting it, My father launched into another ready stream of rubbish. "Look, Paulie. Bloody ref's smiling at me!" he yelled, and I cringed, wishing the ground could swallow me whole.

I backed away from the line of spectators as the teams got into position, finding a space over near the railings separating the car park from the grounds. My brain ran through a list of places I'd rather be right then; anywhere but there.

"Hey sweetheart, how are ya?" Terry Saint approached me, striding from the car park pressing the remote in his hand to lock the expensive BMW. My body stiffened, adding his presence to the list of bad things about the soccer club, but I forced a dutiful smile onto my lips to greet my father-in-law.

"Hi, Uncle Terry, I'm good thanks. You?" He nodded and his eyes strayed to the number one pitch as the whistle blew for the kick off.

"How did the reserves do?" he asked, searching the field and spotting Paulie and my father.

"Lost," I answered, praying he made a beeline for them and released me. "It was close but Mount Albert scored in the dying minutes. The final score was 3:2 to them."

Terry Saint hissed through his teeth, brow knitted. "My Pete would've dug them out of the crap!" he spat. "That boy could kick from anywhere."

My chest tensed and I held my self upright, forcing my head to nod in agreement while my heart demanded I run away screaming. Since his death, Peter Saint had somehow become Saint Peter, a hero of renown instead of a bad-tempered player, scorned by the referees and cringed at by his wife. I said nothing and my father's cousin stared at me, his jaw grinding almost audibly. He looked for affirmation but after my romp with Teina, I no longer felt able to give it.

"Dad's over there," I said, pointing a shaking finger and Terry nodded.

"Where's Mark?"

"Haven't seen him," I said, realising how odd the sentence sounded. "That's weird. He must still be hung-over. His car's in the carpark over there." I pointed and Terry raised a grey eyebrow and pulled a face.

"Better bloody not be! Not on game day. We're paying that joker to see it through. Twat!"

I kept my face neutral, studying the flaccid chins which hung from Terry's jawline. Pete might have developed the wobbling flesh if he hadn't finished life with his body splayed over his car bonnet, covered in shards of windscreen. Lucky escape. For both of us. The chins would have embarrassed him and irritated me.

"How are you keeping? Job going well?" Terry's question oozed politeness, and we both played the game like professionals.

"Fine thanks." I smiled with genuine pleasure at the thought of my class of five and six-year-olds. They were all someone's babies, entrusted into my care for six precious hours a day and I loved each one of them. "I enjoy my job."

"Margaret wishes you'd visit," Terry said, lighting up a cigarette and blowing the smoke away from my face. He pulled a wisp of tobacco from his lip and ground his heels into the grass. "She misses you."

"Yeah. Sorry." I didn't sound it and couldn't elaborate, unable to explain I no longer wished to worship at the shrine of Peter Saint with his mother. I didn't want to light candles and cry over his baby photos. We'd married under duress, pushed into it by Terry and my father in an attempt to tame the free range team captain and produce other little Saints. Eleven of them; enough for a home grown football team. Twenty-five, single and jaded, they'd marched me down the aisle on a carpet of promises and five years later I felt jaded and used. No security, no babies and no happy ever after materialised after the flamboyant ceremony and requisite after match bash at the soccer club. It took everything I owned to pay off the debts Pete left me in his last will and testament, selling the flash house in Devonport to pay the biggest of the bills and settling the rest with my car and a personal loan I'd still be paying for another six months. I stared at the man in front of me, a man I used to respect and felt the hatred rise up like bile. "Actually, I'm not sorry," I said, my eyes blazing.

Terry took a drag on his cigarette and stopped mid pull, staring at me. "What?"

"You heard!" I snapped. "I'm not sorry I don't visit Aunty Margaret. Why don't you both drive across the bridge and visit me in my tiny apartment? Are you afraid it might invoke guilt at the state your son left me in?"

Terry rounded on me with the eyes of a madman. "Don't you dare speak ill of my Pete!"

"Your Pete was a waster!" I spat. I took a step forward, the rage breaking through the veneer of pretence and spewing over into my mouth. My romp with Teina infused me with courage at the realisation someone on the planet desired me. Desired me enough to spend most of the night repeating the conscience pricking error. "Why will you not open your bloody eyes?" My voice rose to a wail and people turned from the side lines to stare.

Terry shook his head and reached out to grab me by the shoulders but the monster broke free from my chest and I opened my mouth to say it, announcing to the world the horror of my life married to Peter Saint. "He was a..." The words gained no traction as Terry Saint's hand came down across my face, the slap ringing out across the soccer ground. A collective gasp rippled along the spectators and a few of the women headed towards us as a brave mob of female solidarity. My cheek and mouth stung with the impact and I tasted metallic blood when I swallowed. I put my hand up to my face and sensed the flesh already swelling into a welt. As the first of the women reached us I turned and ran, sprinting to the car park and nipping through a divide into the bushes onto the main road.

"Ursula, come back!" My cousin Alysha clacked across the car park in her platform shoes and I knew she wouldn't run after me.

"Just leave me alone!" I cried, waving my hand at her as I dodged traffic and crossed two lanes to the centre island. The bus stop loomed on the other side and I cringed, abandoning my father in his wheelchair to the mercy of passers-by, yet again. Someone would drive him back to the rest home, just like they had last night; the night I'd discovered the off field talents of the referee and quashed the sexual ineptitude of my dead husband.

A bus arrived with a hiss of gas from its exhaust, waiting the few seconds for me to run to its open doors. The ride took half an hour through the suburbs of Auckland and my face smarted by the time I let myself into the apartment block, using the lift to get to the third floor. Four flats occupied each level in what used to be the billets for nurses working at the main hospital and despite being crammed in,

I hardly ever saw my neighbours. Loud music issued from the apartment nearest the lift and the heady scent of curry wafted around the lobby, so thick I could have taken a bite out of the air. I let myself into my soulless apartment and closed the door, resting my back against it while I caught my breath.

"You nearly said it," I breathed. A hysterical laugh bubbled up inside my chest and I put my hand over my mouth as I gulped curried air. "Five years of pretending and you almost said it out loud." My chest hitched and misery followed daring as I remembered Uncle Terry's ashen face as he administered the slap. It told me more than years of his placatory words ever had. He knew.

Bile coursed into my throat and I struggled not to retch onto the floorboards in my tiny hallway. I hated Terry and Margaret Saint with a passion which felled me, dropping me to my knees with the strength of it. Did my father know too? Had he any idea what his incestuous plan committed me to? I prayed not, with all the remains of my fractured heart.

Chapter 7

I stood in the bathroom holding a wad of damp cotton wool over the bleeding cut inside my mouth. A red, man sized handprint covered the left side of my face and the ice pack held in my other hand did little to reduce the swelling. "Great!" I hissed at my reflection in the mirror. "Foundation won't cover that up on Monday."

My cell phone buzzed on the lid of the toilet, dancing itself onto the floor with a dull thunk. I ignored it as I had the other multiple times. I lost count after twelve. I lifted the lid of the toilet and flushed the blood stained balls of cotton wool, watching them swirl away like little red ballerinas. I bent and picked my phone off the bathmat where it vibrated itself, contemplating flushing it too. Not one name in my contacts list inspired me with the urge to call them back; not even my father.

I dropped the lid and shoved the phone into my jeans. In the kitchen I grappled another ice pack from the freezer and pushed the limp one in to chill. Perhaps if I iced my face for the next twenty-four hours, I might make it to work on Monday without the endless childish questions about what happened. My eyes teared up at the thought of the hundreds of tender kisses any kind of hurt induced in my captive audience and I loved them for their genuine concern. Every one of the children in my care possessed more worth than any of the adults charged with the unenviable task of loving me for myself.

Nosing in the fridge produced nothing of interest. I fancied crusty bread and cheese but knew the chewing motion would open up the cut inside my mouth and closed the fridge against the prospect of more cotton wool dabbing.

The cell phone buzzed again with a text and feeling I could deal with that, I clicked buttons and read the message. Dad's number gave way to a list of badly spelled swear words and I swallowed, looking for the point of the text. He must have heard about Terry's slap and yet his text contained nothing about my public humiliation. Only complaints.

'Stop bluddy leaving me places!' he grumbled, the message ending with three more unrepeatable swear words.

I closed the message and saw four other flashing envelopes, reading them one at a time.

'What the hell happened?'

'Are you ok?'

'What's going on?'

'I called the cops.'

I groaned in dismay. The four texts came from Alysha and I heard the anxiety in her tone when she got no response. With great reluctance I messaged her back.

'You shouldn't have. I'm fine.'

Her response beamed onto my screen, her shock evident.

'I saw him hit you. He's not getting away with it.'

I rang her, finding the prospect of a lengthy text argument unpleasant. "Why'd you call the cops, Alysha? If I wanted them involved, I'd do it myself."

"No, you wouldn't!" Alysha exclaimed. "The Saint men have been shoving you around your whole life and it's time for it to stop."

"You don't understand," I began and her shrill voice stopped me.

"Like hell I don't understand!" she snapped. "They married you off like they were donating an organ and you've lived with the consequences. I'm sick of watching them treat you like dirt. For goodness' sake speak to the cops when they come looking for you."

"What do you mean?" My voice rose to a shriek. "You didn't give them my address?"

"Of course I did. Make sure you tell them everything."

I slid down the fridge until my bum hit the floor tiles, squeezing the bridge of my nose between thumb and forefinger. "What a mess!"

"A mess they made, Ursula, not you."

"I take it Dad got home." I sighed, wrinkling my nose at his tactless message. "He's not happy; I'm sure I'll never hear the last of that."

"He's a selfish old man. None of them deserve you, babe. You speak to those cops when they show up."

"If they show up." I comforted myself with the thought that Auckland cops had better things to do than arrest a spiteful old man for slapping a relative.

I settled on a tin of tomato soup and regretted it as the vinegar stung my lip. The buzzing of the intercom drove me to the handset, and I lifted it, expecting the dulcet tones of a police officer. Instead I got Margaret Saint, her voice wavering in distress. "I need to talk to you," she said, and I imagined her standing on the front step wringing her hands.

"I'm not up to visitors," I replied and hung up. Peter's mother epitomised everything involved in the words 'helicopter' and 'mother.' She'd blown his nose until the day of his wedding, loaned him cash on demand and probably breast fed him up until his death. I closed my eyes and prayed she went away, otherwise I'd be forced to call the cops myself.

She rang again and again and during a momentary pause, I disconnected the handset and left it dangling from the unit.

I groaned in misery as the hammering began on my front door, suspecting she'd persuaded one of my neighbours to give her entry. I looked through the peep hole and sure enough, Aunty Margaret bounced on the balls of her feet to bang on my door, her thin lips pursed into a straight line and her face set in a look of determination. As I heard other doors on my level bang, I pitied my neighbours enough to swing open the door and face the angry woman on the other side. "Come in!" I said with a decent injection of sarcasm as Margaret pushed past me. The Indian man across the hall shot me a look of consternation and I saw his eyes move across my face to the swollen lip and the bright red hand mark across my cheek. I gave him a smile which didn't reach my eyes and closed the door.

"You set the cops on Terry!" Her voice rose as she faced me, her piggy eyes larger than usual behind the milk bottle bottomed glasses.

I shook my head, wondering if she'd missed the slap mark and faced her down. "No, I didn't. I haven't spoken to the cops. Please leave."

"I'm your mother-in-law!" she barked, putting her pudgy hands on her ample waist and rocking backwards and forwards on her sensible shoes. "You can't throw me out. And you did ring them. They showed up at the club and spoke to Terry."

"Well, they haven't spoken to me!"

Margaret lowered her voice and moderated her tone, wheedling me back into line. "Don't be like this with me, Ursula. We can sort this out between ourselves."

"You knew, didn't you?" I asked, dread creeping up the back of my neck in a slow, prickling line. "Is that why you cooked up a marriage of convenience? It's not a crime to be gay anymore, or didn't you realise?"

Margaret took a step backwards, her face pale with shock. "Gay!" Her eyes bugged and her breath came in snatches, the wind knocked right out of her. "My Pete wasn't gay!"

Tiredness enveloped my whole body, and I turned and strode into my kitchen, slumping in a rickety chair. I rubbed my eyes with my fingers and caught the painful welt on my cheek. "Please don't tell me you really believed he went out drinking on Saturday nights and slept with women." The sadness in my own voice seemed to strip away the last of my resolve. "He kept it secret for the first few years but it ate him up. He picked the wrong guy to bend over to in a toilet near Eden Park and they raped him and took his wallet and phone."

Margaret's hand slipped up to her mouth, her eyes squeezed shut tight, defending herself against my words. I didn't have the energy to spare her anymore. "The debts he left me were from drinking and borrowing money to pay for rent boys. Pete ran through cash like there was no tomorrow and it caught up with him. The house sale cleared most of it but I've still got six months left of a year's loan to finish. I asked you for help and you refused. I owe you nothing so get out of my home."

My mother-in-law gaped and her hands flapped in front of her face. "You're a liar!" she wailed. "He was fine until he met you."

I laughed, the sound low and cruel. "He slept with me twice, Margaret, once on our honeymoon night, probably on your instructions so I couldn't undo the marriage when I found out and once when he was very drunk and you wouldn't shut up about grandchildren. When he called me after the rent boys beat him up, I had myself tested for all the nasties he might have been carrying and I never went near him again." I fixed my dark eyes on her face, animosity for her gone in the relief of my cathartic confession. "It was all about him, Aunty Margaret. He couldn't cope with who he was because you wouldn't let him. If you'd just accepted him when he tried to tell you, he might still be here." I felt sickness rise into my gullet and remembered her spiteful accusation after Pete's funeral. The words felt like acid on my flesh as she'd blamed me for her son's death, stalking after his casket with a belly full of righteous indignation and stonewalling my pleas for help as I sold everything to rid myself of his debt.

"He was fine until he met you," she repeated. "You killed him. His suicide note broke my heart." Her voice rose to a squeak, and I stood, pointing towards the tiny corridor leading to my front door.

"I need you to leave. I haven't spoken to the cops and I don't know if I will. Just get out and leave me alone. I'm done with the Saints and everything you stand for."

Margaret rallied as the tears pricked behind her glassy eyes. She stared at my raised finger and fixed me with an icy stare. "You were born a Saint and you'll die one," she spat.

I shook my head and pitied her, reminding me of my maiden name, the label they sullied with their interference. I daily asked myself why I did it; why I put on a wedding band in good faith and hitched myself into an impossible yolk. Because I was too trusting and already heartbroken; that's why. Peter Saint caught me on the raw and I believed his proclamations of enduring love and the promise of children. Even after I found out about his homosexuality, there'd been understanding, or so I thought. Until the suicide note the cops found in the glove box of his wrecked car. *'I can't do this anymore.'* More fool me.

"I'll speak to your father!" she declared, drawing herself up to her full height and almost eclipsing her face with her ample breasts in the process.

"You do that." I heard the exhaustion in my voice. "I'm finding the burden of Pete's secret hard to bear right now. It'd be best if I told the truth. I can't have everyone thinking his life revolved around the club and bringing on the fresh young players of tomorrow, when really he'd gravitated towards them for entirely different reasons." Even the thought made me sick and guilt flared in my chest at the implied lie. Pete loved his job, and it felt cruel to sully his good work that way.

But it worked. Margaret Saint took a step back and lowered her armoured chest. "You wouldn't?" She didn't sound sure. Her eyes widened and filled with tears and the gentle side of me ached to reassure her I'd exaggerated. My bitch-self pushed to the fore, needing to hurt her for five wasted years of my life; my childbearing years.

"I dunno, Aunty." I shook my head and faked uncertainty for something I'd never do; not in a million years. "Catching the bus to work every day because I sold a nice car to pay your son's debts can make a girl mighty miserable. Living in a shoebox when I owned a perfectly nice house once; that can take its toll too. Then there's that debt I'm still paying which makes me count my outgoings hard enough to stop me living my life; yeah, that makes me so depressed. I've been approached by a magazine wanting an interview. Pete was a real celebrity, especially after being called up to the nationals last year." I sighed. "The fee would wipe out the debt and give me enough for a car, according to what the journo said." I pointed at the door. "Goodbye, Aunty Margaret. Don't come back."

"You're blackmailing me." She said the words in a reverend hush, as though her husband was the only one allowed to box people into nasty corners. My eyes narrowed as I applied the label to myself and took a step into criminality. That's exactly what I'd done; without realising.

I bit my lip and then smiled, wondering why I'd never thought of it before. "I'd like to think of it more as a parting gift from generous in-laws," I said, feeling invincible. I took a step towards her, pointing again at the door and ushering her out of my safe place. She went, looking at me over her shoulder with a newfound respect in her expression. "Oh, by the way." I pointed to my swollen cheek. "I've taken photos of this, should I ever need to use them."

I closed the door and pressed my face against the cold wood as nausea pressed into my throat. The bathroom mirror offered no relief as the jagged shape of Terry's ring showed as a welt under my eye and bruising spread outwards. The All Saints logo showed itself backwards in an ugly circle of red and black and I pressed it, watching the skin turn white and then back to purple as I let go. "What kind of moron wears a ring so the important bit's on the inside?" I asked myself. Uncle Terry, that's who. It was the reason he'd slapped instead of fisted me too. I stared at my reflection and considered the difference between yesterday and today. I looked altered, having leapt a giant moral chasm in less than twenty-four hours and gained the Saint insignia like a brand on my face.

Fornicator and blackmailer. I definitely couldn't go back to church.

Chapter 8

Dad's text disturbed my bath as I soaked in hot bubbles, balancing a book in my damp fingers. '*They won. Ref was shite.*' I pushed my phone from the stool to the bathmat and ignored the next two texts, no longer interested in Pete's legacy. Next week would mark the first Saturday in my entire life when I didn't watch All Saints play. No bus ride to my father's apartment and no sitting in the back of some poor sucker's car as they drew the short straw to take us to the game; my father complaining in the front and me sighing in the back. Freedom.

"Take that Daddio," I murmured and punched the air with my fist, wafting the drifts of snowy bubbles and dropping the library book into the bath. The next half an hour involved lots of swearing, reasonable skill at fishing and then an admission of defeat, as I exited the bath and indulged in a frustrating pass time; patting slices of toilet paper in between each page.

"Just my bloody luck!" I complained, shoving the sodden book in the airing cupboard and praying it wouldn't dry crinkly.

My phone beeped again as I closed the airing cupboard door and padded down the hallway stark naked. When a heavy bang sounded against my front door I screamed, all pretense at a newfound gangster-ship ruined.

"Ursula!" Teina's deep voice sounded from the other side and I squeaked and wrapped my arms around myself. "Open it or I'll stand here all night!" he shouted.

I weighed up my options, wondering why he'd say such a thing. "Wait!" I yelled, dashing into the bathroom for my warm towel, dragging it off the rail and swaddling myself.

Opening the door a crack, I peered through the gap, seeing his tall shape occupying most of the hallway. Dressed in dark trousers and a referee's smart shirt, he stared at me and placed his hand against the door. "Let me in." Authority oozed from his voice and I stepped back and let him enter.

Teina's hair hung on his head in a damp tangle of waves, unbrushed after his shower in the dingy referees' changing room. He smelled of deodorant and pinkness flushed his cheeks after running around for ninety minutes. Taking my jaw in his left hand he examined the marks on my face and hissed in sympathy. "I heard," he said in explanation. His eyes narrowed, and he spoke through gritted teeth. "Bastard. I hope you called the cops. How did he find out?"

I wriggled free of his grasp and hoisted my towel. "No, I haven't called the cops." I shook my head. "Aunty Margaret showed up and pleaded his cause. And no, it wasn't about us, it was over something else."

"You're kidding!" The words exploded from Teina's lips; more statement than exclamation. "What the hell justifies bashing a woman?"

"Just leave it." I turned away and headed towards the bedroom, my wet curls sending icy drips down my spine. I pushed the door closed but Teina followed anyway, slumping on the bed, his olive fingers standing out against the white comforter.

"Talk to the cops," he insisted, and I pursed my lips into a rigid line. "There were witnesses."

"No."

He exhaled and ran his hands through his black hair, biceps bulging against the fabric of the short navy sleeves. I tried to dress beneath the damp towel, my underwear sticking to my skin. As I turned away to fasten my bra, the fluffy fabric dived south and displayed my nakedness. I fought the urge to stamp and scream in frustration, hauling the tired bra over my breasts as fast as I could.

"Stop." Teina's lips grazed my shoulder, and he straightened the straps, his fingers sensuous against my back as he fastened the clasp. His hands warmed the points of my shoulders and he turned me, nestling my face against his chest.

"Ouch," I groaned as the bruise brushed against the hard muscle. He lifted my face with a finger under my chin and sighed. "No, I'm not calling the cops," I asserted, and he raised an eyebrow. "I dealt with it; he won't touch me again."

"And it wasn't because of me?" The question hung between us like a match near a petrol bomb.

"No." I smirked, the action tightening the skin under my eye. "That would be worth both cheeks." The wide grin burst the cut in my mouth and wiped the smile from my face. I hissed and put my hand up to my mouth.

"Is that the bloody logo backwards?" Teina sounded amazed as he peered at the cut beneath my eye and I nodded.

"Yeah. Terry's secret weapon."

He looked away, his eyes narrowed and his mind wrestling with an internal thought which seemed to eat him from the inside out. "How'd he do it?" He studied the mark as I kept my fingers pressed against the cut to stem the blood which pooled its metallic taste in my mouth.

"He has a ring on his finger but he wears it with the pattern on the inside. Lifetime club members get them after they've played so many games."

Teina nodded slowly, his brain working. "Right." He noticed me staring and snapped his attention back to me. "You need ice on that." He snatched my robe off the back of the bedroom door and wrapped me up, shoving my reluctant body ahead of him to the kitchen. Delving in the freezer produced a bag of frozen peas which he split into two separate bags, leaving one and pressing the other to my face. "Swap them over when that one defrosts," he ordered, nosing in the fridge. "You hungry?"

I shook my head and pulled a face. "No. But help yourself. There's stuff for sandwiches or some left over mince. I can make you dinner if you like?"

"Na, just keep the ice on your face. It'll bring the swelling down."

"Ok." I admired his neat bum as he bent with his head in the fridge. The tight trousers accentuated the gentle curves, and I closed my painful eye and squinted to get a better view. Teina glanced back at me and then stood up, reaching for the frozen peas in my hand and hoisting it higher to cover my eye.

"You're gonna have a black eye," he predicted, peering at it with his brow furrowed.

"I'm not going to the cops," I asserted. "He's family, much as I wish he wasn't."

"Hmmmn." Teina wrinkled his nose and delved back into the fridge, emerging with bread, margarine and a pot of jam. He shot me a sideways look as he laid his haul out on the counter in precise order and studied the result. "You might not have much choice in the matter. The woman who serves behind the bar said she'd done it for you."

I nodded. "Alysha. Yeah, she told me." I wrinkled my nose. "They won't come. I haven't made a complaint myself and I won't press charges."

Teina raised one dark eyebrow. "You don't have to. Assault is a criminal offence. If he's got previous, the cops will press their own charges." He widened his eyes with an I-told-you-so look. "Your face will be evidence."

I blinked in horror and he shook his head. "I think you'll end up talking to them whether you want to or not."

"Not," I answered and glanced at the front door, hindered by the packet of peas which obscured my vision. "Will you answer the door and say I'm out?"

Teina smirked. "Don't get me lying for you."

"Can we go to your place instead?" I panicked and dropped the hand holding the peas. "Where do you live? You can hide me."

He stopped buttering the bread and laid the knife down, parallel to the slice. His hesitation strengthened my misgivings, and I dumped the peas next to his hand. "It's ok. I get it." My heart fluttered with dread as I stalked to the bedroom and flung the wardrobe door open. The neck of the sweater caught my cheek as I shoved my head through, yanking my hair out of the hole and letting it tumble over my shoulders and back in damp tresses. I finished buttoning my jeans as Teina arrived in the doorway and leaned against the frame.

"I'm confused," he said, spreading his hands and searching my thunderous face expression with wary eyes. "Yesterday you don't want us to be seen together and today you don't care. Which is it, Ursula?"

"You're married!" I snorted, shoving my feet into socks and sitting on the bed to push them into cowboy boots. My jeans shuddered over the boots and nestled next to my ankles. "That's why you won't take me to your place. I'm such an idiot."

"I'm not married!" he objected, hurt making his eyes sparkle. "I told you I wasn't and I'm not. I don't have a girlfriend either."

"It was too good to be true," I muttered, more to myself than him. "Whoop-de-doo, the fat girl got laid."

Teina's brow knitted in confusion. "You're not fat, Ursula. What're you talking about?"

My laugh sounded cruel, and I bit my sore lip, tasting blood as the cut reopened. I was once.

Fat chicks don't get boyfriends' my dad told me as I sat at the dinner table and filled my face with donuts. At seventeen I decided I didn't care but by twenty-five it was too late. The fat chick morphed into the obese chick and kept going until she was a morbidly obese chick. Dad married me off to Pete believing nobody else would have me, but he hadn't banked on a sterile marriage leading to secret counselling. I learned about Chaotic Eating and recognised myself in the description. Only a few stretch marks bore testament to the old me; a silent reminder not to go back there. Hook's Law threatened me every time I sought to overindulge, knowing physics didn't lie. '*The extension of an elastic object is directly proportional to the force applied to it: $F = k \times e$.*' My skin tone recovered its elasticity once, but there was no guarantee it would again. I had no desire to wear my flesh around my ankles like a pair of wrinkly stockings.

"Sod off!" I snapped at Teina. "Why are you even here? You know everything about me but it's one way. I don't need any more parasites in my life, thanks. I'm not shagging you, so you might as well go." I strode into the kitchen and snatched my keys off the counter, flinging the soggy peas into the dustbin. "Slam the door on your way out!" I called over my shoulder and left, ramming my phone into my jeans pocket.

Chapter 9

I skulked in the alleyway between streets until Alysha arrived, scraping her alloys along the curb as she pulled up. She gasped as I dashed out and climbed into the passenger seat, bobbing down beneath the window line. "Bloody hell! Your face is a right mess!"

"Thanks!" I pursed my lips. "Just drive."

"Where?" Alysha checked her fringe in the rear-view mirror and primped it, fluttering her eyelashes at herself.

"Your house?" I asked, my tone pitiful.

She shook her head. "Craig's home. He'll tell your dad he's seen you. I'm picking that's who you're hiding from."

I thought for a minute. Who was I hiding from? "Yeah," I decided out loud, the memory of Teina's confusion causing an involuntary wince. "Take me to your mum's."

Alysha pulled away from the curb with a squeal of tyres and grinned at my apprehension. "This is exciting," she confessed.

I rolled my eyes and lolled out of view, the seatbelt choking me as she shot around corners too fast. "If you're trying to attract the attention of the cops to force me to give a statement, it won't work," I grumbled.

Alysha narrowed her eyes. "I didn't think of that. Good idea."

"Do it and we're finished!" I threatened. "I'll never speak to you again."

She bit her lip and ignored me, our relationship degenerating into how it was as children, me the sensible cousin and her the tear away. The unfairness of life stung like a tick bite; she snagged the good marriage, and I got dealt the fake.

"Craig did well as captain," Alysha said, eyeing me sideways. "They held a minute's silence before the game for Pete and one in the clubroom after."

"He'd have loved that," I breathed, managing to turn my sarcasm to gratitude in the nick of time. I struggled with the irony of the notion of silence in relation to my husband. He barely shut up when alive and I wondered if they'd been waiting for him to speak from the grave and give the other occupants of Hell a break. I turned the unfeeling snort into a cough.

"You should speak to the cops," Alysha sighed as she slid between two cars on the motorway in a dangerous lane change and I closed my eyes and sank further into the seat. "Terry Saint can't be allowed to get away with that kind of behaviour. It's ugly and I'm tired of it."

"Did they turn up?"

"Yeah. But you'd left so Craig gave them your address. How did you get home?"

"Hitchhiked."

"What?" Alysha swerved as she turned to scrutinise me with disbelief in her eyes. "Liar!" she snapped, almost rear ending the car in front as it braked.

"I caught the bus," I said, my tone acerbic. "Not that anyone bothered to follow me and offer a lift or some sympathy." I touched my cheek and felt the pain flare. "Just hurry up and get me to your mum's place. Nobody will look for me there."

Alysha rolled her eyes. "True dat!"

I relaxed and laid my head back against the leather seat as Alysha lurched her husband's expensive car around Auckland, chattering away about her son, Mikey. I dozed off, scrunched up in the seat and woke to her ceaseless diatribe about Craig's leadership of the first eleven All Saints. "You don't mind, do you?" she asked and jabbed me with her finger to make sure I heard. "I know it was Pete's role but Craig's stoked your dad asked him to captain the squad. He couldn't believe it."

"Yeah," I mumbled. "It's fine. He'll do a good job."

"I'm so relieved," Alysha gushed, and it occurred to me she'd been jabbering about it the whole time I slept. Guilt pricked at my chest, knowing other people still wrangled over Pete's death even though I'd let it go the second I stepped from the cemetery and dusted the soil from my black stilettos. "Life goes on," I added, the callousness leaking through my voice.

"Don't say that!" Alysha snapped. "Pete's death was a tragedy. He'd done so much for you. Think of all the weight you lost while you were married to him and you started running with his help. You've coped with everything far better than we all imagined."

I sighed and rolled my eyes, keeping my face turned towards the side window. I began running to get out of the house and once I started, discovered I liked it. I also enjoyed being thin and didn't intend to get fat again, just in case my father decided to marry the obese chick off to another cousin. Paulie's face wafted across my vision and I shivered. The way he looked at me of late made me wonder if they were cooking up another sham wedding in my honour.

"Wasn't he?" Alysha demanded, and I jumped and turned to face her.

"What?"

"Wasn't he good for you?"

"Who?"

"Pete! He was good for you."

I groaned out loud and contemplated jumping from the moving vehicle. "I'm not talking about Pete, ok?" My voice became a squeak at the end of the sentence and Alysha frowned.

"You never talk about him, Urs. It's not healthy."

"You just said how well I'd done! Make your bloody mind up!"

Alysha tutted and pursed her lips. I knew that look. "It wouldn't be too soon to start dating again," she said, her voice soft. "It's been over six months."

I swivelled my head at speed, wondering what she knew about Teina Fox. "What're you talking about?"

"Paulie!" Alysha smirked. "He said you looked gorgeous last night. We didn't realise you'd left until he searched for you to ask for a dance."

"He's Pete's brother." I spat the words through half-closed lips as my stomach roiled in distaste. Margaret's pudgy face swam past my inner vision and I wound the window down so as not to puke in Craig's work car.

"He's loaded," Alysha commented, an unwitting salesgirl for my father.

"Shut up!" The words spun from my mouth in the wind and I dry retched over the sill. "Bloody shut up!"

Alysha's complexion held a sickening whiteness as she pulled up on my Aunty Pam's driveway. She dived from the car and hammered on her mother's door. "Mum! Please be home! Mum!"

I staggered from the passenger seat, my mind consumed by the thought of Paulie's flaccid lips making a beeline for my face. I hurled in a rose bush on the edge of the driveway and felt the thorns scratch my face in vengeance. The experience seemed freaky enough to be comical. I blew out through tight lips and tried to catch my breath before remembering Paulie's big toes with their painful, oozing in-growing toenails. I hated feet; anyone's feet including my own. The next heave sent me face planting into the rose bushes with abandon.

Chapter 10

Alysha's mother scooped me up, taking my meltdown as yet another stepping stone in her busy day as a nurse at the general hospital. She seated me in her kitchen with an ice pack on my face and a drink of warm lemonade sizzling in a glass next to my hand. Alysha twittered around until Pam got fed up and sent her home.

"Did you put ice on that at home?" Pam asked and I shrugged.

"I only had peas."

"Well, I trust they were frozen and not tinned," she said, shifting the ice pack to one side to examine my bruised cheek. "Are you going to tell me what happened?"

I shook my head and slapped the pack over my cheek, harder than I intended, but I tried not to wince in her peripheral vision as she busied herself at the sink. As she looked away, I screwed up my face and stifled a groan. My cheek felt as though a million needles were embedded under the flesh, being pressed by an unseen hand.

"I know it hurts," Pam said, without turning around. "You don't need to pretend with me."

My shoulders sagged, and I dropped the brave facade. "I said something about Peter and Uncle Terry gave me a slap. It bloody hurts."

"It will do. Drink your lemonade. It'll help settle your stomach."

I sighed and took a measured sip, feeling the cut smart inside my mouth. Pam gave me a nod of approval. "What did you say about Pete?" she asked and I cringed.

"I can't repeat it," I said. "It was mean and I shouldn't have said it."

"Perhaps it was a home truth he needed to hear." She poured hot water over a tea bag and squished it with a spoon, bringing her mug with her as she sat opposite me at the table. "They let that boy run riot; Margaret and Terry. They wouldn't be told. I know he left you in debt." Pam narrowed her eyes and watched me. "We'd all have helped you, sweetie." She leaned forward and stroked my hand with hers and I felt my chest tighten.

"Don't be nice to me, Aunty. It doesn't help and I don't deserve it." My mind wandered back to Terry's face as I threatened his son's good name with my knowledge. I cringed, and she saw.

"I think you've been punished enough, sweetie," she said, her voice soft. "There's nothing you could've done to deserve losing the love of your life."

I gaped and fixed my eyes on a bookcase in the corner, stilling my body and forbidding it to react. I swallowed and waited until I could guarantee the solidity of my voice before speaking. "Yeah, Pete dying was a kick in the guts."

Pam shook her head. "Now we both know I'm not talking about Pete," she said, her tone soft. "Jordan had no right making you marry him. You should've come for help instead of going along with it. Larry always said you were made for each other but I guessed the truth. It wasn't a love match by any standards."

"I didn't see a way out," I whispered. "It's not like I had a queue of hot guys lining up to whisk me up the altar and make cute babies." My eyes strayed to a photo of Alysha and Mikey and Pam tracked my gaze.

"It's not all it's cracked up to be," she said, smoothing her fingers over the top of my hand. "Alysha often looks at you and wishes she could swap lives for a day or two."

I snorted and shook my head. "Don't be ridiculous. She's got Craig and Mikey, a nice house, a decent car and you. Why would she want to swap that for a dingy flat, standing for half an hour on the bus twice a day and the sound of my best friend, the TV night after night?" I heard the resentment in my voice and the vehemence shocked me. Pam kept stroking my hand, not put off by my anger.

"No. She looks at you with your lovely figure, boobs where they're meant to be and a good night's sleep within reach every night. Once you've got Pete's debts sorted your money will be your own and you can spend it on holidays to Fiji or ice cream."

"Probably not the ice cream." I smirked and my lip split again. "Don't want to go back there."

"Yeah, well you need to work with what today brings you, instead of craving what tomorrow might have up its sleeve. There are no guarantees in this world, sweetie. So, you've been stung in the past but it doesn't mean you get to lay down and die. Grab your opportunities and get moving."

I pressed the ice to my cheek and gave a slow nod in acknowledgement of Pam's truths. "Yeah. I felt cheated not getting pregnant. It's probably too late now." I felt the tears prick behind my eyelids and let go, allowing them to surf the contours of my jawbone. I didn't add the minor detail that it took more than two attempts at sex for some women to conceive, figuring she didn't need to know that. Her steady stroking motion against my skin comforted me and I closed my eyes, placing my mother there instead of Pam. I swallowed. "I miss Mum."

"Yeah, I know." Pam's voice wavered too. "She was the best sister anyone could ask for. It wasn't fair; losing her so young."

I nodded, and a tear ran over my fingers and embedded itself in the cloth around the ice pack. Pam leaned forward.

"You said Alysha had me, Ursula. But you've always had me too. I'll be there for you as long as I have breath in my body. It was the last promise I made to Karen before she passed and I mean to keep it." I heard the catch in her voice. "I've done a poor job so far though. She'd be really mad at me. I let your father dispose of you like a possession and I regret that. I wish you'd be honest about why you sold the house and car and at least let me help you."

I shook my head. "It's sorted," I replied, hoping it would be. If not, I'd got the name of the magazine journalist and I'd drag my husband's name through the mud. I knew the journo wouldn't pay me but I'd make sure the Saints went down like a lead balloon. There would be nothing left of Saint Peter's memory by the time I'd finished.

Trouble is, I suspected the only person who'd end up hurting was me.

Chapter 11

Aunty Pam fed me, loved me and cosseted me until Sunday evening when my uncle drove me home to my flat. He stopped on the street outside and waited as I opened the passenger door. "Hey, Ula," he said, his tone serious. "Why don't you move in with us? There's room and Pamela would love it."

I nodded and smiled, picking at the pretty blouse she'd lent me after my shower. "I know, Uncle Larry. She's said it once a week since I sold Pete's house. I just need to find my own way at the moment."

"Well, the offer's there," he said with a wink. "And it won't be going away so we'll keep asking yer."

"Thanks, Uncle Larry." I waved as he drove along the road and wondered if he'd still want me to live with them when he found out I'd blackmailed my mother-in-law and slept with the referee who gave my dead husband his last red card. The notion made me bite down hard on my sore lip, but as my sanity hung in the balance, I made time to see the funny side.

The air inside my apartment felt stale, and I walked around opening windows. My spare keys sat on the kitchen counter and I fingered them, wondering if Teina would ever dare come back after my ugly meltdown. I knew I wouldn't. There were no signs of his sandwich making and I figured at least he was house trained. The flat exemplified my empty life, and I contemplated moving nearer the beach. I missed my marital home in Devonport and wished I'd been able to hold onto it. Walking and running along the beach helped with my fitness and the sea offered a kind of calm not available elsewhere. I stared at the neutral paint in the lounge and imagined renting the sanitised box until I reached retirement. The shiver which worked its way along my spine caused a physical ache and I gave myself a mental and physical shake, focussing on Aunty Pamela's wise words. I recited them to myself as I loaded my washing machine and tidied around, readying myself for school tomorrow. "Work with what today brings you, instead of craving what tomorrow might have up its sleeve." So typical of Aunty Pam's brand of advice, it brought me comfort as evening slipped into night and I crawled into bed.

My last glance in the bathroom mirror didn't bode well, and I doubted makeup could cover the swollen hand mark on my cheek, the cut under my eye or the bruise along my jawbone. I dragged out a tube of foundation and practiced dabbing it over the marks. "Reasonable," I sighed to my reflection, regretting my foolhardiness as I faced the painful prospect of washing it off.

Sleep came late and only after I laid on my back with an education policy manual raised at arm's length. It was boring enough to tire me out but after dropping it on my face twice, I admitted defeat and fell asleep by myself.

It felt as though five minutes after closing my eyes, the deafening blurt of the alarm clock rocked my world and jabbed me from sleep like a jousting knight with a sharpened prong. I groaned and smacked the alarm clock on its already damaged snooze button and sank into the pillows. I executed my first task by counting how many hours it had been since Terry slapped me and praying the healing abilities of my body had worked a miracle while I slept. If I looked in the bathroom mirror and still saw the hand mark, I'd know God resented my absence from church the night before and intended to punish me for my romp with Teina. Stalking to the bathroom, I faced my destiny.

"Not bad," I mused, pressing the area beneath my eye. Less pink and more white, only the nasty cut from Terry's ring remained and the long bruise across my jawline. It gave me hope for a day without awkward explanations. I showered, dressed and applied foundation like any self-respecting plasterer and hoped it wouldn't rub off before home time.

Working with Year 1 children, the day held no guarantees I'd arrive home in the same state I departed.

I breezed into the staffroom at Mount Kearnon Primary School with half an hour to spare and chewing gum on the bottom of my sandal. "Bloody kids!" I grumbled, digging at it with a knife over the sink.

"Stick it in the freezer and it'll peel off," the Year 4 teacher said, yanking my sandal out of my hand and shoving it into the ice compartment of the fridge. She gave me a sympathetic smile and her brow creased as she took a second glance at my cheek.

"My lunch is in there!" the Year 6 teacher grumbled. "Ursula, I don't want your feet all over my sandwiches." His protestations distracted my saviour as she eyed him with disdain.

"Colin, her foot isn't in there; her shoe is." Maddie eyed his portly stomach like a horse breeder studying a disappointing result of interbreeding. "I don't think you'll starve."

"Not the point!" Colin reached in and dragged out my sandal. He flopped it in my face. "Put it in a bag."

With a sigh, I pulled open the drawer next to the sink and numerous shopping bags burst out as though having waited all weekend to break free. I seized one of them and shoved my sandal into it. Maddie snatched it out of my fingers and popped it back into the freezer box, slamming the door with undue force. She pointed an elegant finger towards the seating area and Colin backed away at speed and hastened over to his favourite chair next to the principal's usual spot. He'd marked it by leaving his cell phone on the seat cushion and backed up with confidence, pitching himself over the arm and into the lap of my teacher aide, who'd moved the phone and appropriated the seat.

"You dirty bugger!" she yelled, slapping him on the back of the head. "I'm telling my Bert you made a pass at me." Her Northern English accent rang out like a claxon and the staffroom ground to a halt as everyone stopped brewing tea or chatting to watch the spectacle unfold.

"I did not!" Colin bounced up with incredible energy and knocked a full mug of coffee out of the grounds man's hand, sending the liquid cascading down his own back. The strange little primary school teacher hopped around swearing with a series of words not found in the Oxford dictionary.

"Enough!" Vanessa Cathcart's shriek cut through the air and she levelled her manicured brows at Colin. "See me after briefing!" she said, watching as his complexion passed through a series of interesting reds and settled on fuchsia pink.

Maddie's pretty lips quirked up at the corners and Helen, my teacher aide masked her smugness with a cough and avoided my eye. The principal of our small educational oasis seated herself in her preferred chair and waited while we milled around and settled about her like various shades of scattered confetti. Colin sulked in the far corner and kept his damp shirt pulled away from his hairy back.

"The fire service visit is still happening," Vanessa began, brushing imaginary specks from her clipboard. She glanced across at me. "Unless there's a call out and then they'll have to cancel."

"We're baking cookies for them this morning," Helen interjected, her Birmingham accent like fingernails on a blackboard. "We could always make sure the call out's here." She snorted at her own joke and the rest of the staff pinned serious looks on their faces, betraying her without a second glance.

"Not necessary," Vanessa intoned, saying the words with emphasis. "This is a busy week with lots to get through. I want the Year 2s ready for their provisional testing by Friday and this drama production's taken long enough." Vanessa eyeballed the Year 6 staff with meaning and Colin cringed, adding sweat to his coffee stain. "Show the parents and shut it down." Vanessa jabbed the air with her red finger nail and squinted in his direction. "If they want their children to join the cast of Annie, they can send their darlings to stage school."

Colin nodded and whimpered like a squeaky toy.

"Ursula." The principal's eyes roved towards Helen and then me, dancing across heads as she found my steady gaze. "Is the unfortunate bout of diarrhoea now out of our system?" she asked with deceptive sweetness.

"As far as I can tell," I replied with honesty. "It's not like they give much notice before they…"

"Yes, thank you for your update." Vanessa raised a hand for silence and I swallowed the rest of my sentence. I contemplated asking for a phone number for our newest board member who worked as a lawyer in down town Auckland. It could lead to a potential indictment if I knowingly contaminated a fire crew with the essence of Norovirus, delivered via chocolate chip cookies. I shuddered at the notion of alternatives to the chocolate chips and focussed on Vanessa's moving lips as her red lip gloss moved through the timetable for the week and finished off with rousing congratulations for Maddie, whose impending wedding loomed like an albatross in the near future.

"You're all invited," Maddie said, glancing at Colin and regretting her generosity. Her pointed glance in my direction made me cringe. Another wedding reception sans plus one made me reach for ready excuses before the invitation hit the bottom of my post box.

My mood felt flat after the briefing and I rallied long enough to help Helen set up the classroom for the baking session. "How do you wanna do this?" she asked. "I can get three trays of cookies in the staffroom oven so we could do one group of five each at a time."

"Yeah, good plan." I plopped three spatulas next to mixing bowls on the tiny tables. "Petra's coming in to sit with the others and read a story. She can keep them in the library corner while we make a mess here. How long for each group?"

"Half an hour." Helen shrugged. "Depends on who turns up today."

"Can you manage Lawrie?" I asked, chewing my lip. "If he kicks off, we're screwed."

"He won't kick off," Helen assured me. "We had a chat on Friday and I told him I'd work with someone else if he had another meltdown like last week."

"What did he say?" I asked, picturing the silver-rimmed spectacles and stubborn face, the child's lips pulled into a grimace.

Helen shrugged. "He said he'd try. I know he struggles with his fine motor skills and most of his problem is frustration."

I nodded. "We're so lucky to have you, Helen. There're some days when I know I couldn't manage thirty children and Lawrie by myself." I stared out of the window where three hundred miniature people bounced around larger copies of themselves.

"Yeah, you would." Helen punched me in the arm and draped a mini cooking apron over the back of a chair. "You're awesome. Look at Penny from last year. You managed her just fine, and she's gone off into Year 2 as happy as a sand fly."

I watched Helen's sandy hair swish around her jaw as she bustled to the other side of the classroom and tidied up the library books in her inimitable way, all capability and self-assurance. I smiled at the Year 6 monitor as she dropped the register on my desk and gave me a grin and a wave. Working in a school offered a finite glimpse of time as children arrived as babies who couldn't hold a pencil one minute and went off to intermediate with dyed hair and piercings in what seemed like the blink of an eye. I'd taught at the school for nine years and rued the day when the children of my pupils bounced through the door. I promised myself I wouldn't become one of the fluffy haired old ladies who'd stayed in the same classroom, eating the same sandwiches for lunch their whole lives. Helen turned to face me and cocked her head.

"What's with the musing?" she asked. "And why are you hiding a damn big hand mark under a shed load of foundation cream? You look like you laid it on with a trowel."

"Oh." I touched a finger to my cheek and then removed it; I needed the makeup to remain glued to my face until three-fifteen at the earliest. It didn't matter what my bus compatriots thought of my wounds; it was none of their business. "Stupid incident at the weekend," I said, playing it down. "I got in the way of things and ended up with a slap."

"Who called the cops?" Helen asked, concern on her face.

I shrugged. "My cousin. But they didn't show up, so it's over as far as I'm concerned."

Helen shoved the last library book on its shelf and straightened the bean bags. "All set?" she asked, moving the conversation away from my mishap. I figured she saw my discomfort but knew she'd revisit the subject at the earliest opportunity.

Birds sang in the trees around the playground as autumn leaves scattered to the floor and Helen and I led our merry band of skipping children into the classroom. Their eyes lit up with excitement at the sight of the two tables set up for cooking and the thrill spread like an infection.

Chapter 12

"How many meltdowns can one kid have in a day?" Helen asked with a sigh, watching as Lawrie Hopu sat on the carpet with his arms clasped around his knees. She shovelled her sandwich into her mouth and eyed the back of his head with nervous anticipation.

"Something's not right," I whispered, observing the hunch in his shoulders. "I'll speak to Vanessa at the end of today. The educational psychologist needs to assess him."

"Good luck with that!" Helen snorted. "Those guys are like hen's teeth and I know Melissa in Year 6 has been waiting a year to be seen on the state. The only other way is to pay privately and I can't see our boy's aunty having four hundred dollars in spare cash lying around."

I nodded and wished I had it, figuring it would be a good use of my money. I jerked my head towards the mess on the two tables and whispered to Helen. "If you could run to the staffroom and check the last few trays of cookies, I'll clear up here. He'll be fine for a few minutes."

Helen rolled her eyes and peeked through the wide windows into the playground. "If you're sure. The other babies were quite shaken up when he started throwing stuff around. Emma's sitting on Carly's knee outside the window and Dannie only just stopped crying by the looks of it."

My eyes strayed to the classroom assistant from Year 4, who cuddled one of my children on the bench outside and watched a ball game in progress. Lawrie's body still appeared bunched and tense on the carpet, no energy left in his small frame. I'd never seen a child morph into a Tasmanian Devil; not in nine years of teaching various age groups. It was spectacular and terrifying and neither Helen nor I had the faintest clue what kicked it off.

"Lawrie?" I approached the little boy and waited until he gave me eye contact before smiling. "Feel better?" I asked, noticing the delay before he nodded.

"Bet," he said and his chest hitched. I sat in the miniature chair I used for group teaching and reading stories and held my arms out to him. "Want a cuddle?"

"Cuggle," he parroted, and I saw the powerful need in his eyes. I beckoned with my fingers and he stood, his gait listing to the left as he lurched into my arms, a bundle of fragile bones and overlarge clothing. I settled him on my knee and controlled my breathing, desperate to infuse love into this confusing child. His eyes looked sticky from salt tears and his nose stuck to his sleeve as he swiped across it. Reaching next to me I offered him a tissue and felt my heart crack as he showed ineptitude with the simple task.

"Blow," I said, laughing as he huffed into it and we spent an amusing five minutes with me showing him something Alysha's son learned as a toddler. I cleaned up his face and straightened his hair with my fingers as he sat on my knee with his chest giving an occasional hitch.

"What am I going to do with you?" I whispered, and he nodded.

"Do wiff you."

I pressed him into me and rested my chin on his head and when Helen returned, she found the child peaceful and the classroom still a mess. "You're a soft touch," she mouthed, and I pulled a face at her and stuck my tongue out.

"I need to clear up the mess, Lawrie. Would you like to go outside with Mrs Morris? She needs someone strong to hold her hand and keep her safe."

Lawrie looked at his palm, the tiny fingers splayed out like a rose. "Hand," he repeated. "Ho han."

"Yeah, hold hands." I smiled at him and filled my expression with reassurance. He hopped off my knee and wobbled and I straightened his metal framed glasses on the neat little blob of a nose. "Be a good boy with Mrs Morris."

Lawrie watched me leave the room and I heard the click of the outer door as I strode to the front office. Putting my head around the door frame, I caught the eye of Julie, the school secretary. "Hey, Jules," I said, chewing my bottom lip. "Have the files come from the kindy yet? I wanted the one for Lawrie Hopu, in particular."

Jules wracked her memory, staring at a white space on the ceiling for inspiration. "I don't think so. We've got the others but I remember you asking for that one at the start of term."

"Yeah, I really need it," I replied. "I don't want to go rushing in and call his family for a meeting without all the facts, but my gut tells me there's something going on with that little boy."

"Hmmmn." Julie ran a hand through her blonde hair and nodded. "He lives with his aunty in a state house not very far away. There're heaps of children and the place is a mess. She's on her own and to be fair she works long hours to feed them."

"He doesn't have siblings or cousins here though, does he?" I asked, feeling a headache build as my brow knitted. "I wonder where they go."

"Oh, he does. There's three cousins here and the older ones are at high school. They've got nothing, Ursula; it's really sad. I'm fairly sure Lawrie's mum's in prison and there's an older child farmed out somewhere else." Julie watched me with concern. "I'll ring the kindy while you're in class this afternoon and pop down if I find anything out. I'll also take a wander outside after school and see if I can pick up any gossip, but I doubt it. She keeps to herself and is often rushing off to her next job."

"Thanks. I'll take him out myself and see if I can chat to whoever comes for him."

I strode back to the classroom and tidied up the mess as fast as I could, using cream cleaner to get the impacted cookie dough off the plastic matting. By the time the bell rang for the end of lunch the classroom was its usual orderly self and I had steeled myself for the firemen visiting, a session on the last five letters of the alphabet followed by a story.

The visit from the fire brigade proved a success, with the children squealing at the awful sound of the two-toned siren and the colourful, flashing lights. Helen grumbled about the lack of young firemen although the men looked pumped and muscular. "They only sent the crusty old ones!" she complained and I laughed as the children clambered over the huge truck.

"There isn't one over forty!" I snorted. "Stop being a pervert."

"I wouldn't kick that one out of bed for farting," she conceded and winked at a dark haired man whose tee shirt fought to contain his rippling muscles.

"That's sexist!" I rebuked her under my breath. "You'd have Bert in here waving his fists if someone said that about you."

The fireman ignored Helen and gave me the slowest, laziest wink I'd ever seen and I flushed with embarrassment.

My teacher aide glared sideways at me. "Typical!" she sniffed and went to retrieve one of the little girls who'd managed to get her pinafore caught on the gear stick and embarked on ninja moves to free herself. A sound of ripping material met Helen at the truck door.

At the end of the school day I led Lawrie outside to meet his carer, feeling a tug on my hand as he gravitated towards a fretful looking girl near the back of the playground. With dark hair scraped back into a severe ponytail and a curvy body, she had Polynesian roots and a similarity to Lawrie. I caught Helen's eye as she delivered the other children to their waiting parents, one at a time. "Hi." I made my voice sound bright and the girl glanced around her as though irritated at being singled out.

"What's he done?" she asked, her tone acerbic.

"Nothing." I watched her with my senses on alert. "He wanted me to meet his aunty. Is that you?"

"Not whaea," Lawrie muttered and I maintained my smile, hiding my misgivings.

"I'm his cousin," she answered, relaxing as I kept smiling and stroked a lock of dark hair out of Lawrie's face. "My ma picks up her other kids from their school so I get this one." She chewed her lip and moved from foot to foot. "What's he done?"

"Nothing." I brushed away the earlier meltdown and bent my knees to meet Lawrie's eyes. "Bye, mate," I said to him with gentleness. "See you tomorrow."

"Morrow," he said and gave me a beautiful smile, complete with missing front teeth.

I watched as the girl led him out of the school grounds and away from my protection, wondering what waited for the small boy at home. She didn't reach for his hand and he trooped along next to her, shoulders hunched and eyes raking the ground through his silver-rimmed glasses.

Standing in the playground made me accessible to the other parents and I answered the same question five times about lost items of clothing and heard four excuses relating to incomplete homework.

"They only have to colour a bloody sheet!" Helen grumbled as we packed up for the day and turned off the lights. "You didn't ask them to work out the theory of relativity in their little heads, for goodness sake!"

I shrugged. "We're just trying to form good habits for when they're at high school. It's not compulsory at this age but it helps the class move along faster if they've talked about it at home."

"Don't know how you stay so cheerful," Helen intoned as I closed the classroom door behind me. "They drive me nuts!"

"Perhaps you're in the wrong job." I grinned and she narrowed her eyes at my teasing.

"The kids are fine; it's the parents who need shooting."

I stuck my head in Julie's door but found her talking to an irate parent who waved an allergy leaflet in the air and complained in a nasal, irritating voice. "It's not my fault that kid's got a peanut allergy," she raged. "My son's always had peanut butter in his sandwiches. He won't eat anything else." I raised my eyebrows to ask Julie if she needed help and the slight shake of her head meant the mother was about to be dispatched with good grace and politeness without winning her argument.

Vanessa's attendance at a conference for primary school principals postponed the usual Monday night staff meeting and I caught the bus back to my apartment with sore feet and a sense of relief. My apartment felt even emptier and I ate a wilting salad from the tiny supermarket near my street. I'd just curled up on the sofa with a mindless soap opera when the buzzer sounded for the outer door.

My hand shook as I wielded the receiver and answered, my heart thudding at the thought it might be Teina. I needed to talk to him; not knowing where I stood caused a hard knot in my chest. If he'd lied about having a wife or girlfriend, I needed to hear it so we could go our separate ways instead of hankering after a man I couldn't have. I regretted my juvenile overreaction and needed to say the words out loud.

"We're looking for Ursula Saint," the dismembered voice said and I heard the noises from the street behind him.

"Why?" I asked, keeping my tone short. I'd had too many crank calls, people trying to access the building and a homeless woman with a shopping trolley who tried to get in and sleep in the downstairs lobby.

I heard the male clear his throat and then he replied. "We're with New Zealand Police, Mrs Saint. We'd like to talk to you."

Chapter 13

I hung up the phone and to be on the safe side, used the lift to get downstairs instead of buzzing them in. At the front door stood two intimidating police officers, both over six feet and five inches apiece. My footsteps faltered as I walked towards them and judging by the look they gave each other; I knew they'd seen my hesitation. Feeling like a criminal without having done anything wrong, I opened the front door and allowed them to walk past me. They turned in unison and I stood in the hallway in my bare feet with wariness in my face. "How can I help you?"

They glanced at each other again; the proverbial double act. The family from the ground floor emerged and clattered past with the average noise of two parents and three small children. The smallest child rode on her father's shoulders and he ducked to negotiate the front door lintel without braining her.

"We'd like a chat in private," said the cop with blonder hair than his counterpart and I shrugged.

"Do you have ID?" It sounded ridiculous to ask when they stood before me in police issue uniform, stab resistant vests and chattering radios on their left breasts. Without comment, both reached into their trouser pockets and pulled out wallets with identifying cards in them. The numbers matched those on their epaulets and despite a chronic case of hat-hair on blondie, they looked like their pictures. "We can go up to my flat then," I said, noticing the father of the dark-skinned little family glancing backwards with an anxious look on his face as he closed the front door behind him.

I padded to the lift and it was a silent and awkward ride up to my floor. I used my key to let my new friends into the apartment and then indicated the lounge. "Do you guys want drinks?" I asked out of politeness and they shook their heads. Blondie sat forwards on the sofa and flipped out his pocket book, readying his pen while his companion cleared his throat.

"Can I just stop you?" I asked, raising my hand palm outwards in a universal stop sign to emphasise my point. "I don't want to press charges; it was a family dispute and it's over. He lost his son a few months ago and hasn't got over it yet. The family's really angry at him and I know my aunt rang him and gave him at yelling at which he won't forget in a hurry." I touched my sore face and tried to ignore the cut on the inside of my swollen lip. "We're good thanks."

Blonde cop looked at his darker haired mate and there it was again, the exclusive communication. "Have you been assaulted, Mrs Saint?"

My jaw hung open and I closed it with a snap. "No, I felt lonely so bashed myself about a bit in the hope that someone would visit and I could use the sympathy vote. Why are you here?"

"Not about that." The dark haired man stood up and approached me, his eyes widening at the left over make up covering my cheek, now visible under the glare of my kitchen spotlights. I should've kept them downstairs in the dim lights of the lobby. He stood over me and leaned his hand on my kitchen counter. "Did you report this?"

"No!" I shook my head and frowned. "My cousin did but I don't want to press charges."

"Assault's assault, miss," he said, tilting his head to assess the damage. "Who hit you?"

"Why are you here?" I repeated, backing away and occupying myself with filling the kettle and flicking it on to boil.

"Do you know a man called Mark Lambie?" the blonde cop asked, joining his colleague at the counter but leaving the fake marble surface between me and them. I turned and leaned my bum against the dishwasher.

"Yes, of course I know him," I said. My eyes widened. "Why? What's happened?"

"What makes you think something's happened?" the dark haired man asked and I blanched.

"Because you're asking questions about him." I stared from one to the other and resisted the urge to roll my eyes like a stroppy teenager. "If he's at home right now eating his tea, why are you here asking if I know him?"

When they stared at me with deadpan expressions I reached for my mobile phone and dialled Dad's number. Blondie wasn't quick enough and Dad answered after one ring. It was a lottery whether he kept it in his shirt pocket or the back of his trousers but he'd complained it gave him a dead leg from his wheelchair in the ass pocket, so I banked on him having moved it. "What?" he snapped and I body blocked blondie as he tried to lean over my head.

"What's happened to Mark Lambie?" I asked and even the cops heard his aggravated yell which echoed around my small kitchen. It started with five expletives and continued in the same vein.

"He's done a runner!" he shrieked. "In-the-bloody-season!" He inhaled and I looked at the cops with something like apology as he launched again. "Bleedin' selfish bugger. What the eff does he think he's playing at?"

"Ok, thanks," I squeaked and at blondie's look of pure menace hung up, palming my phone behind my back. I could tell by their look of shared exasperation they hadn't expected me to do that.

"He's missing," I said with assurance. "Dad said."

"What do you know about his disappearance?" the blonde cop said and I blinked and stared at him. I felt tempted to repeat my father's string of dirty words but felt the mood change and didn't want to find myself being processed at the police station in town.

"Dad says he's done a runner and he's cross. The season started on Saturday and Uncle Mark's the coach for the first team."

"Is he your actual uncle?" the dark haired cop asked and I nodded, shook my head and then nodded again.

"I'm not sure. We all grew up calling him Uncle Mark. Dad's generation call him Lambie." *Or Lardarse, Lazy Scheister and Lecherous Lambie*. I kept those to myself.

Blondie leaned his bum against my counter and I realised it rested at the same height as Teina's. The thought gave me a sick feeling and I tried to concentrate. "Mrs Lambie reported her husband missing on Saturday morning when he failed to return from a wedding reception." His eyes flicked over his notebook. "Other members of the wedding party report seeing you go outside with Mr Lambie after the main course."

I nodded, my eyes wide and a sick feeling in my stomach. "That's right. He went outside for a smoke and didn't seem that drunk at first but then he got worse and worse and ended up sitting on the floor. Another guest at the reception helped to get him into their car and we drove him home. We sat him on the doorstep. I don't understand why his wife says he didn't return. We sat him there and rang the doorbell."

"So you didn't see him into the property?"

"To his front door, yes. He threw up all over the grass verge outside and covered himself in it." I wrinkled my nose. "He's really heavy and there were only two of us. We propped him upright against the front door and rang the bell. He seemed fine." My colour rose as I contemplated what might have happened. A vision of Mark wandering into traffic or falling into a waterway made me cringe in my gut. I swallowed. "We should have made sure he was safe, shouldn't we?"

I stepped around the counter and dragged out a dining chair, skirting the two intense males as I slumped into a seat. "Damn!" I said. "I feel terrible. Where could he have gone?"

"Who were you with?" the dark haired cop asked and my stomach took a flying flip and plummeted south.

"I'd never met him before." I shrugged, playing dumb. "He was on his phone in the car park and knew Uncle Mark. He was a guest at the reception and offered Mark a ride home. I helped him to the car and didn't want to go with them, but he said he couldn't manage on his own so I went."

"You got into a car with a stranger?" I deserved the accusatory barb in blondie's voice.

"It was an emergency!" I protested. "And Uncle Mark knew him."

"What's his name?" Blonde cop poised his pen over the notepad and I held my breath. Dumb seemed like a viable option so I maintained the slumped posture and the irritation at my own lack of care for a drunkard.

"Poor Uncle Mark," I sighed, staring at the back view of my front door. "He called the man Foxy, I think. Yes, that was his name; Foxy. Mark definitely knew him."

"So, you dropped Mark Lambie at his house, rang the bell and then what?"

Then what indeed? Oh the glorious benefit of hindsight in spotlighting the errors of one's conduct and the playing out of consequences. I tried not to think of Teina's luscious olive skin or the sweep of his fingers across my thighs in the big double bed. I swallowed. "He dropped me here and left." I wondered if condensing the truth counted as lying and kept my wince as a virtual expression, firmly on the inside of my head.

"He dropped you here and left?" Blondie scribbled in his pad and the dark haired man eyed me with veiled suspicion. "What time was that?"

I shook my head realising I didn't know. We hadn't turned the TV on or timed ourselves at any particular activity. "I have no idea." I sounded surprised even at myself. "We left as the main course finished and drove for maybe twenty minutes to Uncle Mark's place. It took five minutes to get him out of the car because he kept barfing and then five more minutes for him to stagger up the front steps." I raised my eyes to meet blondie's gaze. "Someone in the street must have noticed us. He was pretty obvious and quite loud." I closed my eyes and added up the minutes alone with Teina on the drive home. "Probably another twenty minutes and we were here. Foxy saw me inside and that was it."

"Was it?"

My heart took a tumble as colour flushed into my face and my slow burning temper came to my aid. I stood, not wanting my sluttiness to go in that notebook in the crabbed left handed script. "You want to know why I left the wedding so early?" I asked and both men watched for cracks in my armour, part training but mostly instinct making them stare at the freak show. "I got married in that club house," I spat, raising my voice. "My husband died six months ago and you lot scraped his body off the bonnet of his car." I took a huge breath inwards. "Mark Lambie asked me to go outside while he smoked and I went because I'd had enough of all the congratulations and false smiles. When he needed help I gave it and yes, I didn't go back and eat wedding cake and drink Jack Daniels with a fake grin on my bloody face. Are we done here?" My fists balled by my sides and I strutted to the front door, swinging it wide open.

With a look of mutual acceptance, the police officers mobilised and strolled through the door. Blondie turned, opening his mouth to speak and I jabbed a finger in the general direction of his chest, somewhere above my head. "And you know what? Next time someone's rolling around on the floor because they've had too much alcohol, I'll step over them and call you. How about that?" I slammed the door in a single fluid movement and enjoyed mild satisfaction at the way the sound echoed around the whole lobby and bounced off the metal doors of the lift.

Behind the door I thumped my forehead with the heel of my hand and chastised myself with each and every one of my mother's stock phrases.

"When first we practice to deceive, what a tangled web we weave."

I couldn't admit to my night of passion with Teina, not because I knew he was a referee and a member of the third team on any pitch. Not because my father hated all referees and judging by Saturday's performance, Teina Fox in particular. I couldn't admit it to two serving police officers because I knew it made me look like the usual Friday night slapper who decorated the insides of their cars with puke and took up space in the drunk tank, slinking out with a hang-over and an apology in the crude light of day.

"Yeah, I'm ashamed!" I admitted to the empty flat and to myself. My mother's other favourite phrase chased me into bed that night and I cringed under the weight of her voice.

"Your sins will always find you out."

Chapter 14

I caught Vanessa on Tuesday morning as soon as her heels tapped into the front reception. "I need to speak to you about one of my boys," I said, standing in her way and forcing her to deal with me. She nodded me into her office, her big hair wobbling on her head and dumped her bags on the visitors' chairs, denying me a seat and daring me not to hang around too long.

"Lawrie Hopu is showing signs of significant difficulties with social interactions and learning. He gets angry and confused and doesn't seem to know what's going on half the time. I'd like him assessed."

"Join the queue!" Vanessa scoffed and I saw the frustration in her face. She was as much a victim of the system as Lawrie. "Unless his parents can pay, I'm afraid he's stuck in the line, same as the rest of the poor little buggers." She ran a hand over her eye, smudging her impeccable makeup. "Perhaps we should start a donations page and keep it running for the duration of the school's existence. I can't touch the operational budget for things which are clearly operational and then the ministry ties my hands behind my back in all other matters."

I nodded in sympathy. "I know. But Lawrie's urgent. I don't have his kindy notes yet, but his behaviour is escalating and yesterday he terrified some of the other children with the level of violence he exhibited. Physically restraining him opens up a raft of other problems." I bit my lip and prayed none of the other children mentioned to their nice parents at tea time how Helen picked up the flailing child and squashed him into her wobbling boobs until he couldn't breathe. It wasn't in the operational handbook and forcing a five-year-old to choose between fighting and gasping for air was probably illegal. In Helen's defense, she'd been trying to cuddle him but her large appendages got in the way.

I stepped backwards towards the door and narrowed my eyes at Vanessa. "You'll end up with him and his whānau sitting in here while you suspend or expel him," I said, certainty in my voice. "I'm just trying to head it off."

Vanessa sighed and sank her well-shaped bum into her office chair. "Ok, thanks. I'll get him put on the list for the educational psychologist and talk to someone at the ministry." She shrugged and her neat suit jacket shuddered up and down on her shoulders. "And I'll get Julie to ring the kindy. They know the rules."

I opened my mouth to tell her I'd already asked and then closed it again. Julie would think I'd complained about her but it couldn't be helped. "Thanks." I left Vanessa to her frustrations and sorted out my classroom before school. The deputy principal's role opened up a few weeks ago but the thought of applying made me shudder. I suspected they'd bring someone in from outside; someone who didn't mind no longer having their own class of children, someone happy to push paperwork around a desk and play with the bigger picture view. The management points on my salary and the kudos for a job title of that magnitude failed to sway my opinion. I'd stick with the Lawries, the Jennies and the Carls; children who'd hopefully left my care better than they entered it.

My cell phone rang in my handbag as I sorted out paint pots and water for the morning's activities. "Sorry," I winced with a glance at Helen. "Forgot to mute it."

"Just answer it," she said with a furtive look at the door. "We were both half an hour early; if they can't let you answer the phone for a second, it's a poor show."

I darted into the stock cupboard, phone in hand and hissed a reply into the handset. My father's expletives bit into my ear drum. "I've run out of bloody medication," he rasped. "Get it for me."

"I'm at work, Dad." My tone betrayed my discomfort as Helen clattered around in the classroom.

"Fine! I'll just bloody die then." He let off a stream of other unpleasant works and I clasped the phone to my collar bone in embarrassment.

"Your place is two bus rides away from here, Dad. Isn't that why you employ May-Ling?"

Silence.

"I'll get it after work. I don't want you to die, ok?"

He disconnected, leaving me with the consequences of his frustration. I sighed, knowing his bad-daughter label would stay lodged in my chest all day. Not fair, especially when I had better things to worry about.

"That your dad?" Helen asked, knowing the drill.

I nodded. "Yeah. He gets his prescriptions faxed to the pharmacy just up the road from him and then expects me to take two buses over there and walk it round. He asked before the weekend but it slipped my mind."

"A smack to the head can do that." Helen continued slapping wooden paint brushes onto the table, the splayed bristly ends well past their usefulness. She picked one up and eyed it, attacking the pigs' hair tufts with scissors to make them more uniform. "We need new ones," she commented and I rolled my eyes and turned away.

"No money for that," I sighed. "No money for anything."

"Doesn't that home-help lady live at your dad's?" Helen asked with curiosity in her pudgy face.

I nodded with deliberate slowness. "Yes. She moved in before Christmas. The place is a permanent mess and I keep meaning to phone the company and complain, but he likes her. I pick up the phone to ring them and then end up bottling out. The lady who cleaned and picked up after him before was efficient and got everything done. But he didn't like her as much because she wouldn't let him upset her."

Helen chewed her bottom lip in concentration and trimmed another brush with the rounded scissors. "I'd ring the company. She might try to con him out of his money."

I nodded. "That occurred to me. I'm a coward. Taking May-Ling away would unleash the beast and I'd be over there every night on the bus, tidying and making his dinner. He's so mean and he ran through over ten carers before the last lady told him to wind his neck in. I wish they hadn't moved her on."

"Maybe she left," Helen suggested.

"Nope. She's still with the same company. I've seen her in the supermarket near me with her children and she wears their uniform."

"Weirder and weirder," Helen chirped, snorting as Colin strolled past my door. "Speak of the devil and he shall appear."

I laughed and plopped water into the jugs on the table, knowing as thirty-one children washed their brushes and turned the liquid varying shades of brown, there would be at least two major spills and one catastrophe with a painting.

Sometimes it felt like predicting a car accident but driving the same route, anyway.

The children exhibited excitement beyond the extreme as they made thank you cards for the firemen who'd visited the day before. They wore old shirts over their uniforms to mitigate the damage and made a peculiar sight. I'd cut the sleeves off most of them and the body reached the backs of the children's knees. The shirts came home with me in a carrier bag once a month to wash, reminiscent of the days when Pete wore them and the worst spills were spaghetti juice or coffee. I knew he'd be disgusted at what I'd turned them into; it's probably why I did it.

"This is the fire engine!" screeched a child with glasses and carrot orange hair. He gritted his teeth in excitement and the brush shook his hand as he clenched every muscle in his body.

"Lovely Kane," Helen intoned. "Inside voice. Watch what you're doing with that brush, oh now look what's happened. Go to the sink and wash around your ear, Meredith and wait a minute your shirt's caught in the..." She supervised the first crisis of the morning while I mopped up the second. I'd got the grounds man to make up blocky wooden holders for the water jugs but still the children managed to knock them over. At least it reduced the disasters to under twenty per session.

Helen moved off to deal with Meredith's paint filled ear and I helped Kane redo his fire engine, his chest hitching in grief at the version crumpled into the dustbin. "I like this one better," he announced eventually, his face breaking into a smile.

"Mine's got zombies," Kevin said, huffing and puffing as he scratched the scrubby brush across his paper.

"I don't remember any zombies in the fire engine," I said, keeping my voice level. I'd spoken to his mother about the games she allowed her son to play and the effect it had on his view of the world.

"It keeps 'im quiet!" she'd replied with indignation. "You should try havin' eight kids, missus."

"I don't want to see zombies in your picture," I said with determination. "I want a proper thank you for the lovely firemen before the end of this lesson, otherwise you'll have to stay in and do another one with Mrs Morris at playtime."

"Ar, no!" he exclaimed. "She'll push me into her things and Samuel couldn't breathe last week!"

"I liked it!" Samuel shouted from across the room. "Them's is squishy like a cushion."

"You said yer didn't! Liar!" Kevin yelled and I quelled the noise and the disruption with a well-placed raise of my eyebrows.

"Kevin, get rid of the zombies. The firemen will be offended because none of them looked like they were starving."

"They had big muscles!" crooned a pretty little girl with long, brown pigtails which swished into her painting every time she moved her head. "My mum asked me all about them."

"Did she want to know about the fire engine?" Kane chirped, scrubbing the brush across the dodgy rectangle with green paint.

"Nope, just the firemen."

"What colour's that?" I asked Kane, keeping my voice level as he worked hard to keep the green separate from the red, avoiding the diarrhoea colour of the zombies on the artwork next to him.

"This one?" He shoved his finger into the middle of his fire engine leaving a fingerprint. "Ooh, windows," he mused, beginning to make it look like a cruise ship instead, using all ten of his digits to create holes in the paint.

"Yes, that one." I forced him back on task with my question and he looked at me as though I might be simple.

"It's red, innit!" he scoffed and I glanced at Helen in despair. Colour blind. I added a visit by the nurse with her psychedelic chart to my list of requests and walked around the classroom for the next hour. I righted toppling water jugs, overflowing pallets and doled out poster paint like there was a national shortage.

Helen joined me in the staffroom for morning tea and we sank into the sofas with relief. "Those firemen were jaw-droppingly hot," Helen snorted, "but they'll see their pictures and have a crisis."

"You didn't think they were! You said they were old and crusty."

"They weren't as luscious as last year but they looked tastier than my Bert in his boxer shorts with his belly hanging over the top," Helen sniggered.

"And the green fire engine," I groaned, pushing Bert's semi-dressed image from my mind and wanting to wash my eyeballs. "What will they make of that?"

"That explains heaps," Helen sighed. She slapped my thigh in camaraderie. "Not bad though, love. One poked ear, two poked eyes, only four major spills and one minor one. It's getting better."

"You forgot the fight."

"Ah, yep. Paint brushes at dawn. Parents in, or do we deal with those two ourselves?"

"Ourselves." I gnawed on my bottom lip and contemplated the scary father who came to pick up one of the paint brush jousters. He'd stood over me at the meet and greet during the first week and stared down my blouse without shame. I glanced sideways at Helen with her wobbling boobs of destruction and decided in the interests of health and safety, I should keep her away from him.

The day continued through basic mathematics, more alphabet learning, colouring in alphabet letters, writing our names and a story. I often looked back on the day's achievements and wondered how such basic tasks could seem so exhausting. My father punctuated the lessons with abusive texts which I mainly ignored. I responded to the last one, '*I'm effing dying*,' with, '*Then do it quietly.*'

He didn't respond again, but I smiled at his misspelling of the 'f' word for most of story time. Short sighted old men should be banned from texting. He remained silent for a while and then as I cleared up ready to catch the bus home, he sent his most damaging one of the day.

'*Cops been. Said you killed Mark Lambie.*'

Chapter 15

"You don't have to do this." I sat in Helen's car feeling awkward as she negotiated the traffic towards my father's apartment in Mangere.

"It's fine," she replied, grinning and waving at an aggressive male who honked his horn at her and passed over the centre line to zoom by.

"You know him?"

"Nope," she said with a grin. "But now he's wracking his brain over that nice wave and worrying I'm from his workplace, a friend of his wife's or someone who can damage him later."

The driver settled into the traffic in the right hand lane and gave Helen a beautiful if somewhat fake smile as she went straight ahead.

"I might try that," I said with a giggle and she looked at me sideways.

"From the bus?"

I sighed. "Yeah. From the bus."

We said our goodbyes and she dropped me outside Dad's place. The entrance to the warden controlled apartments displayed local artwork donated by bored local teens. The graffiti truck parked on the verge and the council worker used a power blaster to remove it. I gave him a pleasant smile and he stopped his hose long enough to let me pass. "Spray paint costs a fortune," I said, my expression confused. I pointed towards the fading block capitals depicting someone's wonky name and the man nodded and shrugged.

"So do drugs," he said. "And they still do that an' all."

I went inside wondering about the relevance of his answer and felt glad I was only educating future graffiti artists and not clearing up after them. The lifts smelled of disinfectant and the carpet on Dad's corridor bore some horrific stains. I let myself in using a key and heard a strange noise coming from the lounge. It sounded like someone pumping up an air bed. "I'm early," I said, walking into the dim room with the prescription bag in my hand. "Helen waited for me at the pharm..."

My elderly father sat on the knackered sofa with his trousers round his ankles. His home help, allegedly from the Philippines, sat astride him, naked from the waist down.

They grunted in unison, sex noises filling the room as the fifty-year-old woman raised herself up and down on her knees. I gaped with my mouth open before the bile rose into my throat and caused me to close it. Dropping the bag on the carpet, I turned and marched from the flat, leaving the front door open. I couldn't remove the image from the backs of my eyelids and even hot tears of disgust couldn't lever Dad's open mouthed look of ecstasy from my brain. I shuddered and trembled with horror and nobody sat next to me on the ride back to downtown Auckland in case it proved infectious.

An hour and another bus ride later and I pushed my front door open with my hands full of mail from the box downstairs. The image still floated around my inner vision but I'd replaced it mostly with the red mist of fury. I rang the company who'd organised May-Ling to inform them she'd crossed the line in her caring and met with his case worker. "That's not in her job description," I said, hearing my voice wobble. "I walked in on them and it was hideous. I'd like her removed, please." I stopped myself adding 'surgically', not wanting someone else to suffer nightmares too.

"Mrs Saint." More silence. "Your father terminated his contract with us before Christmas. I have no idea who this May-Ling is; she's nothing to do with us."

I sat on my sofa for a while with my head in my hands. Dad didn't text which could mean a number of things. I liked to imagine he felt great shame, but reality told me either he'd had a massive coronary or worse, was still in the same position I left him in. A spiteful part of me hoped they got stuck like it and the warden called the fire brigade to prise them apart.

I reread his last text; the one which caused me to alarm Helen with my shaky silence and the flicker of fear began again. I wondered if the two police officers told my father their suspicions or if he'd jumped to conclusions. I contemplated ringing the station and confessing to not only abandoning a drunk on his doorstep like he meant nothing more than a newspaper, but also to dashing back to my place and allowing myself to be undressed by a complete stranger.

The cringe came from the inside out and I put my head in my hands. My cousin Jack worked as a cop and anything with my name on it would reach his ears. I didn't want him to know about Teina, even though I knew he couldn't tell the family. The Saints excommunicated him the minute he stepped into his police issue trousers. Saints hated cops almost as much as referees. It was rule number two.

I couldn't spend the evening worrying so instead I called Aunty Pam. She answered the phone with her usual brand of cheer. "What's up, sweet pea?"

I held my breath and then exhaled, splurging all my most recent problems with it. "I found the home help on top of Dad, the cops think I murdered Uncle Mark and I slept with a total stranger."

"I'll be there in thirty minutes," she said, her voice calm and even.

Chapter 16

She made it in twenty because she coerced poor Uncle Larry into dropping her off. Then she sent him to buy pizza.

"She's not really a home help," I complained, my fingers writhing in my lap. "What should I do?"

"Call the police?" Pam asked, gripping my hand in hers.

"No!" My eyes widened until my face hurt. "Then they'll arrest me for killing Uncle Mark! They'll think I hate all old people."

Pam made a dismissive sound with her lips. "I don't care about any of that. I've told Jordan for years to go screw himself so I'm glad he's found someone to help. Don't give him a second thought, Ursula. Stop running around after him; if he's well enough to engage in that kind of afternoon pastime then he doesn't need you at his beck and call."

I nodded, unconvinced. "What if she's after his money?"

Pam snorted. "If she's willing to do that to get it, she's welcome to it."

I put my hand over my mouth. "That would make her a prostitute."

"Who cares?" Pam slapped my leg. "He's not your problem anymore." Her eyes crinkled in the corners. "Before Larry comes back, I want to know everything about this mystery man."

My tears alarmed her and the smirk dropped off her face with rapid speed. Her arms doubled for my mother's embrace and soothed me as if I was Alysha. "It's ok," she whispered. "He didn't hurt you, did he?"

I shook my head. "He was perfect; everything seemed incredible." I wiped my nose on my sleeve. "He came round here after the game because he'd heard about Terry slapping me and I overreacted. He wanted me to talk to the cops, but I didn't want to and panicked. I asked him to take me to his place and when he hesitated, I accused him of being married and haven't seen him since." The tears coursed down my face, taking the heavy foundation with it and Pam winced at the revealed cut and bruising on my cheek.

"You haven't been putting ice on that," she tutted and I sighed as the nurse in her overrode everything else.

"I've had other things on my mind!"

Pam smirked. "I can imagine. What's he like?"

I thought of Teina's easy smile and the way his fingers stroked the hair back from my face. I spoke, mid-sigh. "You remember that thing the vicar says about sex?" I asked, blowing my nose into a tissue. "It's like gluing two bits of corrugated cardboard together and leaving them to dry. Then when you try to pull them apart, both get damaged."

Pam looked at me with an odd expression. "So, was it not good then?"

I leapt up with a groan of exasperation. "It was brilliant, ok? All four times were absolutely amazing! I'm not talking about the mechanics. I'm trying to tell you how I feel at the thought of never seeing him again; like having my guts ripped out."

Larry stood at the open front door clutching two pizza boxes. His mouth hung open and he stared at me with betrayal in his eyes. "You did it four times? Are you trying to make me feel inadequate?"

Pam stood and took the pizza boxes from his hands, patting him on the cheek with a gentle hand. "You're all quality, babe. Once is enough."

Larry appeared mollified and grabbed plates from the cupboard, laying them out on the counter. "Do we know him?" he said and shot me a peculiar look. "How would he know what happened at the game?"

I swallowed, not ready to give up Teina's identity yet. "He heard about it," I lied.

Larry nodded, seeming to accept my answer.

"We'll eat here," I said, pulling up the two bar stools for my guests and standing on the other side, leaning over my plate with my elbows on the counter.

"Stand up straight," Pam rebuked me. "You'll give yourself indigestion."

I resisted the irrational urge to pout and stood up in obedience. Pam nudged Larry with her elbow as he snaffled a huge bite of cheesy pizza into his mouth. "Ursula walked in on Jordan giving the home help something a little extra," she said, her tone so casual he stopped chewing as though he'd misheard.

Realisation dawned on his face and he covered his hand with his mouth and dropped the delectable slice back onto his plate. "I feel sick now," he announced, pushing his plate away.

"It didn't do much for me," I sighed, looking for sympathy. "I need counselling."

"Oh, shut up, you're not five," Pam snorted. "What did you think they were doing? Playing scrabble?"

"You're Mum's sister! You should be upset." My indignation emerged in my tone and drew hurt from Aunty Pam's face.

"Yes, I am. I miss her every day but the only good thing to come out of her marriage to that loser was you. I don't care if he wants to do every dirty chick in greater Auckland, Ursula. I hope he catches something nasty, and it drops off!"

"Pamela!" Larry's warning hand rested on his wife's arm and Pam shook him off with a rough movement.

"Excuse me," she grunted and hopped off her stool, heading for the bathroom with a swish of her floral skirt.

Larry looked at me with apology in his eyes and I swallowed. "She doesn't like Dad?" I whispered as though it was a new concept. My faithful uncle's face creased in amazement and he snorted with laughter, hooting until actual tears ran from his eyes and the stitch made him clutch at his side.

I shook my head in surprise, unable to join in and astounded at how clueless I'd been at noticing the most important things under my nose.

Chapter 17

He stood on the balcony of the club house, leaning with one elbow on the rail. A group of teenage girls ogled his neat backside from a table inside the open doors, giggling to one another behind their hands. Oblivious as always, Jack Saint turned at the sound of my footsteps on the worn deck. "Hi," I grunted, placing both palms on the rail next to him and closing my fingers around the rimu. I imagined our grandfathers hugging the wood and watching the final stages of a close game.

"What's up?" He leaned down and nudged me with his shoulder, turning to get a better look at my grumpy visage.

"Nothing," I lied, shielding my eyes from the setting sun.

"Jack, Maddie fancies you," one of the teenagers called amidst much screeching and the sound of chairs scraping on the floorboards. Jack wrinkled his nose and ignored them, just like he'd done since we were kids.

"Your fan club doesn't age," I grumbled and saw his lips lift in a smirk. It wasn't a great surprise. With a Māori mother and a Pākehā father, Jack Saint Senior's children looked like demi-gods with olive skin and black hair. Jack and his younger brother Alan could pass for models although both avoided the limelight. Jack became a police officer and Alan joined the army; each escaping the Saint regime the only way they knew how.

"Pity," Jack mused. "I'm no more into jail bait than I was then." He lifted his right arm to scratch his nose, and I saw the black cast covering his wrist and forearm.

"What happened?"

He winced. "Fell trying to restrain a drunk teenage girl. Hit my bloody wrist on a low wall and gave myself a green-stick fracture."

"Ouch, sorry." I grinned and jerked my head backwards towards his entourage, who'd moved closer to counteract my proximity to the object of their desire. "Hence the distaste for giggling girlies."

Jack nodded. "Pretty much all the female population gets on my nerves at the moment."

My heart sank, and I stared at him with wariness in my eyes. "Would you rather be on your own?" I glanced at the sideline where my father waved his arms and pitched forward and back in his wheelchair, wishing I'd stuck to my decision and stayed away.

"Present company not included," he said, his dark eyes raking my face. "You've never been like other girls," he mused. "You're different."

Nodding, I focussed on the game, understanding his comment. Jack and I shared a complicated dynamic and always would. He felt like my brother but at the same time, my soul mate. He sneaked under my skin and I his, able to bless and wound each other in equal measure. When he married a girl from my class at the age of seventeen, my heart shattered into a million pieces and I'd eaten myself into a human marshmallow. "How is Lacey?" I asked as the words followed on from my torturous thoughts.

Jack looked at me with a frown. "No idea, Ula," he replied, using his pet name for me.

I shook my head in confusion. "Sorry, I don't understand."

He studied me for a moment as I watched Uncle Terry scrape my father off the pitch and seat him back in his chair. The referee approached in his bright yellow shirt and jabbed his finger into Dad's personal space. "What's that about?"

"The ref called advantage and Jordie disagreed," Jack said, still boring a hole into my right cheek. "As usual."

I nodded, avoiding Jack's gaze, feeling as though I'd missed an important birthday and couldn't worm my guilty way out of trouble. I knew he'd sensed my discomfort when his hand snaked around my shoulder and pulled me into his armpit. I exhaled and relaxed, his familiar scent wafting over my jarred nerves. "It's not like you've had nothing of your own happening," he said, his voice low. "Lacey left me, Ula. Happened a couple of months ago." A vein twitched in his left cheek as he spoke. "She's pregnant by some other guy."

"I'm so sorry," I breathed. "I really am, Jack."

"Yeah," he said. "Me an all." He left his good arm around my shoulder, oblivious to the silent rage of the teenagers and the myriad eyes watching from the club house.

Jack formed an unwitting rearguard as we watched the All Saints second eleven win their first game of the season. The referee kept control of the temperature which hiked in the last half as the opposition tasted defeat and didn't like it. A winger received a red card and an early shower after going in for a dangerous tackle with his studs up. The All Saints player wiped from the pitch with an ankle injury cried tears of pain and anger as he sat on the grass next to Dad's wheelchair with an ice pack on his bare flesh. The mood turned nasty, not helped by my father's lusty voice as he incited a riot and by the time the final whistle came, the opposition supporters left without daring to enter the club house for the after match refreshments waiting for them.

"He's being assessed." Paul Saint's voice cut through my thoughts as I watched the opposition supporters clear up their deckchairs and make their way to the car park.

"Pardon?" I left my body leaning against Jack as I glanced sideways towards the voice. "Who is?"

"The ref." Paulie eyed Jack's olive fingers curling a lock of my hair and furrowed his brow. "Over there under the trees. There's a group of them turned up for the second half."

I looked to where his finger pointed and saw a knot of males standing together on the furthest edge of the grounds. To their left a man stood alone with a clip board and the referee and his two assistants made a beeline for him, their flags flapping in the breeze. I shrugged. "So what? The ref played it fair. I thought he was good." I looked up at Jack for confirmation but he kept his eyes directed at the knot of males and I stared at the underside of his chin for a second before looking back at Paulie. "Didn't you?"

"He was ok," my cousin replied, agitated by Jack's presence. Paulie leaned across me, his shoulder brushing my temple as he spoke to Jack. "Yer dad's looking for you," he said, his eyes hard.

"I've got eyes in my head," Jack replied, protecting my face with his outstretched hand. "Watch Ursula." Narrowing his eyes, Jack's face adopted a hardness which I associated with his work. He took a step back, pulling me with him before turning and brushing Paulie's chin with his shoulder as he moved me through the doors and into the club house.

"What's with all the macho stuff?" I asked as Jack pushed me ahead of him past the bar and into the corridor beyond.

I glanced back and saw Paulie giving us acid stares from the balcony.

"You don't wanna know," Jack sighed and slipped his arm around my shoulder again. "Take me for a drink."

"The bar's back there," I giggled but he wouldn't let me turn, propelling me onwards to the exit. I popped through the front doors and onto the steps without looking and ran with a smack into a hard chest. For a second it winded me and strong hands gripped my wrist to stop me pitching down the concrete stairs to ground level.

"Sorry!" I gushed, my chest hurting as I fought to catch my breath. I looked up into Teina Fox's dark eyes and felt my words abandon me. Four other men stood behind him on the stairs as though queuing to collect an award and I gulped and recognised them as referees I'd seen at other games. I shook Teina's grip off my wrists and moved past the knot of men, skipping down the stairs with a haste which promised greater disaster. Jack nodded to Teina and followed me, catching up outside the building.

"Wait up!" he said, striding after me and catching hold of my hand. "What's wrong?"

"Nothing!" I snapped. "I'm fine."

"Where d'ya wanna go?" Jack asked, his eyes searching my face. He wrestled car keys from his front pocket, struggling against the plaster cast and dangled them in front of my face. "You can drive."

I took the keys with a shrug and headed towards the car park, peering in the windows of the downstairs hall as we skirted the building. "You didn't come to the wedding," I stated, my tone accusing and Jack held up his cast.

"Too busy getting plastered," he said with a smirk.

"Yeah, well I missed you." My tone sounded cross. If Jack had been there like he promised, I wouldn't have gone outside with Mark Lambie, met Teina or done something I might live to regret. Still might live to regret. I bit my lip and tried to forget how much fun we'd had and the ache it induced between my thighs which took until Tuesday to heal. I groaned with exasperation. As soon as I felt repentant enough to brave church, a dirty thought about Teina ruined it.

"What's with you?" Jack pressed, his beautiful face creased in concentration. "Something's wrong."

"Just get in the car!" I snatched the keys and deactivated the central locking on his station wagon and he grinned and clambered into the passenger side.

"Ursula." Terry Saint's voice sent a shiver of fear down my spine which felt like icy water. I turned and pushed my bum against the car boot as he approached me, his gait slow and wary.

"Touch me again and I'll scream," I threatened, holding my hand out in front of me. "Jack's in the car. I only have to shout him."

"Don't be stupid!" he snapped. "I won't hurt ya. It was a spur-of-the-moment thing and I'm sorry. I didn't mean for it to happen but the things you said about Pete; he's dead, Ursula. Let it go, please?"

I shrugged and backed around Jack's car, edging towards the wing nearest to the driver's door. "The cops haven't come looking for me yet. I haven't decided what to say."

"Say nothing," he growled, keeping his voice low. "I've sorted out a car with Hemi down at the BMW garage. You can pick it up tomorrow. Your dad gave me your account number and I've given you enough to clear that loan. Don't do anything stupid, girl and we'll call it quits."

"You've what?" My frightened brain struggled to take in his words. He'd paid up. The blackmail worked.

"You heard!" Terry snapped. "But one wrong word, girl and I'll break you. For good this time." He whirled around and disappeared, his heels clicking on the concrete as he rounded the building. My heart raced in my chest and I found a wave of sickness. Another one.

In Jack's car I wrestled with the settings of the seat, mirrors and steering wheel while he laid with his head back against the head rest. "You look like crap," I remarked when I'd adapted the car to my miniscule height. "More like a cup of tea and bed than going out drinking."

Jack rolled his head to face me, one eye squinted closed. "You're probably right. Alcohol and pain killers aren't a good idea, anyway." He sighed. "I just didn't want to go home to an empty house."

"You can stay at mine," I offered, feeling a flare of compassion in my chest for his plight. "I know what loneliness is like."

"I know you do," he conceded, facing forwards. "Sorry I didn't realise until now."

"Why would you?" I asked with a sigh. "Everything in your garden was rosy; I thought it still was. My private Hell was exactly that; mine."

"Yeah, but I haven't been there for you. Pete dying coincided with my marriage falling apart and I got busy and selfish. I'm sorry Ula."

"It's fine." I started the engine and released the handbrake. "Where to then?"

Chapter 18

Jack was right when he said alcohol and painkillers don't mix. I'd drunk him under the table by the end of the second glass of sherry, which was all I could find in the back of the kitchen cupboard. I settled him in the spare bed and took his shoes off, not sure I wanted to cope with another naked male in my personal space. He cut a pitiful figure in the single bed; his tee shirt rucked up and his feet poking off the end of the mattress. I covered him up and put myself to bed, after assembling my marking by the front door ready to grab in the morning before school.

I dreamed about Jack and Lacey, arguing over his refusal to have children. She screamed at him in her peach wedding dress and in my dream, I stood up and clapped, inserting myself between them with a sense of glee as I shoved his wedding band on my own fat finger. The beautiful band of gold wedged itself between the first and second knuckle and I looked down and saw all the soft rolls which used to encase my body. Panicking, I sat up in bed, sweat blistering across my forehead.

The digital numbers on the alarm clock betrayed the midnight hour as I cast around in my confusion and a familiar noise drew my attention to the hallway. The light knocking echoed in the darkness. I slipped from my warm bed and padded along the carpet, standing on tip toes to peek through the peep hole. Teina Fox leaned against the wall opposite, hands thrust deep into his pockets and one foot resting on the wall behind him. As I watched, he appeared to give up and turned to leave.

"It's late!" I squeaked, whipping the front door open. "How did you get in downstairs?"

He faced me, his eyes tired and his pale blue shirt undone at the collar. He looked rumpled and careworn. "You told me to slam the door on my way out the other day but I didn't see if you grabbed any keys. I took the ones off the hook by the door but couldn't find you. I drove around a bit and then tidied up here and went home. I meant to come back but got called into work. This is my first chance to come over." His arms snaked around my waist and he pulled me into him. "You ignored me at the soccer ground." Wounded ego leaked through his voice as he ran his hand underneath my pajama top and touched my soft skin.

"You're a lawyer," I said, my voice muffled in his shoulder. "Why would you get called into work?"

"I just did," he said. "Trust me."

I rolled my eyes, recognising one of my father's stock phrases. He usually said it at the exact moment I'd be better off mistrusting him, the words uttered from desperation or a guilty conscience.

Teina's lips sought my neck, and he nuzzled beneath my hair. I opened my mouth to speak, and he covered my lips with his. "I know, I know," he breathed. "You don't want anyone to know about us."

"There's an 'us' then?" I asked, my heart skipping in my chest. His dark, sultry eyes studied my face, and he lifted his hands and pushed them into my long hair, snagging against the messy ponytail at the back of my head.

"Yes, there's an 'us' and no, you won't get rid of me as easily as you might think."

"I don't want to get rid of you," I murmured, enjoying his kisses on my face and the hardness of the body pressed against mine. "I'm a self-saboteur."

He snuffed out a low chuckle. "Yeah. I can believe that." He bit the underside of my jaw before pressing his forehead to mine. "I've never met anyone like you." His greater height meant he craned his neck to look me in the eye and I wrinkled my nose and pushed my fingers under his dark jacket. I teased his shirt out of his pants and he groaned and stepped away, holding me at arm's length. "I need to go, babe. I just brought your keys back."

Disappointment felt like a knife in my chest and I pursed my lips. In defeat, I held my hand out for my spare keys and Teina placed them into my palm, his fingers brushing my skin. We both felt the connection, and he held my gaze, letting his fingers wander onto the soft skin of my wrist and quirking his lips upwards when I shivered. He took a step forward and wrapped his arms around my back, crushing me into his strong chest. I sighed into the sense of safety he brought and let my fingers wander under his jacket again, caressing the smooth fabric of his shirt in the small of his back. I remembered the guilty ache between my thighs and turned my face up to him, inhaling as Teina's warm lips pressed against my cheek and travelled across to settle on my mouth in a breathtaking kiss. "Sorry about before. Are we good now?" he asked, breaking away and nuzzling in my hair.

"Come in and I'll show you," I whispered, wondering how I could explain away Jack's existence in my spare bedroom.

Teina's lips left a kiss on my forehead and he gave me one last squeeze before letting go. "Not tonight, babe," he replied, his voice a low hush. His thumb ran under my left eye in a soft arc and tracked down my cheeks to rub my bottom lip. "Why did you go to the game tonight? I didn't expect you'd be there after Saturday."

I shrugged. "Wasn't going to but Uncle Larry offered me a ride. I get fed up of my own company." Surprised at my own admission, my cheeks coloured and my obvious discomfort embarrassed me.

Teina caressed my cheek with tenderness and his eyes softened to the colour of treacle. "There's a storm coming Ms Saint," he whispered, shaking his head in a slow movement. "I don't want you caught in it."

I screwed up my features in confusion, regretting how it made my face looked squished. But by the time I'd straightened out my dignity, Teina had already mentally vacated my presence. "What storm?" I demanded and he put his finger up to his lips and shook his head.

"Be careful, Ursula," he said and turned away, ignoring the lift and striding towards the door to the stairs.

"Did the cops ask you about Mark Lambie?" I hissed after him and he turned for a second; just long enough to nod.

"Yeah. Just tell them the truth."

I swallowed and shook my head but he didn't see, already gone with the click of the door into the stair well.

His absence left a disquieting vacuum in the hallway and a cool breeze accentuated my sense of isolation. I tracked it to an open window at the end of the hall and padded across to close it. I used the excuse of fixing the dodgy catch closed to watch for Teina's exit, hoping for one more glimpse of him before I returned to my loneliness. "What else could I tell them?" I mused.

Feeling the vibration of the downstairs door click shut, I pressed my face against the glass and watched as Teina skipped down the front steps, his hands jammed into his pockets. The aftershave he transferred to my face from his, seemed to shroud me in his essence as I watched the top of his dark head move onto the street. He checked left and right before crossing the road, although no traffic moved around my silent neighbourhood at that hour. I scoured the street for his car, looking for its sleek outline under the street lamps but saw only familiar vehicles with their glowing residents' passes glinting in the eerie darkness.

A vehicle slid along the street, pulling to a stop next to Teina. From above, the saloon looked long and glossy, it's colour indeterminable in the street glow. He slipped into the passenger seat and the car waited for a heartbeat before moving off and turning left along a street running perpendicular to mine. It moved in short, jerky runs as the speed increased and the vehicle pushed through its gears, as though the driver's foot was a little too keen on the gas pedal. It paused at the junction ahead and indicated left to head back to the motorway and I realised how little I knew of Teina Fox. He'd given me no contact number or address; a secret, mystery lover whom I possessed no way of reaching. I gaped in surprise as Teina's car did an emergency stop after beginning its journey onto the main road and a white van sped by much too fast. My hand fixed itself across my mouth at the realisation I'd almost witnessed a nasty crash.

The colour drained from my face as the familiar blue and red lights flashed on in the rear window and the long car took off after the van. I gripped the window sill until my fingers ached and concentrated on breathing in and out at regular intervals, desperate to push out the feeling of faintness which started from my chest and worked its message to my brain.

"Ula?" Jack's voice forced me upright and I turned with a look of confusion plastered over my face. "Why are you out here?" His hair stuck up on one side and he looked handsome in a rugged way, carrying his broken wrist close to his body. He stood on my pathetic doormat in his socks, his jeans hanging low having parted company with his tee shirt to display a muscular abdomen covered in silky olive skin.

"Why would a lawyer get into an unmarked cop car?" I asked, my voice echoing in the hallway. I shook my head and ran a hand over my eyes, letting the swearword slip from my lips.

Jack tilted his head to one side and gave me a look of fondness. "You're sleepwalking, Ula," he said, putting me into the basket with all the other cute crazies he dealt with most days. "Come back to bed." He held his arms out to me and I padded towards him, glancing back out of the window. With a clunk, the dodgy catch released itself and the unmistakable sound of a police siren drifted through the gap. Jack glanced through the glass, instinct piquing a cop's interest in the plight of brothers in arms. Seeing only a reflection of the dimly lit hall, I watched him brush it off and beckon me with his good hand. "Come on, sweets," he crooned, brotherly affection in his eyes. "I forgot you did the whole sleepwalking thing." He enfolded me into his chest and kissed the top of my head. "I'll get you a drink and settle you back in bed."

My bed felt cold and unwelcoming as I pushed myself beneath the covers. I heard Jack in the kitchen fighting the microwave one-handed. As good as his word, he brought me the overcooked milk and I scraped the skin away with my fingernail, finding it burning hot on top but cool and gloopy near the bottom of the mug. I sipped, trying not to pull a face at my cousin's botched kindness. Jack settled on Pete's side of the bed, stretching out and laying his head back against the headboard. It felt like we were children again, the solidarity spreading between us like fine copper threads. "I remember when you sleepwalked into the garden at Terry's place," Jack said, his tone light. "Alan stopped you falling in the pool."

I nodded, remembering the shocked sensation of the cold water on my toes as I walked down the first step. The boys hid my near accident from the adults, covering it up as high jinks, cuzzies together having a laugh when Margaret found us and sent us all to bed in disgrace. My sleepwalking became legendary within our generation of the Saint family and proved a source of much teasing and embarrassment growing up. Within the annals of my memory were visions of waking up with a shock, as my mother walked me round and round the cold tiles of the kitchen at our house in Mount Eden. She would find me in the strangest places, looking for things which weren't lost or trying to leave the house in my pajamas. I missed my mother with a familiar ache and tears welled from somewhere near my heart. I suppressed them, not bothering to correct Jack in his inaccurate recollections.

"We're like a pair of odd shoes," Jack sighed, sympathy in his eyes for my unshed tears. He held his good arm out and I put my mug on the bedside table and scooted over, snuggling into his chest. Instinct stopped me explaining about Teina's visit and I let my gentle cousin believe I still grieved for Pete, my mother and our broken marriages.

My alarm woke us at six, clanging into the silence and making us both jump. Jack's cast rested over my thigh and he spooned me from behind, his chin on my shoulder and his body pressed in close. I leaned forward and his face slipped onto my pillow with a groan so I couldn't lay back and resume the comfortable cuddle. I shifted sideways and looked at him. "Do you have work today."

"No." He spoke into the pillow, his voice muffled. Raising the cast, he waved it in my face. "They gave me this week off to recover. I'll go back on light duties next week."

"When does the cast come off?" I asked, yawning and stretching my arms above my head to touch the headboard.

"Three weeks, then they check the stitches from the surgery."

"You had surgery?" I turned to him in surprise.

"Course. The bone stuck through my forearm like a bloody shipwreck."

"No wonder it hurts," I conceded. "Sounds awful."

Jack grunted and rested his head on my shoulder. "Everything's awful," he sighed. "My life's a heap of crap."

I put my arms around him and stroked his hair. "Only temporarily," I soothed. "It'll work out. It just feels bad right now."

Jack's cast felt scratchy against my bare stomach as the pajama top rode up and his fingers stroked the soft skin. "My wife screwed another guy to get pregnant," he said, his voice a low growl. "How can that work out?"

I frowned, not understanding. "So, is she still with him?" I asked and Jack shook his head, his hair tickling my neck.

"No. She thought I'd accept another man's baby just to please her. What kind of crazy logic is that?"

"Don't understand." I hugged him harder and felt the exasperation in the tightness of his body.

"I fire blanks; I can't have kids," he hissed.

"Oh. I assumed you didn't want them," I replied. "You always said you didn't."

"It was unlikely I could. Lacey knew that right from the start and accepted it. Then all of a sudden, she wants a baby so much she finds a guy and gets herself pregnant." Jack's head shake grazed my shoulder. "Bloody hell! This is so messed up."

"Do you still love her?" I asked, feeling the pent up emotion through his muscles.

"I'll always love her," he sighed. "But I can't forgive what she did."

"Did the chemotherapy for that tumour in your knee cause it?" I asked and Jack nodded against my shoulder. "Sorry," I whispered. "I didn't know."

Jack swallowed and his fingers moved against my flesh, sending shivers of excitement to my brain. His cast felt scratchy and rough as his hand moved upwards so his fingers cupped my breast. He shifted, his interest growing and I allowed myself to be fooled by childhood desire and fantasy as he moved across me, balancing himself over me on his elbows. His clothed body felt taut and hard against mine and his kisses on my neck left damp trails of ecstasy. The old me would have relished his sexual attentions and given anything he demanded with a willingness born of idol worship. He could have used and abused me and I would have been grateful enough to thank him for it.

I lay still and analysed myself with a coolness which surprised me as my childhood crush nibbled my breast through my pajama top. The fingers of his good hand grappled with the elastic of my shorts and began to tug as his lips found mine. His kiss held desperation, stale sherry and sleep, but in his eyes I saw pain.

"No!" I pushed at Jack's chest and it felt an age before he stopped and rolled onto his back. I sat up and hugged my knees, his fingers brushing against the small of my back. I wavered, his gentle movements causing erotic sensations to addle my brain.

"Why?" he whispered.

"I just can't." My feet hit the floor and I stood, gathering my fallen hair into a ponytail behind me and yanking a scrunchie from the dresser when I couldn't find the other one, suspecting it would be in the hall where Teina dislodged it. At the thought of him, I felt a stab of guilt and left the room, ignoring Jack's use of my name. In the kitchen I slugged a glass of water and then another, as though ridding myself of the taste of Jack's kisses.

He followed me and leaned against the doorframe, his eyes downcast in misery. "I feel like I should apologise," he mused, his tone heavy with regret. "But I'm not sorry."

"You're married!" I exclaimed. "I'm not interested in messy relationships with married men. My life is complicated enough."

"It should've been you and me who got married, Ula, not you and Pete."

I slammed the glass down on the counter, hearing the tinny click as a crack began in the outer layer and worked its way up to the rim. "Are you freaking kidding me?" My voice sounded ugly as a screech and Jack took a step backwards. "You never liked me in that way!"

"Of course I bloody did!" he bit, his face angry. "Always! I wanted to take you to the school ball in fifth form and your dad threatened to break my legs! So I took Lacey instead and the rest is history. Jordan promised it would never happen so I gave up. The day you married Pete, I got so drunk at the reception, I don't remember the next two days." Jack hovered in the doorway, repelled by my expression of painful astonishment.

"Dad did what?"

"I thought you knew." Jack's crossed the distance in two strides and his arms wrapped around me, tightening into a powerful hold. He kissed my forehead and dragged his lips down the side of my face in a hail of kisses. "It was always you; I didn't want anyone else."

"But Lacey! You married Lacey!"

"I know." Jack leaned back and watched the horror in my expression. "I'm sorry."

"You broke my heart!" I slammed my fist into his chest and he grunted. Tears of fury pricked behind my eyes and I hit him again. "I loved you and didn't know how to say it. One minute you're everything to me and the next, you're marrying Lacey!"

Jack gripped both my wrists with his left one to stop me pounding on his chest. My angry shrieks turned to miserable wails as he held me and rocked me against his body. "I'm sorry, Ula," he breathed, "I'm so sorry. I thought you knew and didn't care."

"Didn't care?" My chest heaved. "That afternoon when you kissed me, I thought I'd never been happier." I freed my left hand and hit him again. "Then you asked Lacey to the ball and two seconds later you were married."

Jack's lips against mine felt like an answer to prayer and I wished I could send us both back in time to our teens and start again. Maybe we could've saved ourselves a whole heap of trouble. He pushed his hands into my hair and ran me up against the pantry door, the handle digging into my spine. His cast felt heavy on my shoulder as he stroked my cheek, his other smoothing the skin over my hips and pushing at my pajama shorts. I leaned in to his kiss, sharing the frantic wave of emotion and surfing the crest like a frightened novice.

He lifted me with a hiss of pain at his broken wrist and sat me on the counter, fitting his hips between my legs. His good hand roved over my body, making me feel stripped and vulnerable and despite the excitement and craving, I remembered Teina's gentle, energetic lovemaking. The memory jarred me and I pressed my mouth against Jack's collar bone, abdicating from his kiss and experiencing a stab of regret which began in my gut and moved through my chest. The realisation bit me with force and I knew it wouldn't work. Fifteen years made a world of difference in my perception and even though I loved Jack no less than I did during our only teenage fumble, I couldn't see us together.

"Stop, Jack. Stop."

I felt his rapid heartbeat through my own chest and his ragged puffs of breath made his body tremble. His dark eyes channelled betrayal as he glared at me with thwarted desire.

I fixed my arms around his neck and held him, pulling him into a tight embrace and leaving no room for lust or sex. "It's too late," I whispered into his ear. "We're not kids anymore."

I expected anger, not brokenness and his reaction destroyed me. He shook in my arms and soaked my hair with his tears, clinging on to my waist as though he'd be snatched away if he let go. "What should I do?" he sniffed, keeping his face averted and his arms clamped around me as he struggled to find his equilibrium. "I feel so lost."

"I don't know, Jack," I whispered, rubbing his back. "You need to speak to Lacey, not me."

"I loved you so much," he breathed, stroking my cheek with shaking fingers. His eyelashes looked glossy and damp from his tears and his bedhead accentuated his fragility.

"I wish I'd known," I said, sadness enveloping me in a shroud of lost opportunities and a life lived on the dreadful stage of Plan B. "Everything would've been so different." I smiled through the pain and searched for the elusive rainbow. "I wouldn't have become a fat chick."

Jack wrinkled his nose. "I never noticed." He looked down at my slender waist and neat breasts and gave me a wink filled with fake bravado. "You're pretty hot now though. Sure you don't fancy a quick one for old time's sake?"

My mouth opened in horror and Jack covered it with his lips. When he stepped back and let go of me, regret coursed through my veins at the shift in our combined universe. I rested my hands on his shoulders and slipped off the counter, bracing myself against his body as my feet found the floor. "Did you love Pete?" he asked, stroking my cheek with tender fingers.

I shook my head and admitted my life's worst secret. "No. I married him because my father made me and he left me with more debt than I knew how to solve. He didn't love me, nor I him. We were thrown together for the Saint's convenience; the fat spinster and the one man who would bring the Saint's into disrepute for his whoring." I felt a stab of guilt at the pain in Jack's face and as he opened his mouth, I placed my index finger over his lips. "And no, he didn't stop whoring and no, he didn't get it from me either."

I glanced at the clock and saw the hands move past the half hour. "I've got work," I said, dashing from the kitchen. "Grab some breakfast while I have a shower."

Chapter 19

Thursday turned to custard from the moment the children entered the building. A windy day always guaranteed drama but the tiny tornadoes whipping up leaves and debris in a sheltered corner of the playground wound them up into a frenzy of emotion. Helen dealt with two spats in the line on the way in and I ended up with a sobbing child on my knee during registration, hemorrhaging tears and snot onto my blouse until it soaked through to my skin. "Come on, Lawrie," I said, keeping my voice light. "Help me take the register." I shifted so I could see the names written on the left of the floppy book. "I'll call them out and you point to them."

The child spent a happy five minutes pointing to random parts of the page while I called out names and received a polite, "Good morning Mrs Saint," from those present. To my surprise Lawrie fixed on his own name before I got to it, turning with a beatific smile on his face.

"A mornin' a Saint," he said, his face eager as I nodded and shook his hand as Helen had done the other children. A formal acknowledgement of their existence seemed to set them up for the day as they greeted me and her with good eye contact and a smile. If I taught them nothing else, it would be social skills and a damn good handshake; firm but not finger crushing. We were getting there. I needed to remember they were only five-years-old as I kept my expectations high and drove them on to better things than the sad lives some of them endured.

Jack texted me and I read it at lunchtime. '*Can I stay with you for a while?*' he asked and I chewed my lip and wondered about the wisdom of it. I bought a sandwich from the dairy next to the school and wandered around the playground during my duty, answering after a colleague relieved me.

'*Depends,*' I said, hoping he understood my reservations.

'*Yeah, I get it. Hands off,*' came his reply.

'*Ok then. Spare keys are on the hook in the kitchen.*'

He didn't reply but once I finished work I travelled to the BMW garage where I'd been five months before, forced to sell my lovely car at a loss and bussing home with a bag full of cash and a wounded heart. Hemi greeted me at the front gate, almost bowling me over in his enthusiasm. "Hey, Mrs Saint!" he trilled from twenty metres away. "I've got a treat for you."

Relief coursed through my veins as I'd spent the whole bus ride anticipating difficulty and running through a conversation which began with him knowing nothing about Terry's promise. "I spoke to Mr Saint," he said, allaying my fears. "We've picked out just the thing."

I tried not to cringe and prepared my face to mask disappointment when presented with a barely roadworthy heap of metal. So fixed on looking for something disguised as a skip on wheels, I missed the direction he took me until I stood next to a cornflower blue SUV, complete with alloys and a leather interior. The motif on the front claimed it was a German built BMW but I didn't dare hope. "Are you sure?" I asked. "I thought it would be less..."

"Less colourful, I know," Hemi gushed. "But Mr Saint said you'd love it. It's taxed and the warrant of fitness starts from today. It's only four years old so it'll do you for a while. I like to think of it as eye catching and only someone as classy as you could pull it off." He waxed lyrical for a further ten minutes, despite not having to sell it to me. Uncle Terry was right. I loved it.

"It looks expensive." I chewed my lip. "Is it legal?"

Hemi Brown paused in his diatribe and fixed warm dark eyes on my face. His lips quirked upwards as he feigned offence. "I don't sell knock off shit!" he squawked, his voice reaching girly heights at the end of the sentence. "It's all legit, bro', I promise. It's got an AA report and everything."

In his forties but still wearing his trousers so low I could see his shorts underneath, he did a peculiar skippy dance that made me snort. "I suppose if it was nicked, someone would notice it fairly fast." I imagined myself driving it and my heart gave a leap of pleasure. My old car was black and this would be part of my new start. I felt like a sex maniac when I thought of Teina in a near naked state and perhaps the car best fitted the sinful woman I'd become. The vicar had his work cut out to bring me back on the straight and narrow. "Let me see the AA certificate and have a test drive," I said. "Then I'll sort out insurance."

"It's all done, missus," Hemi said, hiking his trousers up as he increased gear to cover the forecourt. "I just gotta give youse da keys."

"How?" I ran to catch up with him. "You need my driver history to insure me."

"I had it remember?" He winked at me and eyed me up and down with slow precision. "From your last purchase with Hemi and Bros Vehicle Services."

It all sounded dodgy to me, but when he handed me the insurance cover note for my old company with the stamp saying PAID over the invoice number, I had to believe him. "So, no test drive then?" I asked as he handed me two sets of keys.

"Na," he said. "We're closing now. Me and the boys is goin' fishing. You'll be right."

He explained the rudiments of the vehicle and waved me off as I slid into the traffic like a cupcake in a feast of brownies. I stuck out in my expensive cornflower blue BMW, but the feeling verged on exhilaration as I cruised home in a quarter of the time it took on the bus. I'd always owned a parking space in the underground garage and slid into it, just as the father from downstairs crept around the corner in his beige station wagon. "Oh," he called through his passenger window as I emerged and activated the central locking. "I park." His broken English made me cock my head to aid understanding and the man pointed at my space. He hovered in place as though expecting me to jump back in my SUV and move it for him.

I glanced at the wall where the big number 12 corresponding with my apartment number, was spray painted in white at least half a metre high. "It's my space," I said. "I've got a car again now so I'll be using it."

"What? What?" he said, his face pale in the dim lighting of the garage. He stared at me as though his current misfortunes were my fault.

"You can't park there," I replied and sauntered past. His wheels screeched as he took off at speed in a temper, rounding the pillars at the end fast enough to spin the back tyres. He met me back on the small crossing in front of the lifts, squealing to a halt as though having contemplated killing me for my space. My euphoria melted from my heart and trickled into my feet and I hated him for ruining my lovely afternoon and the shininess of my gift. His window was still open and he glared at me through it. Anger bubbled to the surface and I crossed to his driver's window and heard my own voice emerge from between my lips, strong and true. "You really don't want to mess with me," I said through gritted teeth. I heard my father in the veiled threat and it surprised me, but not enough to dispense with the power it offered. I put my hand on his windowsill and watched him flinch. "I can see your brain working," I said, my voice cold. "You'll try to beat me home tomorrow to get my space and assume I'll just call the apartment supervisor. He'll do nothing and you'll have reclaimed something that wasn't yours to begin with." I leaned down, temper heating up my eyes until it felt as though they blazed in my face. "I don't recommend you engaging in a game like that." I held up my fingers and counted his options off for him. "Rent another space, park outside or get rid of a vehicle. And while we're at it, I might like a donation towards the six months of parking you've had because I forgot to cancel my rental agreement." My eyes glared and I watched him shrink at my vehemence. I felt angry enough to rip his head from his shoulders and he knew it. "Don't. Mess. With. Me." I said, enunciating each word before stepping away. I jerked my head to the right, wanting him to move first, so I didn't present him with the opportunity to accidentally slip his clutch and mow me down. He sped off and up the ramp, waiting for the roll gate to rise before speeding off onto the street.

My heart pounded in my chest and my breath came in snatches. It occurred to me I didn't know who I was anymore. And I hadn't forgotten to cancel the rental. The tiny portion of my apartment fee covering the garage parking space had been my way of holding onto the past. I could pretend I would one day fill the space with a vehicle; that my life wasn't entirely a failure. Today was the day.

"Hey, Ula. How was your day?" Jack asked, rising from the couch and rubbing his eyes. "You're very late. I forgot to ask if you had a staff meeting."

"Not tonight." I twirled the car keys in my pocket, clinking them and enjoying the sound. "I picked up my new car."

In the process of opening the fridge, Jack whirled around with an excited look on his face. "Truly?" He bit his lip and reminded me of the tousle haired boy who delighted in anything new amongst the cousins. Jack always had to press and poke and try things, pushing them to their limit while the new owner watched in horror.

"No way!" I answered the unasked question and jerked my head towards the cast on his arm and he shrugged. "If it's an automatic, I'll be fine. I'm still driving mine."

"I bet you're not supposed to!" I scoffed. "Your insurance might have something to say about it."

"I bought a cooked chicken and salad for dinner," he said, running a hand along his bristly jaw. "But I wanna see your car now."

Pride flared in my heart and then faded as I thought about how to explain its sudden appearance. "It's nothing special. I've finished paying Pete's debts so treated myself. I'm sick of the bus."

"Pete's debts were that big?" Jack looked around and I saw the pennies drop into the slot in his brain as he considered my reduced circumstances in a different light. "I knew there were some, but not massive ones. Why didn't you ask for help?"

I shrugged and busied myself with the kettle, pressing buttons to make it boil and slapping a bag of green tea into a mug. "Nobody else's business."

Jack ran his hand up my back and his fingers fondled the curls in my ponytail. "It's my business, Ula."

"I don't think your wife would've felt the same way." I turned and leaned my bum against the pantry cupboard, detaching myself from Jack's touch and the look of longing in his eyes. He swallowed and I broke the moment, jangling the keys. "Do you wanna see it?" A look of mischief in my face made him laugh.

"Hell yeah!"

Chapter 20

He raved with enthusiasm as only Jack Saint could, walking around the entire vehicle and admiring the colour, the shape and the smart leather interior. "This is radical!" he gushed, fingering the BMW logo on the rear. He opened the boot and closed it again. "Must've cost you a fortune!"

I swallowed and smiled. "I fell in love with it."

"Where'd you get it?" Jack's words filled me with misgiving and I whispered Hemi's name in a muffled squeak which the cavernous parking garage picked up and echoed around my head.

"Ah yeah." Jack didn't sound surprised. "He supplies lots of the cars for All Saints and their minivan for games. You need to be a bit careful but he generally flies on the right side of the law."

"Generally?" The foreboding in my voice alerted him to my discomfort and he closed the rear passenger door and put a comforting arm around my shoulder.

"Want me to check it out?"

He responded to my nod by reaching for his cell phone one-handed and making a hushed call, leaning against the wall staring at my front bumper. His low voice echoed as a steady rumble and my heart clenched, not wanting the vehicle to prove stolen or written off in some hideous fatal accident and glued together in a dodgy chop shop. I opened the boot and busied myself making checks I should have done in Hemi's presence, sighing with relief at the brand new spare tyre, nestled under the rear rug. I poked around and found a crow bar, jack and tool bag in a panel over the rear wheel arch.

"All good." Jack made me jump as he appeared behind me, his face smiling with approval. "I asked a mate at Mangere to check it out and it's fine. Nothing wrong at all. Congratulations." He pressed his lips to my forehead and lingered over the kiss, disappointed when I pulled away.

"I'll drive," I said, dodging past him and closing the boot. "You can buy me dinner."

Jack griped about having already bought dinner and I slapped his leg and laughed at him as we left the parking garage. My downstairs neighbour waited for me to exit and headed off down the ramp as I watched him in my rear-view mirror. "I bet he nicks my space." I hovered in the small roadway and Jack screwed his head round to watch the tail lights disappear into the dim car park and the latticed roll door close with a series of metallic clicks and clunks.

"Don't you rent it?" Jack asked, watching my face flush with dread. I nodded and he watched me for a second. "Trouble?"

I indicated left and merged with the steady traffic, explaining my dilemma. "I haven't been down there since I got rid of the old car, so didn't realise he'd been using my space. He got rather upset when I wouldn't move out of it earlier and I kind of threatened him."

"You what?" Jack's merry laughter destroyed the last vestiges of my confidence.

"Yeah, thanks for that!" I spat, heading downtown and deliberately aiming for the most expensive restaurants on Quay Street as revenge.

"I just can't imagine it," he mused, watching me sideways through narrowed eyes.

"It wasn't my finest hour," I grumbled, pressing too hard on the accelerator and scaring him enough to make him face forward.

Jack's idea of dinner out ended up as fish and chips on the beach. We sat side by side in a patch of sand as the sun removed its light by degrees and darkness shrouded us in simplicity. "You have the rest," I said, wiping my greasy fingers on a tissue from my pocket. "I'm stuffed."

"Me too." Jack crumpled the wrapper and balled it next to him, fixing his eyes on the water as it sent white waves onto the Mission Bay sand. "Have you settled in East Tamaki?" he asked. "Don't you miss Devonport and the sea being so close?"

"Of course I do. Moving from a beautiful house near the beach to an apartment block wasn't in the grand plan for my life. It was pure necessity."

"Because of the debts you mentioned?"

"Yeah. They didn't die with Pete; just became repayable with immediate effect and I didn't have the money."

"What kind of debts were they?" he asked and I saw the flicker of a cop's interest.

I sighed and listed them one at a time, crossing the seventy-thousand-dollar mark with a memory of the sick feeling the number caused. "Online gambling attributed some of it but he'd done other, really odd things with cash loans that were never accounted for. He'd got into a mess and selling up and modifying my lifestyle seemed the only quick way out."

"Until now."

Jack's words stilled me and I realised how incongruous the opulent car must appear. "Yeah. I had a year left on the last of the loans and they agreed to let me pay monthly. I've lived like a monk and cleared it early." The lie tripped off my tongue like an Olympic diver.

"Weren't there penalties for that?" Jack asked, his gaze intense.

I hid my cringe as much as possible. "Worth it just to have them off my back. Can we not talk about my private finances anymore?" My voice sounded pleading and needy.

"Ok." Jack put his arm around me and pulled me close. I felt the comfort of his strong arm muscles and the hardness of his ribs as I nestled in. But I'd seen something else in his eyes; something really worrying. He'd watched me with the eyes of a cop, one who could spot a lie at fifty paces and wanted to chase it down like a hungry lion. He stopped because I asked him but it hadn't left his sphere of thought and hung there whenever he caught my eye. I couldn't tell Jack about Terry's gift because of the dirty way I'd earned it, threatening him with his son's indiscretions. Nor was he aware of Peter Saint's sexual preferences.

The thing in my cousin's eyes looked like something different. The suspicion ran deeper than me finishing a loan or coming into money and as the evening wore on and we spent more time together, I realised he thought I'd done something criminal; something which might attach to him and his career. Neither of us raised it as we dumped our rubbish in a public bin and spread white sand all over the carpets of my new SUV. But it hung over us like a mantle.

My brain felt rattled by the time I crept under the roll door into the parking garage and the sentence roiled round and round in my thoughts. "What the hell does he think I've done?"

Chapter 21

I put the handbrake on and stared at my neighbour's car, nestled between a pillar and the vehicle next to him.

"I thought you said you threatened him," Jack said, watching my face as an embarrassing blush crept into my cheeks.

"Well, it was obviously really effective and terrified him." I didn't hold back on the barb in my tone.

"I'll go see him. Where does he live?" Jack wrestled with the door handle and hefted himself out.

"Ground floor," I sighed. "It's messed up because his wife has 12a, which would be mine if I had a partner but their other space is number 2 near the exit."

"If there was a 2a, wouldn't they have both?"

"There isn't a 2a." I glanced behind me at the empty bay where his car should be. "The ground floor flats have a second space outside in the car park. The landlord thinks it's easier for them to walk outside. He leased the mother the park next to me on the understanding I didn't need it." I chewed my lip. "I guess if I complain he'll intervene and revoke the second space, but getting hold of him through the land agent is impossible."

"Take his space for now," Jack said, pointing to the empty number 2. "Reverse in and then you can drive straight out."

"I haven't reversed it yet!" I squeaked. "I'll ding it."

Jack snorted out a laugh. "It's got so many bloody sensors; it could probably park itself! Get on with it, woman!" He strolled off towards the lifts, ignoring the button in favour of the stairs. He was right about the reversing sensors. The automated BMW voice told me everything I needed to know and then repeated it at least eleven times in case I was either hard of hearing or suffered from short-term memory loss. The big SUV slid into the ample space under the guidance of the smooth Australian male voice and I left the gear stick in reverse, just to hear him say, "Half a metre of clearance to the rear," just one more time.

I brushed sand off the mats from the foot well into the open space in front of the car, waiting for Jack to return. I gulped when he strode out of the lift with my neighbour, who sported a child on his shoulders. "This is Ahmed," Jack said, introducing us like strangers. He pointed to the man's shoulders. "And this is Liliane."

I watched through eyes filled with wariness as the man's face remained blank. Jack turned to me. "Liliane can't walk. She's got Cerebral Palsy. Ahmed's wife explained the problem. They need to park the cars together so that in the morning, Ahmed can carry Liliane downstairs and then help his wife with the younger kids. He takes Liliane to school, but he needs to help his wife load in the other children or they run around down here and it's usually busy by the time they leave."

I looked at the man's blank face and felt my heart squeeze in my chest. I taught primary school children and he was trying to keep his own safe. "I'm so sorry," I gushed, noticing how the little girl's legs hung at odd angles on her father's chest and she clung to a clump of his hair as though it was a natural riding position. I looked to Jack for a solution and watched him in cop-mode, negotiating using his hands. "Ursula can have this space, and you take hers?" he said, pointing to my car and then to the man's battered station wagon.

Ahmed nodded, a huge up and down action which almost pitched the child off his shoulders. "Ee!" he said with enthusiasm. "Ee."

I pointed over at the locked cabinets above the parking space and mimed the turning of a key. "I've got stuff in there," I said, directing my concern to Jack. "I'll need to get it out."

Jack jabbed his finger at the cabinet above my vehicle and Ahmed shook his head and wagged his finger. "La sha," he said and shrugged, forcing the girl to use both hands and adopt another clump of the tufty black hair.

"He's got nothing in there," Jack confirmed. He pointed towards the cabinet over number 12 and the man nodded again with vigor. Rushing across, he unlocked the vehicle, dumping the little girl into the passenger seat and running around to the driver's side. He jammed a key from his pocket into the ignition and dropped the car forward so Jack and I could scoot behind. I used the key from my fob to open the heavy doors and together we unloaded the cupboard.

"Don't hurt yourself," I said to Jack, watching him struggle to use his broken wrist. "I'll do it. I meant to clear this stuff out months ago but kept putting it off."

Ahmed ferried items to the bottom of the lift and the men held the door open using one of the stacker boxes while we pushed the rest over the corrugated metal surface. When the cupboard was empty, Ahmed dropped his car back into place, reattached his daughter to his shoulders and smiled as I handed over the key. He swapped it for the one matching the cupboard behind my vehicle and we parted as friends, despite my need to repeat my apology another eighty times.

"He doesn't speak English," Jack said under his breath and I nodded.

"I still shouldn't have been so mean." I looked at him with curiosity. "What language does he speak?"

"Arabic." Jack didn't miss a beat. "He brought his family over from Syria."

I groaned and rolled my eyes. Teina Fox had lit a fire in my belly which seemed determined to erupt from my mouth. I contemplated his hold on my soul and wished I could believe it was all bad.

On the third floor, Jack jammed the lift doors again and pushed items out with his foot while I hauled them over to the front door. I unlocked the apartment while he removed the stacker box and let the lift go about its business. "What is it?" Jack asked and I shrugged.

"Pete's," I said, my voice reflecting my remembered exhaustion of the weeks after his death and the hurried exit from our shared home. "I got rid of most things I couldn't sell but these boxes contain random things I didn't have time to look through. I'll give most of it to Terry and Margaret to deal with."

"Don't you want to look through it first?" Jack nudged a dusty box with his toe, a policeman's curiosity in his eyes.

"Not really." Aware I sounded far too dismissive, I added a smile. "I've got work in the morning and I'm tired. Thanks for dinner."

"Hey. Thanks for the company." Jack wrapped me in his arms and I fought the tug on my heart strings which promised how easy it would be to fall into his bed and pick up the fragile threads of our teenage connection. I yearned for companionship and solidarity and Jack offered all those things. Then I thought of Lacey and how easily my childhood crush replaced me without a minute's argument and the feeling passed. I avoided his lips and closed myself into my bedroom, falling asleep as soon as my head hit the pillow.

Chapter 22

"**I**s Mark Lambie still missing?" I asked Jack the next morning as I shoved toast into my mouth and applied mascara at the same time. He looked up at me from his position on the lounge floor amidst the detritus from Pete's life and shrugged.

"Haven't heard anything. Guess so."

"I wonder where he's gone," I mused, shoving the lid on my mascara and ramming it back into the cutlery drawer. The compact mirror snapped shut in my fingers after a final examination of my makeup and I pushed it into my handbag. "He was just a bit drunk when we dropped him off."

"We?" Sharp as a knife was our Jack and I swallowed and hesitated a moment too long.

"A guy from the club gave us a ride to Mark's place and then dropped me home. He seemed nice enough but neither of us wanted to be puked on so leaving Mark on the doormat was a mutual decision."

"What was his name?" Jack's hair stuck up on end and a line of dust created a black smudge on his forehead. He hadn't shaved and still wore yesterday's clothes.

"Bloody hell, Jack!" I exclaimed. "Twenty questions! Check with your mates; I told them everything. How'd you expect me to remember some stranger a week later?"

I pointed at the mess on my lounge floor. "I want that stuff put away by the time I get home. I never want to see Pete's junk again; do you understand?" I couldn't reign in my vehemence and knew that Jack's perception would see right through my protestations. "Please put it back in the boxes for his parents," I demanded.

He sloped off to the bathroom, leaving me to clear up the kitchen after my foray and I walked through to the lounge to peer over the mess. There were notebooks and odd bits of clothing scattered in a large arc around Jack's absent body and my eyes came to rest on a laptop next to the sofa.

"Ooh!" I swooped down and seized it, hefting it into my arms. I couldn't see a charger nearby but my eyes lit up. Pete's old Apple Mac had to stay plugged in or it died and I needed a replacement. I turned it bottom upwards and checked the manufacturer's logo, realising with a skip of pleasure it looked the same as the one in my class. "I'll charge the laptop at work," I called down the hallway towards the closed bathroom door.

"What?" Jack replied and I ignored him, leaving the apartment before my wily cousin could put his finger on my sore spot through his investigation of Pete's possessions. Admitting I'd been duped into marrying a closet homosexual wasn't a source of shame in itself, but having Jack know I'd considered pregnancy by him acceptable, increased my bloom of embarrassment to fever pitch as I entered the parking garage. Nor did I want further questions about Teina Fox, which would end up with an admission of our night of unbridled passion and the fact I still thought of him almost constantly; hankering for more of the same.

The cornflower blue BMW lit my face with instant effect. Excitement bubbled at the realisation I wouldn't have to wait by the bus stop in driving rain or sit for hours while it crawled a circuitous route through the city taking us all home. The perfectly engineered hunk of blue metal would cut my journey time into a third and overnight, I'd become my own boss again.

The sunny day fit my wonderful mood and I buzzed down the motorway towards school, windows down and the radio blaring like a teenager. When a severe looking man in a Jeep cut me up on the turn towards Takapuna, I used Helen's tactic and waved. He looked uncomfortable, his olive face flushing a deep red and then to my amusement, waggled his fingers back at me.

I plugged the laptop into my charger in the corner of the classroom and left it there, teaching the children with my usual brand of enthusiasm and backed up by Helen's bad cop routine. My first chance to open it arrived at morning tea time when Vanessa called an emergency meeting with the management team and kicked everyone else out of the staffroom.

"What's that about?" Helen asked, retreating to the classroom with her coffee and sandwich. "She threw us out!"

"No idea," I mused. "Probably money, it usually is."

Helen grunted and went outside, sitting on the bench under my window surrounded by adoring children. I listened to the tenderness in her voice and saw her feeding her sandwich to the hungriest of the class like a mother sparrow feeding torn off meat to baby birds.

When curiosity dictated I should fire it up, the laptop behaved as though closed mid-task only the day before and not abandoned for half a year. The screen opened onto a chat room page with a thumbnail picture of a saxophone at the top. The name of the profile owner was 'Musician', with a header photo depicting a landscape scene of a Devonport park. I'd been to it with Pete heaps of times in the days when we walked together and communicated like married adults. There were over four thousand notifications pending in a box in the corner and a speech bubble demanding attention for over seventy missed conversation prompts.

I opened up the private message box and flicked through, assuming most of the profile names were fake, although a few looked genuine. '*I missed you tonight, baby,*' one remarked, the date of the message set four years earlier. My breakfast rolled in my stomach at the thought of who might have typed the message or why he missed my dead husband. I closed the lid of the machine as Helen brought the class back indoors like a string of baby chicks bouncing behind her.

The laptop pulled at me the whole day, luring me over during lunch time and causing me to miss an important announcement in the staffroom.

"Vanessa's bloody leaving!" Helen raged afterwards, hissing under her breath. "She said if the ministry doesn't give a shit, why should she?"

I commiserated and waited until she went outside before scrolling back through message after message, sorting out the indecent from the blatantly lewd with a calm which surprised me. I should've felt worse, glimpsing this private view into Pete's secret world and hearing the voices of his many and varied sexual partners through the typed text. Yet it affected me less than I'd believed. Some of the messages were graphic and included photographs and after the horror of the first few, I couldn't look, getting the gist and closing down those boxes in rapid succession.

Unused to social media and technologically naïve, it never occurred to me that my actions would draw online attention, or that the other members in the conversations would receive a notification when their message was read. I hadn't banked on the flurry of response or the sudden influx of notifications which heralded a barrage of questions.

'Hey, baby, where've you been?'

'Big boy! We need to meet up xoxo'

'I've missed you so much!'

'I heard you were dead.'

Seeing the messages pop up in the browser, I read the first line and resisted clicking on them, not interested in the rest of their dialogue. I worked through the remainder, reading them quickly and then right clicking the mouse to mark them unread, hoping nobody would notice. My heart pounded and I cursed my mistake. The tiny picture of the saxophone remained greyed out, but the messages kept coming. Looking at the name, 'Musician' as Pete's profile made me sad, reminding me of his gentle guitar strumming during better times.

One conversation caught my attention because the first line said, *'Don't do it.'* It tugged on my curiosity and drove me forward, working out how to open the whole conversation without marking the message as read. My heart gave an unexpected jolt in my chest as I recognised a different kind of relationship in play. This person spoke to my husband without the dirty sexual references and their conversation seemed at times, like an agony of revelation. When I read my own name on the screen, I knew I'd have to read it all.

The conversation began five years previously, during the early months of our sham marriage. I swallowed and picked at the ridged scab which made a poor job of keeping my heart safe, hoping I could find some inner catharsis in truth. I should've known better.

'I need to tell Ursula the truth. This isn't fair on her.'

'Don't you dare! Keep her happy, give her a kid and nobody needs to know.'

'But it's killing me. Don't you care?'

'No. You know how the world feels about people like us. Do you honestly think the lads on a Saturday will get naked in the changing room once they know? They'll be too scared to bend down for the soap. Don't do it.'

'Life's not like that anymore. The lads will be fine. I've got taste too. I don't automatically fancy every dude I see.'

'Don't do it!'

'I can't live a lie anymore. It's not fair on Ursula. She doesn't deserve this.'

'Don't. I'm telling you. Don't.'

I felt sick to my stomach. Pete wanted to tell me and this confidante convinced him not to. I would remain ignorant for a further two and a half years after that sentence was typed, believing myself ugly and working hard to slim down and create a more appealing bed fellow for a man who just wasn't interested in women. I revolted him and the realisation made the fragile love I'd fostered for him turn to ash in my mouth. The other party to the conversation typed under the name 'Plus One' and I hated him for denying me the truth, a bubbling, broiling emotion which fostered an ache in my temples.

I slammed the laptop lid and left it charging under my desk, teaching my babies mathematics, full words in phonetics and reading an extended story as the heavy clocked ticked on the wall above the door. But it drew me like a sickness, filling me with the need to know more. At every opportunity I slunk back to the chat room, making sure I showed up as 'offline' each time, so I could go back through the four-year conversation from the start.

'How do you live the lie? How does your wife not know?' Pete asked.

'I can't let her. She has no idea.'

'But Ursula wants a baby. I should just tell her and let her find someone else to get pregnant with. I could support her and a kid financially. I wouldn't mind.'

'No. Father your own child.'

'I CAN'T!'

The sentence pained me as I read it, remembering my husband's stellar efforts on our wedding night. Alcohol made him sappy and I wondered if he took some other mind bending drug as he'd flipped me over and taken me from behind, his roughness a surprise after a courtship of gallantry and chastity. Sore and disappointed, it felt all wrong and I'd hoped things would improve. I shook my head at my own blindness back then.

'Pretend she's someone else.'

I stared in disbelief at the words, the cruelty leaving an arrow trace through my heart. I put my hand up to my mouth and bit down on the inside of my fingers, no longer able to read the coldness in the other person's advice. It explained the method behind the only other time Pete made love to me, not that it could be called that. Fumbled and brutal after the only time Peter Saint received a red card on the pitch, I never ever asked for his clemency again. He'd balanced on his elbows above me with his eyes misted by rage, grinding for ages until I cried with relief at being allowed off the bed and into the safety of the bathroom. I realised then that a child wouldn't fix our marriage and stopped asking. Figuring I'd made a terrible error of judgement, I buried myself in my work, keeping up a great pretence for family and friends and heading towards my thirties with a broken spirit.

Somehow despite my horror, Pete's secret conversation brought me comfort with its clarifying flare of hindsight. The problem was him, not me. I could go on. He couldn't. I thought of Teina's gentle ministrations and my lips quirked at the memory of pleasures I hadn't known possible before him. I used the feelings he created in the pit of my stomach to overwrite the nastiness of sex with Pete and the misery of my marriage, planting Teina's loving as a garden of flowers in my mind to cover up the barren, empty ground. I'd slept with a referee and not just any. I'd danced on Peter Saint's grave using the man who dealt him a red card with a strong, outstretched arm and a fixed smile on his face. What's more; I'd enjoyed it.

Chapter 23

I laid in bed late on Saturday with my cell phone on silent. I suspected my father would text his fat little fingers off trying to force me to go to the game in the afternoon and planned ahead, having unplugged the landline the night before.

Jack stuck his head around my bedroom door at lunchtime, grinning as I sat ensconced in my duvet with stacks of lesson plans scattered around me. "What you up to?" he asked.

"School stuff," I said and ran a hand through my tangled fringe. "Where were you last night?"

"Out, Mum!" he said with sarcasm.

"Are you going out again now?" I asked.

He nodded. "Yeah. Hey, you know the boxes of stuff we brought upstairs? What happened to the laptop?"

I shrugged. "It was knackered. Wouldn't turn on."

Disappointment scudded across Jack's handsome face like cloud cover. "Oh. I wanted it."

"Sorry." I feigned indifference, feeling the temperature hike between us but not understanding why.

"What did you do with it?" he pressed and I frowned.

"It doesn't matter if it's broken!"

"I might be able to get it working," he persisted. "I'll pay you for it."

"For a knackered laptop!" I scoffed. "Don't be ridiculous."

"I'd really like it," he repeated and I detected the hard edge in his voice.

I stared at him and tried to read his face expression, coming up empty when usually I knew his inner thoughts as though they were my own. "You should have said something," I sighed, picking up a picture of a bunny rabbit shaped from the letter 'b' and pretending to examine it. His eyes bore into the side of my face. "It's gone now, sorry."

"But where did you put it?" he demanded and I narrowed my eyes.

"Jack, stop!" I thumped the rabbit onto the bed and saw it bend in half with a ruinous crease. "Bloody hell, man! Go into town and score yourself one that works. The Easter sales are still on for goodness sake."

I closed my eyes and heard him leave, confused by the nonsensical argument. The front door slammed and I heaved a sigh of relief as the tension left with him, blowing out as rapidly as it blew in. Unable to concentrate, I kneeled on the floor next to my bed and reached underneath. The laptop slid into my fingers, inviting me to experience more of Peter Saint's confidences. The home screen showed a full battery and I closed the lid again, rolling up the charger and sitting it on top. "Not today," I told it. "I'm not in the mood."

Clearing a passage through my clothes in the wardrobe, I sought the safe buried into the wall and tapped in the code. The dim light revealed my passport and other important documents and I wedged the laptop into the slender space, just managing to fit it in and close the door. The charger proved too much of a stretch and I hid it in my underwear drawer. I projected thoughts of gratitude towards the architects of the ugly nurses' home who employed extreme foresight in some matters and ineptitude in others. The safe in each apartment counted as the former and the lack of a separate toilet and bath as the latter.

I heated a tub of noodles in the microwave as Jack slammed his way back into the flat and flung his backside into a bar stool. "Want some?" I waggled the fork at him and he shook his head.

"I need to talk to you," he said, his tone serious.

"Sounds important." I shovelled noodles into my mouth from the tub, feeling decadent for a Saturday afternoon. "You not going to the game?"

Jack snorted. "I never go to the games."

"Liar! You were there on Wednesday night!"

He rolled his eyes. "To see you! Dad sent the Saint-minions out looking for me, remember?"

I shook my head. I didn't remember.

"Paulie!" Jack huffed, exasperation in his voice. "He said Dad wanted to see me. That's code for 'he wants to hurt you and throw your body to the fishes.'"

"To say hello!" My voice sounded muffled through the noodles. "Not to throw you out of the grounds."

Jack still looked fed up, so I stashed the fork in the dishwasher and washed the tub out under the tap. "I'm not going either," I said, feeling like a rebel. I dropped the tub into the bucket under the sink for recycling. "I might go and support the girls tomorrow though. That will really upset Dad." My chuckle sounded all revenge and no mirth and I didn't like how that looked on me.

"I need to get on," I said, heading for the door into the hall. Jack moved quicker than I gave him credit for and barred my way.

"I said I need to talk to you!" His eyes held an unfamiliar intensity and unnerved me as he gripped my shoulder in his good hand. I couldn't seem to shake him off.

"I'm not interested. We've had this discussion and if you can't accept it, you need to leave." I pushed at his chest and felt him rock on his heels but as I raised my hand to repeat the movement harder, he gripped my wrist.

"Not that, Ula! This is different. I need that laptop; Pete's laptop."

I put my head back and groaned. "No! Leave it. It's gone, that's final. Get out of my way."

When he failed to move, I kicked him in the shin, hurting my bare foot more than his leg. Enraged, I attempted to grab his nuts and we ended up collapsing to the kitchen floor where we grappled around on the tiles. It didn't end well for me against a much stronger opponent, even one with a broken wrist and he pinned me down with sickening ease, holding my flailing wrists above my head one-handed and suppressing my kicks with the weight of his body. "Ula, stop!" he shouted. "I'm serious!"

I lay still and played dead, refusing to look at him or respond to his questions about the laptop. Even when he lifted my shirt and tickled me, I giggled like a child but didn't crack. He also gave up before I did, proving little had changed since our childhood. Leaning up on one elbow with his leg stretched out across mine, Jack Saint gave me a look of blistering lust. "I hate you," he said with a sigh and I giggled again.

"No, you don't. You just always want what you can't have."

"True dat," he sighed and laid his head on my shoulder. I put my arm around his neck and cuddled him close, spotting a lonely, dried up pea which had made its escape under the fridge months ago.

"Go and see Lacey," I advised him. "Did you ever give her the chance to explain?"

"She shagged someone else!" Indignation filled his voice.

"Just hear her out," I begged, amazed at my own level of investment. "It might surprise you."

"I'll wear you down instead," he joked, making a grab for my breast and catching my ribs with the edge of his cast. I kneed him in the nuts and he doubled over, allowing me to make my escape without hindrance.

"About the laptop," he called after me and I slammed my bedroom door and locked it, refusing to listen to him anymore.

In true Jack-style, he didn't give up, ambushing me every time I left my room until I shouted at him and told him to leave. He didn't.

"This is why you and I would never work!" I yelled finally. "You don't know when to shut up."

"Ok, ok," he conceded, holding his hands in front of him. "I'll tell you everything, Ula. But you can't repeat it or I'll lose my job."

"What?" I stopped with the wine glass half raised to my lips, filled to the brim with the nice stuff Jack funded on our impromptu beach picnic.

"Promise." His eyes begged me for mercy as he took the wine stem from my fingers and laid the glass on the counter. I nodded, the action feeble against the momentum of some unseen force in the room which channelled itself through

Jack's brown eyes. He watched for a moment and then took my hands in his. "I think you need to sit down," he said.

Chapter 24

"They're watching me too?" My voice rose a notch and I heard my heart send blood rushing too fast into my brain. I felt dizzy with fear. "For how long?"

"A few months now. I've literally fallen into this mess face first." Jack curled his top lip as though suffering garlic reflux and sighed. "All these years I've kept my distance from the Saints and their mess and now I'm in it up to my eyeballs."

"I'm in it up to my eyeballs too," I whined, twisting my fingers together in my lap. "How did this happen?"

"No idea," he replied, running gentle fingers up and down my back in a soothing motion. "I knew nothing about it until last week. There's been gossip at the station and one of the guys who ran me to hospital did some legwork for the detective heading up the case."

"Start at the beginning," I pleaded. "I don't understand."

Jack kissed my temple and then ran a pink tongue over his full lips, picking his words with care. My brain felt foggy with confusion and nothing made sense. "Someone tipped off a detective last season, claiming a gambling syndicate operated within the premier soccer league. The informant said All Saints were at the centre of it with two other clubs. The betting service lays the odds and takes money from members of the public who choose which club will win or lose that week. There are bets for anything; the range is incredible and hardened gamblers will place bets on what time the sun comes up each day if they can find a bookie to take it. Anyone can bet on anything if they're willing to risk their money; who scores the goals; what minute a goal will be scored in; the final score or the number of red or yellow cards given. It's all up for grabs. This Asian Handicap system has caused heaps of problems in European soccer because there's no draw; only win or lose."

"Why didn't I know about any of that," I mused. "I scored some goals last season. Do you think the four people on average who showed up for our games were gamblers?"

Jack kissed my head again and crushed me closer. "Sorry. I don't know if they bet on women's soccer," he said, sounding regretful.

"Typical!" I snorted. I pushed myself away from him so I could watch his face. "Is it illegal to bet on soccer?"

Jack frowned. "No, but it's illegal to rig the games so that certain gamblers get massive payouts. That's cheating."

"So this detective somewhere thinks All Saints are cheating?" My eyes widened and I couldn't stop the laugh which emerged. "Oh my gosh! Could they throw them out of the premiership?" I imagined my father's disgrace and wondered if he'd allow his wheelchair to be rolled onto the grass of a first or second division pitch.

Jack maintained his serious face, ignoring my sniggering. "They'd be thrown out of New Zealand football, Ula. And anyone associated with All Saints. A team a few years ago in Europe were kicked out of the Champions' League for throwing a final."

"Oh." It didn't sound so funny anymore. "That's really bad. Who told the detective? Can't they be more specific about who's doing it so the detective can catch them red handed?" My eyes widened. "Is it possible All Saints cheated in the final last season?" My voice rose to a squeak. "But they won."

Jack stroked my fringe back from my face and his words sounded like nails on a blackboard. "They'll sort it out, baby. But they can't talk to the informant anymore, Ula. He died in a car accident, hours after meeting with the detective." His eyes told me everything his lips couldn't as he held me in a firm embrace.

"Pete." My voice sounded dull and flat against the sounds of traffic in the street outside and my body felt numb beside the hardness of Jack's muscular body. "Pete informed."

I shoved Jack from me, hearing a hiss as my flailing caught his wrist. I stood and backed away, shaking my head. "Is that why you're here?" I demanded. "Pretending you're horny and wanting to rekindle something which never got started?" I sounded hysterical. "You're trying to make detective and I'm your means to an end."

"No, Ula." Jack stood. He waved his arms at my lounge and sparse furnishings and shook his head. "Me, my current situation; it's all real. My life sucks and I came here hoping that..." He stopped before his feet went into his mouth and he choked on his own words. I had no plans to resuscitate him. "I wondered if we had a chance but yes, my ulterior motive is to protect you. There were millions of dollars at stake and the syndicate won't stop if they're onto a good thing. You can be sure they'll run the scam again this year."

"So, Pete wasn't involved?" I asked, covering my face with my hands. "He didn't cheat?" I remembered his playing style and fierce competitiveness. I couldn't bear to think it might have been an act. Pete's soccer was the only thing about him which still seemed truthful in the face of everything else.

"They don't know." Jack approached me, his arms by his sides. "Maybe he found out and wanted it stopped or perhaps he'd been involved at the start and wanted out; who knows?"

"I don't want to believe it," I said, wrapping my arms around myself. "So the cops are watching everyone; me, Dad, Uncle Terry, all of us?"

Jack winced and nodded. "Yeah."

"Oh my gosh, no." I bent double and grabbed my knees, waiting for the faintness to stop as the floor tiles whirled around in my peripheral vision. "I just bought a fifty grand car and paid off a ten grand loan early."

"I know." Jack patted my back and forced me upright, leading me back into the lounge and helping as my legs collapsed onto the sofa. "That's why I asked so many questions about it."

"I can't tell you." My eyes filled with tears. "And I don't even know where he got the money in the first place. It might've been dodgy." I resisted the urge to bawl like a baby but my chest gave in early, like always, spitting ugly sobs into Jack's denim shirt while my nose left telltale trails of snot.

Chapter 25

I tried so hard to understand the information Jack bombarded me with. His earnest face drove me to increase the brain space available for such ridiculous notions as gambling. I'd never met a rich gambler and my parents instilled into me the futility of such pastimes. My father's definitive sentence on betting was; "The only winner is the bookie."

Fixing a valiant smile on my lips to show I cared and using my best listening face, I sat through an hour of arm waving, hasty diagrams and prevented Jack explaining overs and unders using a whiteboard pen on my lounge window. "I need a drink," I sighed, switching to a more social form of addiction to vent my frustration.

"In a minute," he promised and carried on.

"You said that ten minutes ago!" I griped. "How is this helping me? Your colleague is probably watching me drive around in a cornflower blue SUV and assuming I've taken a bribe! Or someone close to me has. Or worse, that Pete hid money and I've just unearthed it. What am I going to do, Jack? You're not helping."

He ignored my whining and explained the Asian Handicap system. "It's like this." He waved his cast and lurched for the whiteboard pen, snatching it up and attacking the centre pane of glass which faced onto my slender balcony. A forgotten tomato plant waved floppy tendrils at me and begged for water in my peripheral vision. Who was it kidding? It produced one tomato and a bird stole that. I turned my attention back to the mess Jack enthused over my windows.

"With Asian Handicap, a gambler betting during a live game decides how many goals could be scored from the moment he places his bet. The odds on this type of gambling are lower so it's harder to make much money, but it's a popular way to bet at the moment. The favourite is handicapped by the bookmaker. For example, the opposition were the underdog in last season's cup final. So All Saints would have been handicapped by -0.5 or another figure deemed appropriate. Their handicap is added to the underdog's score at the end, so in that case, All Saints would need to beat them by at least one goal to win because they'd start down -0.5 before they even ran on the pitch. The odds can even be split across both teams if the gambler feels confident."

"How do you know this stuff?" I groaned, face planting into the sofa cushions. "I just need to know if I'm gonna be arrested so I can hand myself in instead of traumatising my class."

"Drama queen!" Jack snorted. He turned back to the window, writing left handed in a loopy scrawl which hiccoughed at the window frame and continued into the next pane. "With overs and unders, you bet on goals scored in the ninety minutes of play, including injury time but excluding extra time. For instance..." Jack drew a wonky table behind the left curtain and I craned my neck to see if he'd marked the fabric with his flailing pen. "You pick a score, say 2:1 to All Saints. Then you look at the total goal line and decide if you want to bet over or under. Over 2.5 with a score of 2:1 would give you a win. Under 2:1 would be a loss. The split line bet divides your stake between the two teams. For instance..."

"No!" I stood up, desperation etched on my face. "I can't take anymore."

"But I haven't finished," Jack sulked. "I still need to explain 1 x 2 fixed odds."

I ran to my room and slammed the door, hurling myself face down on the bed. My cop-cousin didn't understand my dilemma and if he did, he didn't care. He seemed more interested in expounding on his superior knowledge and driving me deeper into my black hole. I needed to speak to Uncle Terry. I should've thanked him when I picked up my car and hadn't; avoiding contact with him. I pulled my cell phone from my jeans pocket and stared at it, imagining the conversation.

'Thanks for the lovely car you picked out, Uncle. I love it. And I paid off my loan with the cash you wired into my bank.'

'Sod off.'

'Oh, while you're on the phone, please can you tell me where you got the money from? I'm a bit concerned it might be from match fixing.' I groaned and pulled a pillow over my face, breathing in the scent of floral fabric softener.

"Ula?" Jack's voice sounded soft and muffled through the pillow and the bed dipped as he sat next to me. "Where did you get the money?"

"I can't tell you." My hair stuck out like antennae as I pulled the pillow off my face. "It came from someone in the family."

"Not a Saint?" Jack groaned and flopped backwards on the bed, the marker pen raised in his left hand. "You've got real problems, babe."

"Stop it! I know what it means, Jack. The cops will think I took a payoff."

Jack turned on his side. The dark locks tumbled into his eyes and I watched his brain tick over on auto while he pondered the issue. "Why don't we visit Mark Lambie's wife?" His face lit with a smile of genius. "She's family so there's nothing wrong with that but we might find something out. You can do the vacuuming or something."

"Gee, thanks so much!" I didn't bother withholding my sarcasm. "You can mow the grass."

Jack held up his plaster cast in victory and I rolled my eyes at the ceiling.

Half an hour later we pulled up outside Mark Lambie's house in my cornflower blue SUV. I made sure I parked well away from the verge which he'd decorated with vomit, in case it still lurked in the grass. "Why are we here?" I asked, nerves emptying my brain before we even got out of the car.

Jack gaped. "To work out what happened to Lambie!" he snapped. "I'll do all the talking. You vacuum or make the beds and I'll see what I can find out."

"Can't you just ask someone at the station?" My fingers tapped an annoying beat on the steering wheel. "Your colleagues have already asked all the questions available."

His face softened. "You think she'll growl you for leaving him?"

"Wouldn't you?" I ran my hands through my hair and my mind wandered to the All Saint's game currently playing out in Albany. Curiosity bloomed and I tried to guess the half-time score. Jack's fingers closed around mine and he pulled them out of my hair with tenderness. "Ula, it's fine. There's lots of things I'd do differently if I could go back in time." His words held too much poignancy and I leapt from the car with fake enthusiasm.

"Come on then." I forced out a breezy encouragement. "Are we doing this or what?"

Chapter 26

"Come in!" a wavering voice called as I knocked on the door for the third time. "It's open."

Jack turned the handle and pressed the wooden door inward, stepping over the threshold into the hallway. Shelves ran the full length of the space, reaching from floor to ceiling and covered in china animals; a housekeeping nightmare. I yanked on Jack's sleeve as we deposited our shoes next to the doormat. "Don't wanna dust that lot!" I hissed, jerking my head towards the delicate ornaments. "I'm too clumsy."

His eyes channelled pure amusement and I dug him in the ribs, knowing he wouldn't retaliate here. He'd get me later. "It's just us, Aunty," he called, raising his voice. "Jack and Ursula Saint."

I knew he savoured our joined names on his tongue and the look he gave me smouldered in his eyes. My heart skipped a beat and I repeated the coupling in my head. It sounded nice once. Years on, it left me feeling hollow and my thoughts turned to Teina. Apart from his late-night visit mid-week he'd been absent, yet he occupied my thoughts with constancy and my body with guilty yearning.

"Come on." Jack took my reluctant fingers in his and pulled me along the hall, bypassing a lounge and kitchen to left and right. The final doorway at the end of the narrow space opened into a sunny bedroom and a hospital bed occupied most of the floor.

A hand went up to my mouth at the sight of the woman collapsed on the bed and Jack squeezed my fingers as propriety abandoned me. "I'm sorry!" I wailed as my chest gave a powerful hitch. To everyone's surprise, including my own, hot tears erupted from my eyes and leaked down my cheeks as my crime revealed itself. I'd left a friend on his own doorstep without helping him inside and rung the bell as though this poor lady had a chance of answering it. My unwitting selfishness slapped me in the face and even sharing the blame with an absent Teina did nothing to lessen the force of emotion. "I'm a horrible person!" I sobbed and pushed my face into Jack's chest.

He tutted and held me, kissing the top of my head. I heard a murmured conversation between him and the woman in the bed but the words evaded me, a distant rumble under the sound of my own tears. By the time I finished wiping my eyes and nose on my cousin's chest, his tee shirt sported a darker band at face height. Guiding me to a chair next to the bed and pushing me into it, Jack pulled the soaked fabric away from his skin with a look of disgust. "Sorry," I sniffed and cranked up for another round of guilt fuelled self-pity.

"Don't start again," he asked with a plea. "It's fine. I'll make a drink and find you a tissue." Jack nodded to Mrs Lambie and exited the room, leaving me to my fate.

"Sit here." Dora patted the side of her bed and scooted over to allow room. As I edged onto the mattress she grabbed my hand, her fingers containing surprising strength as she squeezed. "Don't fret so," she said, her eyes kind. "I don't blame you." A soft covering of downy hair dusted her head, growing through white as snow even though I remembered her with dark brown locks only six months ago at Pete's funeral.

"But I should've helped him in," I whispered. "He'd covered himself in sick and it got harder and harder to avoid. I rang the bell and assumed..." My voice faded along with my excuses.

"It's ok," Dora said, her voice soft and soothing. "He's a silly old duffer to get so drunk."

"But he wasn't!" Confusion clouded my expression as I cast my mind back. "We went outside so he could have a cigarette. He knew I felt alone and wasn't coping so he invited me to go with him. We chatted for a while and he got worse and worse." My eyes widened. "He bumped his head on the club house as he fell but it didn't look that bad."

Jack entered the room with two mugs of strong tea in one hand and I wrinkled my nose at the dark, stewed colour. He jabbed it towards me, slopping some on his jeans. "I made you one, Aunty," he said, his voice earnest. "Can you manage the mug?"

Dora shook her head and waggled her free hand towards a beaker on a trolley next to the bed. A long straw protruded upwards from it and Jack nodded and retreated to fill it with tea. "Did you tell the cops what you just told me?" she asked, her eyes keen.

I shrugged. "I don't know, Aunty. It's a bit of a blur." I chewed my lip. "I thought they came to ask about Uncle Terry slapping me, so it caught me by surprise."

"Yeah, I heard about what Terry did. I hope the cops arrested him." Her face clouded. "You need to tell them my Mark hit his head," she said, her voice soft. "Maybe that's why he started throwing up." Hope blossomed in her eyes and I sighed.

"It's incidental, Aunty. He'd already started reeling before that. He slugged a glass of whiskey before we left the table and it's occurred to me since that perhaps somebody put something else in it."

"Drugs?" Jack leaned against the doorframe with the beaker in his hand. His brow furrowed and he nodded with a slow movement. "Yeah. It would explain his sudden decline and perhaps the vomiting. I wonder if the cops took samples from the puke outside."

I closed my eyes and tried not to think about it. Jack held the beaker out for Dora and put the straw in her mouth. "Rohypnol can show up in blood and urine but we'd need Mark for that. I'm not sure about puke that's sat on the verge for over a week."

"The date-rape drug?" My eyes widened in horror and I choked on my tea. "Why would someone want to do that to Uncle Mark?"

Dora coughed and tea spluttered from her lips. Jack dragged the straw away and mopped at her mouth with the tissues he brought me. "Geez, sorry Aunty." He darted a dark look in my direction. "It won't be that. He's wandered off somewhere and got lost. He'll be home soon."

To our surprise, Dora Lambie scoffed. "Huh! Who am I kidding? He's gone off with his mistress. I should've expected it, but thought he'd have the decency to wait until I'd climbed into my casket."

My jaw hung open and I swallowed. "What?" The mug of tea tipped sideways in my fingers and Jack confiscated it, balancing it in his sore hand.

A tear slipped down Dora's cheek and I snatched up the toilet roll and unwound a length, bending over her to dab at the hollow face and feeling her bones through it. "Don't cry, Aunty. We didn't come to make things worse."

"You haven't." She gathered herself, taking a deep inhale and shuddering. "I've known about his bit-on-the-side since before Christmas. I haven't got long left; guess Mark couldn't wait." She sniffed and her betrayal resonated deep inside me, twanging a loose thread in my undealt with pain.

"Bastard!" I spat and Jack stared at me in surprise. I patted Dora's thin hand. "What can we do to help?"

She sighed, her chest caving on the inwards breath. "I'd like to see him one more time, I think. He's had different women over the years but I'd like to be able to release him. If she makes him happy, who am I to deny him some comfort?"

"Aunt Dora!" I stood up, leaving a dent in the bed. Jack lurched for my rigid body, not understanding my horror. "You can't let him get away with this. You're sick and he should be here with you, not seeing other women!"

"Ula, leave it!" Jack hissed and fixed his arm around my shoulder. He winced as I tried to pull away and caught the cast.

"I hope you told the cops," I said, my eyes pleading with her and all sympathy for Mark's plight gone. "I hope you told them what a cheating, lying bastard he is."

"Ula!" Jack's horror brought me to my senses and I stopped struggling. "Ula, stop!"

"I told them," Dora sighed. "They went to see her, but she doesn't know where he is. She's probably lying."

"Where is she?" I demanded. "I'll sort her out!"

Dora's blue eyes turned towards me and her words left a chill in my spine. "Her name's May-Ling, sweetie. She's your father's carer."

My jaw hung loose, giving me an unattractive gape. Jack shook me hard and stared from Dora to me with dismay in his expression. "That Asian chick?" He screwed up his face. "I think you're mistaken, Aunty. They're probably just friends."

Dora snorted and opened her mouth to speak. The sound of the front door closing silenced us all.

"Hey, Dora. I'm back!" A short woman with a wide smile bustled down the hallway and entered the room, bringing the sunshine with her. "Kia ora, my friend," she breezed, pushing past us to plant a kiss on Dora's cheek. Her Māori heritage leaked through every pore, jolly and filled with a love of life which infected even me, despite the emotion boiling in my stomach. I pressed my fingers over my lips to prevent me blurting it and smiled as Dora's new guest shook hands all round and offered us more tea.

"Na, we have to be going, Aunty," Jack said, his calm body language an antithesis to mine. He called the new lady, Aunty too, the most natural thing in the world for him with his mother's heritage. I realised how lovely it sounded and wished I'd grown up in a spirit of acceptance, instead of with such a racist, bigoted father.

Dora accepted a kiss from both of us and raised brows with only a few stray hairs growing back. "Could you check on the progress of things, Jack?"

He faltered, not keen to press his nose into an investigation his colleagues would deliberately keep away from him because of the family connection. "I'll try, Aunty," he said. "But I don't think they'll tell me. It's too close to home."

Dora nodded once and squeezed his hand. "Thank you, boy."

Outside on the pavement I could hardly keep still, waiting until Jack closed the door behind him and skipped down the front steps. "Bloody May-Ling!" I raised my voice and his eyes widened in surprise.

"Who is she? Dora said she's your dad's carer. What does that mean?"

My eyes bulged and my gag reflex made my eyes water with impressive speed. "It means I walked in on her and Dad...doing it." I fixed my eyes on the big, blue sky overhead and concentrated on the winding cirrus clouds drifting in a lazy line. Anything to avoid the memory of May-Ling sitting in my father's lap naked from the waist down.

"Euwgh!" Jack squeezed his eyes tight shut and then opened them again. He shook his head and the distaste left his expression. "I've seen worse," he said, his tone philosophical, the jaded sights of his profession already ingrained on his eyeballs. He put his good arm around me and steered me across the road to the car. "Now we've got another problem then."

"Oh, goody!" I unlocked the car and leaned against it. "How?"

Jack pursed his lips. "What if May-Ling was knocking off both of them and they fell out over it?"

"You think Dad killed Uncle Mark?" I felt the colour drain from my face.

Jack shook his head. "Wasn't he at the wedding with you?"

"Yes, but I left. Mark gave us both a ride, so Dad had to find someone to give him a lift to Mark's place and arrive just after we dropped him off. Dad can get from the bed to his chair but he wouldn't manage the path and stairs up to Mark's porch. I don't think he killed him." I shook my hair and it tumbled down my back in dark ringlets. "And what would the driver do? Sit there while Dad bumped off his love rival? Or do it for him?"

"Depends who it was," Jack mused and I shrugged.

"Maybe they share her," he suggested and I made vomit noises and tried not to throw up for real.

"That's prostitution. Are you gonna tell your colleagues?" I chewed my lip and imagined repeating my story to the two cops who visited me. I knew I'd flush bright red under their scrutiny. Or throw up.

"I think I have to," Jack replied. He walked around the back of the car and climbed into the passenger seat. He watched as I clambered up next to him, his eyes boring into the side of my face.

"What?" I snapped and he laughed.

"I need to speak to your dad first."

My head shook from the first mention of Jordan Saint and continued like a clockwork toy with the key stuck. "You'll do that on your own, mate! I don't want to see him ever again!"

My vehemence made Jack screw his head sideways to stare at me.

"You don't mean that!"

"I bloody do! He's done it this time. Dirty old man." The head shaking began again, accompanied by violent shudders of misery. "My mum would be knocked sick by his behaviour this last few years. He's a nasty, selfish old man who ruins other people's lives just because he can." I glared at Jack. "I'm happy to drop you at his place, but I'm not going in."

"Fine!" Jack belted himself up and sat facing forward. "But I need to talk to him before I go to the station and tell them what we just found out."

Chapter 27

I sat outside and waited while Jack traipsed upstairs to my father's apartment alone. When he'd walked around to the driver's side and tried to make me accompany him, I locked the doors. He licked my window out of spite and I waited until he went out of sight before getting out and shining the glass with a tissue from my pocket.

"There you are!" The male voice made me jump and I tippled forwards, connecting with the side of my car. Brian Montana loomed behind me, his soft, Polynesian skin like caramel in the late sunshine. I smiled with relief.

"Hey, coach. How ya doin'?" I stuck out my hand and he shook it in his giant paw, leaning in to press his nose to mine in a hongi. He closed his eyes for a fraction of a second, opening them long enough to read my soul like an open book.

"Good, number nine," he said, referring to me as always. "Been tryin' to call you."

"Oh." I thought about the phone in my glove box, turned off to avoid my father's many calls. He'd enjoyed an orgasm without dying so he could quit calling me every time he got a sniffle. "It's not working." Almost the truth; it couldn't work unless I switched it on.

"I need you tomorrow," he said, fixing brown eyes on mine and watching me hold my breath.

"I can't," I began, but he raised his hand.

"No excuses, number nine. My right wing has gaps and you're it."

"I'm not playing this year!" My voice hiked up a notch. "We had a conversation at Christmas and you agreed."

"Only to shut you up." Brian snorted. "Do as you're told. Game's at nine. Be there an hour early to run through some drills."

"But I haven't trained!" I hated the whine I heard in my tone and Brian grabbed me in a bear hug, enfolding my face and torso into his giant chest.

"You look all right to me," his voice rumbled. "Be there. We need ya."

He let me go and I wobbled on my feet from the temporary suffocation. "I don't know where my soccer boots are."

His laugh echoed in the car park, bouncing off the other vehicles like a pin ball. "Crap!" he snorted. "Yeah, ya do. See you tomorrow." He turned and set off for the apartment block, waving over his shoulder. "Gonna raak up yer dad now."

"Good luck with that!" I watched Brian skid to a halt and stare back at me, a confused look on his face. Fearing he might return for an explanation, I bounced into my car and locked the doors, hiding behind the tinted glass like a fugitive.

An hour later, I sat with my legs crossed, busting for the toilet as Jack sauntered through the front doors with a grin on his lips. "Haha," he sniggered as I deactivated the central locking. "You got called up for The Priestesses."

"Shut yer face!" I snapped, gunning the engine. "I need a wee and it's your fault."

"Could've come in." He fixed his seat belt in place and halted the irritating warning alarm from the dashboard. "Nice to catch up with Brian."

"I didn't think they'd talk to you," I grumbled and jumped at Jack's peel of laughter.

"Is that why you agreed to drive me? You're so transparent, Ula! Your dad behaved like a gentleman, actually." He glanced at me sideways when I didn't reply, eager to be back on my good side. "Sorry. The time flew, especially after Brian arrived."

"Did you get to ask him about his little house guest." I couldn't keep the bile out of my voice.

"Didn't need to say much," Jack replied, looking at me sideways. "You didn't know they were married, did you?"

The BMW possessed incredible brakes and the stopping distance proved beyond my wildest dreams. The emergency stop I pulled would have sent Jack through the windscreen if he wasn't belted in. He swore up a blue streak in my vehicle and I opened the windows after I'd pulled off the main road and parked in an affluent Auckland suburb. "Your language is vile," I commented, looking in the rear-view mirror at my white complexion and frightened brown eyes, focussing on getting my heart rate to slow. I'd almost been rear-ended and it scared me.

"You left tyre marks!" Jack squeaked, his eyes terrified.

"Because of what you said!" I gritted my teeth and balled my fists, willing the prickling tears not to betray me. "They can't be married."

Jack rolled his eyes. "Sorry, sorry. Ula, that was an awful way to find out. I thought you knew and just wanted to cause trouble."

"Get out." I pressed the button on the dash and the doors unlocked. "Get out, Jack."

"No." He clung to his seat belt as though I might rip it off him and a red mist descended over my vision. He believed I'd be spiteful enough to set the cops on my father just for fun.

"Get. Out." I separated the words and felt my heart pounding blood through my ears. My breath caught in my chest and rage consumed me. When Jack refused to budge after being thumped twice, I fixed my palm over the centre of the steering wheel and pushed.

In addition to great brakes, the BMW owned a super-sized horn. It blared out into the suburb and echoed off buildings like a claxon. Other drivers turned to stare and a woman walking her dog stopped on the pavement across the road. Jack tried to move my hand but his broken wrist caught the gear stick as he raised the cast and he hissed in pain. "Get out!" I screamed like a maniac and fear lit his eyes in the realisation I meant it.

The horn continued without pause, attracting the attention of every human eye in the street and with a look of betrayal, Jack climbed out of my car.

I left him standing on the pavement clutching his broken wrist in his other hand with a look of disbelief on his face. Clumping my foot on the gas, I forced my way into the stream of traffic, letting the tears streak down my face in the privacy of my vehicle. My hands shook and I drove the wrong way along a one-way street by accident before arriving home and sitting in the parking garage in my car. I howled then like a baby, wailing into the empty space and leaving my dignity on the seat. I missed my mother and knew she'd be appalled by May-Ling and their mutually convenient union.

My father's cruelty cut me to the quick and when I'd cried myself into a state of sullen anger, I grabbed my phone from the glove box and turned it on. Sixty-four messages and thirty missed calls flashed on the screen and I emptied the box without reading or listening to any of them. Then I blocked Dad's number and resisted selecting the option to receive a text if he tried to contact me. His reign over my life ended there, in a dirty parking garage under an apartment block inhabited by people who were down on their luck. He'd put me there and he'd have no part in watching me clamber out.

Chapter 28

Jack didn't come home and I wasn't bothered. I'd put the chain across the front door anyway and planned to ignore him. I dwelled on my behaviour far too much over the cooking sherry and made myself maudlin and depressed. Sobbing some more, I watched myself cry in the bathroom mirror, which was silly but entertaining. I couldn't make it look attractive like an actress' gentle tears because I screwed my face up too much and my nose bulged.

Jack's betrayal seemed almost worse than Dad's. I thought he knew me but he didn't. Or maybe he did and I didn't like what his assumption revealed. My reaction told him I knew nothing about my new stepmother but it scored deep gashes in my soul that he could believe I'd set him up by taking him to see Jordan and saying nothing. I washed my face with cold water, poured the cooking sherry down the sink when

I spotted flies in the bottom and went to bed with Pete's laptop. It's not like anything he said from the grave could destroy my mood much more.

I deduced the other person in the most interesting set of conversations must be someone familiar. Whoever it was knew me.

'She's a sweet chick. Just have babies with her and it will be ok. That's what I did.'

'Yeah, she's lovely. I fell on my feet with her. It was a great idea.'

At first I wondered about my father but his atrocious spelling would have outed him within the first sentence. Who else took part in the planning and organisation of my fake marriage? I considered all of them and drew a blank. My husband and his friend talked about soccer with an expert's eye which narrowed out more people. I glossed over Pete's father as the writer. I'd seen how he spoke to Pete and the written conversation contained too much affection and the kind of advice delivered by someone who cared. It couldn't be the same man who slapped me in public. I felt the writer to be male and his affinity with the gay community ruled out even more candidates, including Aunty Margaret. I seemed no nearer to solving his identity after two hours of drunken reading and alternate sobbing than when I started.

But I knew Pete in death more than I ever had in life. He cared about me in a way I hadn't realised and it affected me. It brought healing to know I wasn't his stooge and he spoke about his anger towards me in ways which made sense. I'd been his public saviour and his private jailer. I gave him a veneer of respectability whilst removing his freedom.

'I look at her sometimes and wish she knew. I think she'd understand. We could come to an arrangement where I got her pregnant and we lived together as friends. I like her. She's cute and funny. We just want different things.'

I dwelled on whether I would have remained satisfied with such a half-life. At work, I saw women every day who put everything into their only child and kept nothing back. When the teenage stage hit and their love fell on deaf ears, they shattered like unfired pottery.

I skimmed the conversation which took place over four years, covering the attack on my husband in an Auckland toilet and my subsequent entry into his double life. I gained nothing new from the exchange and let the messages scroll past my tired eyes until the end when it finished with a message sent to Pete the day he died. It remained greyed out and I hovered over it, not wanting to change it from 'unread' to 'read'.

'Don't do anything stupid,' it said.

My heart quailed at the timing of the message, sent as my husband's body flew through his windscreen and sent fragments of glass into his handsome face. The suicide note sneaked to the front of my mind again and left me reeling. But the online message seemed out of place and strange, as though another discussion had crept into the mix, left over from a phone conversation or something said face to face which jarred with the usual harmless banter of the chat room. It related to nothing spoke of previously.

Thoughts of Pete's death rolled my stomach and I turned my brain by an act of will towards Teina, savouring his smile and the way he'd loved me, expunging the damage from my marriage of convenience and the lack of confidence it wrought in my personality.

I craved Teina then; in my mouth, my body and most of all in my head. I used the laptop to search for residential addresses listed under *T. Fox* and lawyers with his name as partner or associate. My fingers moved over the keyboard, desperate to find him and bring him running. Nothing. Nothing relevant, anyway. There were two hundred addresses in New Zealand inhabited by a *Fox* and twelve of them attributed to *T. Fox*, but none of those lived in Auckland. I found one lawyer by the name of Fox but unless he worked as a woman during the week, it wasn't him.

Laying back against my pillows in the empty bed, I stretched my finger towards the power button and acknowledged my readiness for sleep. Then it happened. The screen made a peculiar noise and an icon flashed in the top right corner. I sat up straight and peered at it, using the mouse to click out of the online address book. I closed out of the nonsensical spreadsheet I'd also glanced over, not understanding the numbers next to team listings, but having toyed with it being something to do with the gambling scam. With everything else closed or minimised, it left only Pete's conversation with the stranger and I stared in horror at the flashing box on the screen where a new message sat waiting.

'Pete?'

I held my breath and scrolled around the screen, looking for the box at the top where I always checked I hadn't changed anything. Panic sped up my pulse as I tried to work out what I'd done wrong. "Think! Think!" I urged myself. "Pete never saw the last message and it was a different colour; grey. It was grey. I didn't change it. I clicked nothing!" I stared at the screen, where the final unread message looked the same colour as the blue ones above. In my clicking around with addresses and searches, I'd somehow marked it as 'read' and the chat room sent a notification to the sender.

"I kept it showing as offline!" I shrieked, but the laptop screen flickered without concern for my blunder. The drop-down-box on the right showed a thumbnail of the saxophone image and the word, 'online'.

'Who is this?'

I heard the indignation hidden within those three small words and it dawned on me that Pete's friend knew his real identity. He hadn't called him, 'Musician', but 'Pete.' If they knew my husband, they also knew whoever read the six-month-old message wasn't him.

Chapter 29

It took less than a second to click Pete's profile to show him offline, but the threat remained and haunted my dreams all night. I woke up countless times sweating, imagining a faceless spectre hovering over me waiting to smother the life from my body. The laptop sat next to my bed and it remained silent, logged off and charging. I wasn't sure I'd have the courage to open the lid again and contemplated dumping it in the estuary during the early hours of the morning as I cowered under the sheets afraid.

Up and dressed by six, I sat at the kitchen counter in my soccer kit, dark smudges of sleep deprivation beneath my eyes and my unruly hair knotted into a high ponytail. Shaking fingers hugged the mug of tea in front of me. In the calm light of a new day I regretted my reaction to Jack's wrong assumption, but didn't know how to put it right.

My landline rang and I picked it up, the product of a gut reaction. Jordan Saint's guttural tones spewed from the handset. "What the eff's going on with you, lazy bloody woman! I nearly ended up in hospital with my heart yesterday and you..."

The click of the handset docking killed the irritating voice and I felt an overwhelming satisfaction. I waited for guilt to catch me up but nothing came. "Get your wife to look after you now," I said to the empty room and dumped my mug in the dishwasher.

Driving my gorgeous car caused a smile to touch my lips. I loved it more each time I climbed into the driver's seat, relishing independence and freedom. I reached the All Saints' ground in twenty minutes without the usual traffic volume present on every other day of the week. Parking outside the locked gates I waited, finding myself early.

"Yey! Ursula, oh wow! So glad you're here!" Two of my team mates arrived, hugging me and gushing their gratitude. "Amanda fell last week and twisted her knee after a bad tackle. She's having physio but might need an operation." Leonie glanced at me sideways. "I'm glad you're back."

"Just filling in," I said, holding up my hands. "I haven't trained and I don't want to be a regular team member."

"But we miss you." Alice moved closer and lowered her voice. "We hoped you'd take up the Captaincy this year."

"Leave her." Leonie nudged her team mate's arm and widened her eyes in warning.

I fixed a smile on my face and knew their minds had gone straight to my husband's death. "I didn't quit because of Pete," I said, keeping the smile in place. "It was for lots of reasons. I felt I needed a break and until this week, I didn't own a car. I caught the bus everywhere."

"Someone said that," Alice gasped. "But what happened to your car?"

"Alice!" Leonie shoved her hard and gave me a look of apology. "We haven't been talking about you, Ursula. Promise."

"It's fine." I leaned back against my car and made a decision to scotch the rumours. "Pete didn't have life insurance and left a lot of debts. I guess he didn't expected to die right then. I sold the house and my car and it's been quite hard." I jerked my head towards the BMW and fixed the smile back on my face. "I'm all square now though. I've worked my way out of it and things will be better."

The girls mirrored my enthusiasm and admired the car until Brian arrived, grinning at my presence. "I'm glad you showed up," he said, unlocking the gates and embracing me. He pressed his lips to my forehead like a benevolent father and I detected a sense of relief in the action. Once on the training ground, he morphed into slave driver mixed with Roman centurion and flogged us to death in a warm up which left my knees trembling.

"I'm done!" I groaned, laying flat on my back on the grass. "I've got nothing left for the game."

"Get up, girl!" Brian snapped and nudged my boot with his foot. "Should've come to training last week."

I opened my mouth to protest, but he walked away, still bemoaning my lack of commitment. "And the week before and the week before that."

"Ignore him," Leonie said, helping me up. "He's thrilled you're back. Anyone can see that."

I nodded and looked around me at the other ten players, all younger than me by at least five years. Alice wore the captain's band around her upper arm and I felt pleased for her, knowing my decision to decline the honour last year was the right one. Pete's death and the subsequent revelations which unfolded around my head left me numb inside and I wasn't in a good place when Brian made the announcement at the end-of-year party.

The opposition gathered on the pitch in a huddle and I switched to player mode, joining the tight-knit circle of women and healing in their solidarity. The customary pre-game chant filled me with a sense of wellbeing and the aches and pains faded into background noise.

"Let's go!" Brian yelled, ramping up the excitement. He tapped me on the shoulder. "Right back, number nine," he said, patting me on the back as I ran out onto the pitch. "Don't get hurt; we've no reserves. Good to have you here," he added, his lips quirking as he issued orders to the other girls.

The turf felt good under my boots and I closed my eyes and savoured the scent of earth and severed grass roots. The female referee seemed to glow in her yellow shirt, the sun reflecting off the fabric like a blinding display of glory. My red and black stripes hugged every curve of my torso like a glove and as the whistle blew to start the game, I felt more alive than I had for ages.

My opponent drove hard for the ball, out running me on every challenge until I grew frustrated with my poor fitness. A bitter spirit took root and I legged her up in a nasty tackle, intended to break her run. She crushed me beneath her as she fell, winding me and scraping her studs down the inside of my thigh. "Serves you right!" she snapped, standing and smirking as the referee arrived, a yellow card raised above her head.

"Do that again and it's an early shower," she said, her tone clipped. Red hair tumbled either side of her face and I saw she meant business. My ears rang from the powerful whistle blow which communicated her disapproval and I apologised and stood up.

"Calm down, number nine!" Brian yelled from the sideline. "You just cost your club fifty bucks!"

I stood back from the free kick and gave myself a stiff talking to, settling into my game and pushing myself to keep up with my opponent. We battled hard, but I kept it fair on my part, recognising how easily the nasty spirit stepped in to compensate for my inadequacy. I matched her along the sideline as she took the ball up towards our goal, closing her down until she lost the ball over the white line.

Alice indicated I should take it and I chased it, flicking it up into my hands with my foot. I noticed the assessor then, using his ballpoint pen to mark a sheet resting on his clipboard. He stood on the other side of the pitch from the spectators and club members, keeping his distance to observe the performance of the referee with a calm eye.

I hesitated and swallowed, a metre away from him with the ball pinned between my fingers. Teina Fox smirked and offered a lazy wink. "I think they want the ball back," he said, jerking his head towards a frantic Brian yelling from the other side of the ground.

Swallowing, I threw the ball, messing up the movement and not pulling the ball far enough behind my head before I let it go. The whistle blew and Alice looked at me in confusion. "Sorry," I mouthed, not daring to glance back towards Teina. My heart pounded in my chest and I couldn't work out whether embarrassment or lust induced it.

The referee let the game run on, not heavy on her whistle but decisive and clear when she needed to be. I experienced flares of jealousy at the thought of her sitting next to Teina in the cramped referees' changing room, pouring over her scores and chatting over his detailed observations. I felt an idiot for my behaviour and worked hard to control the varying emotions, deciding somewhere between half time and the final ten minutes that soccer was no longer my game.

Then everything turned to custard. Alice went down in a terrible clatter with the goalie and didn't get up. The goalkeeper wobbled around for a minute and promised she was okay but Alice stayed on the ground. Brian ran over with ice and a spectator from the opposition declared himself a doctor. Alice woke with a headache and the men helped her, limping from the pitch.

"Ten men!" Leonie yelled, rallying the troops. "We can do this. Let's keep it a nil all draw, girls."

We seemed to go down like skittles and the referee called advantage more times than she blew the whistle. Flattened, we got up and ran, hogging the ball and desperate for the taste of victory. I sent Leonie a freakily accurate cross and she drove the ball into the back of the opposition's net, two minutes before the final whistle. It felt a hollow victory as her opponent studded the back of her leg from knee to ankle and she fell in the penalty box.

I could hear Brian swearing from the other side of the pitch and even the referee's whistle and awarding of a penalty did little to assuage his temper. "Take it number nine!" he screamed at me and I shook my head and backed away. Last year I might have but not anymore. Someone else commanded the Ursula Saint confidence because it sure as hell wasn't me. I turned my back so I couldn't hear his bellowing and Leonie stepped up and took the shot. I knew the ball hit its mark by the cheer which went up along the sidelines. A glance towards Teina saw him writing something on his clipboard but he paused long enough to catch my eye. I'd never wanted to be somewhere else quite so badly as that moment and I hung out for the final whistle, resenting the referee for the extra three minutes she tacked on for injury time.

I shook hands with the referee and the other players and apologised to the girl I'd fouled. "Sorry. You were the better player and it irked me. I deserved the card."

"Hey, no worries," she said, shaking my hand. "It's nice to see you back. We heard you weren't playing."

I shrugged, a familiar sick feeling rising into my stomach. "Just standing in. I won't be playing again."

She nodded, not really caring as her team mates trooped off and she ran to catch them up. I followed my team towards the changing rooms, dreading Brian's dissection of the game in the after-match drink in the club house. The girls celebrated their victory and tried to include me, but every minute felt like an age of torture. I snagged the first shower and dressed quickly, listening to their loud chatter and evading their voiced assumption that I would join them in the club house.

"You might get the man of the match award," one of the defenders commented, towel drying her hair as I tied my shoelaces and stuffed my kit into a bag. "You played well. We've missed you."

I wrinkled my nose. "Nah, I don't think so. I played like an idiot." I kept my head down, sensing the unease inside the room heighten to painful levels. Collecting my gear together, I waved my arm to encompass the team without getting eye contact with anyone. "See ya girls, have a great rest of the season."

Before they could release the giant exhale they collectively held, I left the room and bolted. The yellow shirt of the referee trotted off in the distance, still cladding her sweaty body. I shuddered and felt glad I wouldn't have to car pool with her. I strode away from the home team's lair and skirted the muted commiserations from the away team which I heard through the open windows. Steam gushed through the vents as the women showered more thoroughly than the men seemed capable of. Passing the officials' changing rooms I remembered Teina's presence on the pitch and my heart gave an involuntary skip. I glanced towards the tree he'd stood next to at the other side of the second best pitch and squinted against the bright sunlight. Blinded for a second, I put my hand up to shield my face and let out a squeak as a strong pair of arms seized me around the waist and yanked me sideways.

I spun into the room, dropping my kit bag and readying my confidence to take an angry pounding from Brian for my poor game. The door gave a sharp click and Teina grinned at me, darting forward and wrapping his arms around me. "Well, Ms Saint, fancy meeting you here," he whispered, pushing his face into my neck and inhaling shower gel and shampoo. My soaked hair hung limp along my shoulders, creating a damp patch on my dress and sending drips down my back. A line of water soaked into the spaghetti straps and slithered into my bra. Teina traced it with a lazy finger and then lifted my chin so he could look into my eyes.

"Bad game, Ms Saint?" he asked, covering my rude answer with a kiss. When I turned my face to the side he dragged his lips along the tendon in my neck and nibbled the skin with gentle caresses. I felt my resolve weaken and tried to dig in and find my sense of dignity.

"Sod off!" I scowled and Teina grinned, that smug, self-righteous expression which infuriated me at the same time as felling me on the spot. I bent to retrieve my kit bag and his eyes flicked to the stud marks on my inner thigh as my dress rode up. I saw a momentary flash of sympathy and then it drifted away, replaced by the hard veneer.

"That's what you get for pulling a tackle like that," he said, his face coy and unreadable.

"Thank you so much for your wonderful wisdom." I injected enough sarcasm into my voice to make it sting and then side stepped him, aiming for the door. Quicker than me, he moved to block my exit.

"Your heart wasn't it in," he said and his perception made me wince. "What happened?"

I shrugged. "I don't want to play anymore. Everything that's happened with my family and the club has made it too hard. This place, it sickens me." I looked around at the dingy officials' room, at the lack of respect the club offered men and women who volunteered so All Saints pitches could be filled with the game they loved and it brought it home to me; the club and I were as done as my father and me.

"Referee," he said as though it made perfect sense.

I struggled with the bitter laugh which erupted from my chest. "Yeah. That might just finish Jordan Saint off for good. I should consider it."

Teina cocked his head and knitted his brow, studying me through sultry brown eyes. I stood in the tiny changing room clutching my bag like an island swamped by storm water; going under with painful slowness.

"Come here, Ms Saint," he whispered, holding his arms out towards me. I stared at the neat white shirt, ironed as though pressed onto the muscular body and wanted to run into his arms and bury my face in his strong chest and breathe him in. I knew what lurked beneath his clothes and I ached to hide in this awful room with no windows and recreate what last weekend brought, but I couldn't. It wasn't right.

My resistance caused him pain and I read it in the dark brown eyes, regretting it with all my nerve endings. I shook my head and ran a hand over my eyes, squeezing the bridge of my nose between thumb and forefinger. "My life's about to tip up," I said, my voice soft. "It'll be toxic for anyone around me. You're best out of it."

I pushed past him with unchecked roughness and left the room, closing the door behind me with a resounding click.

My tennis shoes tripped over bumps in the grass as I ran to the car park by cutting across a scrubby lawn. The right lace came undone and almost legged me up as I bolted and I reached my car more through luck than judgement, cursing the gardener who neglected anything not classed as pitch and taking the shoelace manufacturer's name in vain as well.

My car fired up first time and I sped from the ground, determined it would be my last time on the property. My father's fifty percent share in the club meant nothing to me and I worked to swallow down the threatening bile at my betrayal of a revered family legacy. I saw Teina's dark shape in the doorway of the officials' room and cut off any emotional connection between us, determined to leave the soccer world and its complications behind me.

I parked under the building and went upstairs in the lift, standing in the corridor outside my apartment with a peculiar sense of foreboding. I made no noise with the keys and pushed the door open with soundless precision, listening for intruders. My heart pounded with the realisation I'd abandoned the laptop next to the bed and not hidden it in the safe, leaving Pete's guilt in the open for all of New Zealand to gawp at. I held my breath and sent up a silent plea for clemency, not expecting to receive it. Jack's shoes nestled next to my work sandals by the front door and I entered with mixed feelings of relief and dismay. I crept along the hallway in bare feet and startled him as he sat on my bed.

The laptop balanced open on his knee and he tapped keys with a look of frustration.

"Looking for something?" I asked, my tone acerbic. "Is this your game now, Jack? Grabbing promotion by turning over your family."

"No!" He shook his tousled head and hurt flitted across his eyes. "You lied. I thought you'd dumped this."

"Yeah. You also thought I'd set my father up as a murderer to get him back for marrying a floozy and that was wrong too."

"I'm sorry about that." Jack laid the laptop on the bed cover as though it was fragile and stood, his face pained. "I believe you didn't know your dad married May-Ling, Ula. I said a stupid thing and I'm sorry."

"Pete was gay." I put the sentence out in the air with a casualness that sounded jarring. I might have said Pete liked ice cream or Pete hated cats with more expression. Still, it left Jack gaping like a mullet.

"What? No way!" His handsome features communicated his belief that I'd finally cracked and he needed to call the men in white coats to carry me to the psychiatric ward. I doubted his loyalty would stretch to visits there.

"Yeah." My face remained calm and I rose onto tip toes; the way I'd walked as a child before soccer boots and stilettos. "Bent as a five bob note."

Jack shook his head and gestured towards the laptop. "What's the password, Ula? I need to take this into work and they'll ask me."

I laughed, a cruel, sardonic sound, eerie without mirth. "I just told you my husband didn't love me, didn't fancy me and used my body twice in a five-year marriage. I say 'used' because I can't claim either of us enjoyed the experience. And all you can say is, 'What's his password,' so you can take his deepest, darkest secrets to the police station and claim your booby prize."

"Ula, don't do this," he said, his eyes widening at the coldness in my eyes. "We need to sort this out and quickly, before they come after you."

"Go away, Jack," I said with a sigh, turning on my heel. "You make me sick."

I left the front door of my apartment open, figuring Jack would leave with the laptop soon, anyway. Ignoring the lift, I sprang down the stairs, tempted to pitch myself over the railing and end my miserable life once and for all. It was a momentary thought, but enough to bring me to my senses as I pushed through the exit from the stairwell and met my reflection in the front door glass with a look of horror. A cold, hard woman stared back at me and I recognised my father in the angular lines and lack of emotion in the eyes. "It finally happened," I snapped. "You became a Saint! Congratulations!"

Chapter 30

The balmy air outside met me like a wall of heat and took my breath away. My cornflower blue car sat forgotten in the bowels of the apartment building as I began to walk, only my driving licence and car keys in my possession. I wondered who would miss me if I kept walking and never returned, unable to mention any significant names. Aunty Pam's face swam before me in my inner vision and I pushed it away. She wasn't her sister. She wasn't my mother. And it was Karen Lansdown-Saint who I really wanted. I needed her cool hands on my forehead and gentle overtones of sympathy. I hated her too then because she'd left me and stifled a sob with my hand as I smelled the estuary and homed in on it like a beacon calling me.

I stepped off the curb without looking; a tragedy waiting to happen on a weekday, but still risky on a Sunday afternoon. The car screeched to a halt with centimetres to spare and I held my breath and felt my chest lock.

"Ursula!" Teina's biceps rippled under his shirt as he shook me and a tear squeezed out of my left eye and pitched down my cheek. I watched the concern on his face change to fear. "What's happened?"

"I'm sorry, I'm sorry. She just step' out." The tiny Asian man driving the big red Ferrari danced around in my peripheral vision like a fly trying to get inside a candy shop. His accent mangled the words and a bubble of hysterical laughter threatened to pop in my gut. "I could have kilt you," he said, his anger growing. "You need lock up. My car worth more to repair than you!"

Teina turned towards him and stood up straight, maintaining a one-handed grip on my arm. "Hey, buddy. Move along or I'll give you something to repair."

"Hass-hole." The little man scuttled back to his throbbing engine and ground the gears in a hurried getaway. His ruination of a simple cuss word made me splutter and thinking I was about to launch into tears, Teina buried my face in his chest and hustled me towards the car park at the side of my building. He kept one arm behind my back and his large hand spread out across my cheek, covering my ear and mashing my other cheek into his shirt. It occurred to me as we reached his car that the destination might still be the mental hospital.

"I don't want to go!" I snapped, pushing at Teina with my hands and succeeding only in causing him to face me head on. "You can't lock me up."

"What?" His face held confusion mixed with amusement. "Last time I checked, being almost splattered by a Ferrari wasn't an offence."

"I'm not mad," I insisted, realising by implication I'd made myself look exactly that.

Teina planted a kiss on my forehead and squeezed my upper arms in his comforting grip. "Get in the damn car, Ms Saint. I'm sorry it's nothing flasher than a Ford but you'll look better inside than on the front as a mascot."

I sighed as he bundled me into the passenger seat and closed the door, all the fight gone out of me. My muscles ached and the stud welts on my thigh throbbed like a strobe. "Feels like a bloody knife wound," I groaned, touching the heat around the raised blue bruises and wincing. Teina raised his eyebrow at the undignified flash of thigh and underwear and his lips moved into a quizzical line.

"You know what that feels like?" he asked and I closed my eyes against my own stupidity.

"No. So what? I can imagine, can't I?" I heaved out a puff of exasperated air and he grinned, unfazed by my bad attitude.

"You're a shocker!" he laughed and started the engine. "I don't know why I bother with you."

He pulled out onto the main road, smirking at my reply of, "Well, why do you?"

Choosing to ignore it, he headed south, onto the motorway, putting Auckland's sprawling metropolis in his rear-view mirror.

We didn't speak for half an hour while I alternately sulked and inspected my war wound. Teina stopped the car at the Bombay services and filled up with gas. He got out to pay and then turned the car around to park outside the cafe. "I need coffee," he announced, opening my door and holding out his hand.

I declined food but accepted the coffee he bought with gratitude, sipping while he ate a steak and cheese pie and watched me through a veil of dark eyelashes. "Do you know why it's called the Bombays?" he asked and I frowned at the odd question.

"No. It's stupid," I said, maintaining a grumpy expression. I looked through the glass at the busy car park and hid the fact I'd asked myself the same question hundreds of times as I passed through the area, on a bus going to some remote soccer game.

"Do you wanna know?" he asked, his eyes teasing. I did, but not enough to beg for it.

"Not bothered," I answered and he bit his lip and masked his amusement.

He clasped his ankles around my foot under the table and moved his head until I couldn't avoid his eyes any longer.

"Are you gonna sulk all afternoon or do I need to take you into the bathroom and sort you out?"

My eyes widened and I looked around the cafe in embarrassment, wondering if he meant the threat. Nobody looked in our direction at his lewd suggestion and I relaxed. "Take me into the bathroom," I said and Teina looked surprised, scraping his chair back.

"Okay."

"No!" I hissed and he laughed, mischief in his eyes coupled with victory at having foiled my bluff.

"It's nothing to do with India," he said, pulling his chair back under the table and scooting forward to reach for my hands. "This area used to be called Williamson's Clearing, but he subdivided the land ready for a group of new settlers arriving on a ship called The Bombay. They decided to call the new town Bombay."

"Oh." I frowned in disappointment. "I thought it was more exciting than that."

Teina smiled and blinked his long lashes. He glanced upwards with a smile as the waitress collected his empty plate and our cups and she smiled back. A flash of jealousy cast an ugly shadow across my soul and I put my head down to avoid Teina's eyes. His hands felt warm on my fingers, massaging the rigid bones with gentle, sensuous strokes. "Can we go to the bathroom and get it over with?" I asked, making my voice sound dull and bored.

Far from being irritated, Teina smiled with his eyes and shook his head. "I've got other plans for you, Ms Saint."

I looked up into his eyes and felt the lurch in my gut as my heart invested a little bit more in this intriguing male. His lips quirked upwards revealing a long scar buried in the stubble next to his jawline and I resisted the urge to reach out and stroke it, wanting to feel his cheek beneath my fingers. My lips parted and I watched as his eyes flicked down to my mouth and then upwards, the tension heavy between us. "Come on," he said, his voice soft as he tugged me out of my seat. "We've a way to go yet."

I used the bathroom alone and found Teina waiting by his car. The hand dryer wouldn't work and I flapped my arms to get the water off as I walked towards him, my dress sashaying around my thighs. He leaned with his neat bum on the passenger door of his vehicle, arms folded and eyes watching me. Perfect teeth nibbled his bottom lip and I felt like an organ in a specimen jar. "Where are we going?" I asked, leaning next to him and noticing the way his hair curled above his ears. It struck me as endearing and I reached out a hand and stroked the soft locks.

"Somewhere nice," he said, smoothing his fingers along the underside of my forearm and narrowing sultry eyes as I shivered in response.

"As long as it's away from the city," I said with a sigh. "Maybe drop me somewhere and I'll start again under a different name."

"That bad?" Teina asked, fixing his arm around my shoulder. He kissed my temple and I snuggled into his armpit, enjoying the sun on my neck and the soft scent of his aftershave drifting around my head. "What happened on the pitch?" he asked, his voice tender and I wondered if he cared or if professional curiosity drove his question.

I shrugged, dislodging his arm and pulling on his hand to put it back. "Brian coerced me into playing but I've got a lot going on at the moment. I didn't want to play this season but then I felt I had no choice. I haven't trained so I'm not as fit as I need to be, he put me in an unfamiliar position to fill a gap and I got lost. When I made that tackle I saw something in myself I didn't like. I won't play again."

"Become a referee." Teina sounded serious and I imagined my father's horror as I ran out onto the pitch wearing a ref's shirt. It would serve him right.

"Maybe," I mused. "Not right now though. Staying out of prison is more important at the moment."

I felt Teina's body tense and my heart quickened in fear. His body's reaction told me he wouldn't be visiting. "It doesn't matter." I put my hand on the door handle and ignored the look of dread on his face. "Are we going to this mystery place, or what?"

Teina turned off in Ngaruawahia and took the back roads west to the coast. I smelled the sea even before we got there, letting its scent blow in the open window and caress my face. We passed through magnificent bush and narrow, winding roads until the small town of Raglan opened before us like a flower. I laid back in the seat, stretched out and relaxed in the different environment. The town looked sweet and bustled with life, slower paced and less frantic than Auckland's perpetual movement.

Teina parked near a church off the beaten track and locked up his car. I felt a frisson of excitement as he held out his hand and I watched as my tiny paw fitted into it, our fingers interlocking. Happiness budded but the usual stab of fear squashed it, reminding me to enjoy the moment because it wouldn't last. Life would crowd in and ruin any chance of extended pleasure. I squeezed Teina's fingers and decided to live moment by moment for a while. I could confess my sins to the prison chaplain.

Chapter 31

The black sand of the west coast never ceased to surprise me, no matter how many times I saw it. Rich in iron ore it sparkled, retaining the heat of the sun and burning exposed flesh with its glass like quality. Teina led me down through the main street, packed with small shops and day trippers eating at small tables outside cafes. The area hummed with the steady buzz of satisfied humanity, backed by the lulling sound of the sea slapping against rocks in the harbour.

Teina clasped my hand in his and we strolled with companionable ease, further cementing a bond which began with lust but showed signs of progressing into something more permanent. His fingers around mine felt right and a heavy sense of foreboding grew in my chest. It couldn't last. Nothing good happened to people like me. My heavy sigh drew Teina's attention and he slipped an arm around my shoulders, pulling me close. "What's wrong?"

I lifted my face and sought his lips, pausing my footsteps while we kissed. "It feels too good to be true," I whispered, waiting for a family with buckets, spades and grizzling children to pass on the narrow street. "I'll go home and all this will be a distant memory."

I swallowed and cast my eyes around, soaking up the essence of the moment, wanting it to sustain me with sights and smells when the rug-puller yanked the carpet from under me and sent my ass tumbling to the hard ground. Teina steered me to the left of a shop doorway and pinned me to the wall with both hands either side of my shoulders. "You're a conundrum, Ms Saint," he said, his voice for my ears only. "How can I make it better?"

"You can't." The words came out in a rush, tinged with bitterness. "I'm toxic, Teina. I ruin everything I touch."

He ran his finger down my cheek and brushed the pad across my lips. "It can't be that bad, Ursula."

"It is." I forced myself to smile. "But I don't want it to spoil today."

Teina studied me through those penetrating dark eyes and I felt my soul being laid bare. His lips twitched and he leaned closer. "Promise you'll come to me if you need help?" he asked and I swallowed and nodded. We both felt the sharp edges of the lie as it spun out into the sunshine with effortless grace; knowing I wouldn't.

I closed my eyes to mask the fear, suspecting the cops would be waiting for me when I got home. The laptop would be sitting in an Auckland police station being examined by men who didn't know Pete, didn't care about his privacy and fostered no desire to safeguard my dignity. They'd bag it, tag it and drag it out in a court case once they'd got to grips with the complicated spreadsheets. Terry would feel betrayed and demand his money back as Pete's homosexuality became common knowledge at the club. I snorted out a jaded laugh and Teina's brow knitted.

"What?"

I shook my head, regretting my lapse of control. "I love my new car," I said, biting my lip to stop the inner pain. "But I'm certain I won't get to keep it." Even if Terry didn't want it back, the chances were it was part of pecuniary gains from illegal activities and I'd lose it anyway.

Teina tutted and drew my face into his shirt. "Then we'll sort it," he said, with confidence.

"You gonna be my chauffeur?" I joked and he smiled.

"You'd have to admit to your family that we're in a relationship."

I swallowed and uttered the hardest words I'd ever said. "I don't have a family."

Teina winced as though I'd slapped him and shook his head. "Don't say that. Family's all we come into this life with."

"I don't want mine." I gritted my teeth. "Dad's taken me for a fool and I'll never speak to him again. They've all stood by and watched me suffer and done nothing to help. I hate them."

"No you don't," he said, tightening his arm around my shoulders and steering me towards a cafe. He didn't let go until he'd planted my bum in a seat and shoved a menu under my nose. "Eat something. You burned off breakfast on the pitch."

"I didn't eat breakfast." I pushed a finger around the menu choices, my appetite non-existent.

"I'll order for you then," Teina replied, responding to the waitress with ready choices. She blushed pink at his smile and I excused myself as a sense of threat sliced through the air, hiding in the bathroom to avoid my own inadequacy.

Leaning on the sink, I stared at myself in the mirror. Long, dark curls tumbled down my back, a fuzzy halo hovering above where the wind had whipped it into a mess. My straighter fringe dangled in front of eyes which looked sad and filled with foreboding beneath their black lashes. I washed my face in cold water and patted down the loose tendrils of hair, neatening my appearance and trying to match the strong, graceful man who waited for his lunch and an unworthy companion. It dawned on me that he'd referred to our union as a relationship and I'd missed the cue, seeing only problems without solutions.

I sat at the table, glancing around me with unease. Teina studied me with calm interest, breeding a greater sense of panic in my heart. It couldn't last; it was an illusion. Everything about him seemed too good to be true. "We should go," I said, casting my glance towards the open door and shifting in my seat.

"No." He placed his hand over mine and kept it in place. "The food will be here in a minute and I need to eat."

I nodded and let his fingers caress mine, wrestling with feelings of lust alternating with guilt. The vicar at the local Anglican church taught about the sins which kept Jesus writhing on a cross, greed, sex outside marriage and theft. There were others, but I focussed on those of mine which he suffered for. I wanted to keep the car but knew I would lose it. I wanted to go to bed with Teina and be able to blame stale wine for my enjoyment of his body, but the truth was I didn't need alcohol to lose myself in him. I laid the issue of theft on my own shoulders. I wasn't involved with any gambling ring at the soccer club but the loan Terry finished early made me a recipient of the proceeds by implication. I declared myself guilty in God's court and waited for the gavel to fall on my head.

The waitress brought two plates of scrambled eggs to the table and I stared at mine. Teina leaned over and sliced off a piece of toast with his cutlery, pressing it between my lips. "Want me to feed ya?" he asked and I smirked.

"Idiot!" I picked up my cutlery and ate the egg, scraping it away from the bread. "You have a food fetish," I commented, watching him tuck into his plate.

"Have to be," he said. "I'm diabetic. Insulin and regular meals. Best way to stay alive."

"Oh." I leaned forward and showed an interest. "There's a little boy at school with diabetes. My teacher aide takes him to do his bloods before meals and I keep chocolate in my drawer for him, just in case." I jerked my head towards his hands. "I didn't see you do your bloods."

Teina winked. "That's because I'm fast." He pulled a pouch from his trouser pocket and laid it on the table. I recognised it as a diabetes kit. "I've been doing it so long, it's second nature. I tested my bloods while you were in the bathroom and gave myself a shot in my stomach."

I glanced around the cafe at the other diners, expecting covert, curious looks. Nobody looked in our direction. "Didn't they see you do it?" I leaned closer.

"Na. I turned towards the corner. That's why I sat here." Teina poured us a glass of water each and I realised the flaw made me warm to him even more. The attraction hung between us like a fog and I slipped off my shoe and laid my bare foot over his crossed ankles under the table.

I finished the egg and left the toast, copying Teina and drinking the iced water instead of coffee. The day moved along regardless of our temporary halt and when I pulled

Teina's hand towards me to look at his watch, my eyes widened at realising three o'clock approached.

"I haven't seen the sea yet," I said, imagining the cool surf brushing over my toes.

"Let's do it," he replied and stood, stuffing the dark pouch back into his pocket and retrieving his wallet.

I grabbed at his wrist as he passed, feeling the strong tendons and sinews beneath my fingers. "I'll pay you back," I said, my face communicating sincerity. "I promise."

"No need." Teina shook his head and brushed his lips over mine. His sexy smile lit his face and left my stomach pitching into my shoes as I fell even more under his spell.

The harbour bridge teemed with people as day visitors and tourists left the black beach and headed back into town to their vehicles. We walked against the flow, pausing to watch daring teenagers clamber onto the railing in the centre of the bridge and dive off. Their squeals and splashes added to the sense of excitement in the air.

Teina kept hold of my hand as we walked along the beach, waiting while I slipped out of my tennis shoes and knotted the laces. He laughed as I hung them around my neck to free up my hands. "How long have you reffed?" I asked, dancing through the shallow waves as Teina strolled along the dry sand in his polished shoes.

"About ten years," he replied, calling over the sea noises. "I started after I stopped playing."

"You must have started young," I commented, bending to pick up a shell and frowning as my shoes bashed my knees and dipped in the water.

"You think?" He chuckled to himself and I rejoined him, trying to guess his age. His muscular frame seemed deceptive and his wavy hair flipped into his eyes as he walked along, hands stuffed into his pockets. I halted in front of him and stopped him walking, pulling his left hand out of his pocket and placing the heart shaped shell into his palm.

"How old are you?" Curiosity showed in my face.

"Thirty-eight," he answered and I watched the shutters come down over his face. The age gap made him afraid but for me it brought comfort. His steady, assured demeanor and the air of maturity fit with the older man image and satisfied my need to be cosseted and nurtured. I closed his fingers around the shell and lifted my face for a kiss.

"That's so hot," I breathed onto his cheek. I wrapped my arms around him, pulling him closer into my body and offering reassurance in a curious role reversal.

His face smiled with relief and I noticed the crow's feet at the corners of his eyes. "It doesn't put you off?" he asked, sounding like a man who'd held his breath too long.

"Not at all." I kissed him again, pressing my tongue between his lips and feeling the sexual tension between us heighten. "I like it. It explains why you're so commanding on the pitch. You must be an amazing lawyer." I released him and took his right hand, stepping along next to him.

His face showed confusion and he seemed lost for words. "Right," he said.

We walked for ages, Teina watching me with amusement as I played in the sea and explored the tarry sand with childish enjoyment. By the time we reached Ngarunui Beach, favoured by surfers and boogie boarders, the sun was lessening its furious grip on the hot sand and I could walk on the drier surface next to Teina. The beach looked deserted apart from the die-hards and it felt peaceful and calm. A few brave souls surfed the unpredictable waves with wind sails puffed out above them and families gathered children and belongings and headed home. We sat with a dark dune behind us and watched the tide creep towards us.

"Do you defend criminals?" My voice wobbled beneath the weight of a gnawing fear. I watched the water encroach and recede, wondering how much longer I had before life engulfed me for real and washed me away on a white crest.

Teina turned towards me, kicking sand over my feet with his movement. "Ursula, I don't think you quite…"

I held up my hand, silencing him. "It's okay." I released him from the rejection and knelt up, pressing my lips over his. He met my kiss and used his arms to brace himself against the pressure of my body. I pushed and he lifted his hands off the sand, laying backwards and sighing as I covered him full length. His palms felt gritty on my skin as he caressed my back and I straddled him, getting hotter and more frantic as we kissed. My hands spread sandy sparkles through his dark hair and I groaned as his roved inside my dress and fingered the outer edge of my underwear.

"What you doin'?" The voice made me jump and Teina's body went still. I slid off sideways and Teina cleared his throat and spread my skirt over his crotch, revealing my knickers to the small child stood on top of the dune. I wrestled the fabric back out of his fingers and he sat up using his stomach muscles and wrapped his arms around his knees. I shielded my eyes and looked up at the little boy, fixing an appropriate smile on my face.

"Hello."

"My sister an' her boyfriend's been doin' that." The child wiped his nose on his hand and pointed at Teina. "Me dad's just give 'im a slap."

"Oh." I snorted and Teina shoved my leg. "We're going home now," I said, hoping the child would get the hint and leave. I rolled my eyes at Teina and his body rocked with silent laughter. I stood up and sand coursed down my legs, feeling as though it had gotten everywhere. I hauled Teina up whilst trying not to laugh and the small boy watched us walk away.

"That was close." Teina winced and caught my hand in his, lifting it to his lips.

"Which part?" I laughed out loud and then glanced behind me at the sentry watching our progress up the beach. "The bit where you got horny in a public place, or the bit where we got caught?"

"I got horny?" Teina shoved me in jest and I giggled and set off running along the sand. I heard him breathing behind me, controlled puffs of air which put his extreme fitness on display. After a few hundred metres my lungs burned and my legs felt like jelly. I stopped and bent to clutch my knees, squealing as Teina caught me up in strong arms and swung me around. He set me down on the wet sand and spun me, pulling me into his chest. His lips felt soft against my neck and he ran his hands through my hair, snagging his fingers in the tangled curls.

"What is this, Ms Saint?" he whispered, resting his forehead against mine.

"I'm not sure." I answered truthfully but our return to Auckland hung over me like a dark cloud. My carefree mood evaporated and I grew tense, not wanting the day to end but knowing it had to.

Chapter 32

The journey home seemed to take less time and we touched the fringes of crowded Auckland in under two hours. "Thanks for today," I said, leaning across the centre console and kissing Teina. He parked under a street lamp and the light glinted off his hair leaving streaks of silvery white.

"Sorry you lost your shoes," he said with a grin, running his fingers up the side of my neck and watching their lascivious progress. "I think I know when it happened."

"Me too." I smiled, remembering the kiss and where it might have gone. I imagined my canvas shoes sitting on the sand where they slithered unnoticed, the child still watching over them in the darkness.

I froze at the sight of the police car sitting further up the road, its fluorescent colours muted in the darkness. I didn't want Teina to see my demise and kissed him again one last time, hungry to communicate my affection. "I could love you," I whispered, dreaming of a life I'd never have and he opened his mouth in surprise. "Bye, Teina," I said, sliding out of the car barefoot. "Think well of me."

"Ursula!" he called, alarm in his voice. I slammed the door and skipped up the front steps, jabbing my key in the lock and trying not to look at his confused face in the reflection on the glass of the front door.

The lift cranked upstairs, taking an age to reach the third floor amidst worrying judders and shakes which failed to stem my growing sense of foreboding. I pushed the front door open and held my breath, fingering the hem of my dress in trembling fingers like a child as the two policemen rose from my sofa. Jack looked at me with regret in his eyes. "I'm sorry, Ula. I had no choice."

"There's always a choice." I stared at him, the numbness turning my face blank. I glanced down at my toes, seeing the black sand particles clinging to my skin. Raglan and Teina's kisses seemed an age ago.

"Where've you been?" Jack demanded, putting his hands on his hips. I glared at him and wondered how I'd ever loved his charm and easy good looks. He hadn't fought for me then and he wouldn't now.

"Out with a friend." I stood my ground and turned my gaze towards the police officers, uniformed and awkward in my space. My eyebrow raised in expectation. "What do you want?"

"We need to speak to you about a laptop which our officer here brought into the station." The cop had a gentle manner and looked older than his colleague.

"What laptop?" I shook my head, feigning ignorance.

Both cops' eyes darted to Jack and back to me. "It was found here, miss. In your possession. It relates to enquiries currently being made about a fraud."

I put my hands on my hips and shrugged. "Was it a grey laptop?" I drew a rectangle with my fingers. "About so big?"

"It would be best if you came down to the station, miss," the younger cop said, his voice calm and passive, aimed at soothing the silly woman in the room. "The detective leading the case will speak to you there."

"Fine." My heart beat fast but I acted like a West End superstar and gave a polite smile. "The first time I saw the laptop, he had it." I pointed at Jack. "After we fell out and he left, I picked it up and put it in my bedroom next to the bed. I can't get into it; I don't know the password but my fingerprints will be on the keyboard where I tried."

"He brought it here?" The other cop looked at Jack in confusion. "He said you already had it."

I shook my head with confidence. "No. It arrived with him. I'd never seen it before I found him looking at it."

"Ula!" The shock on Jack's face gave me the ultimate in satisfaction and I didn't regret a single word of it. I justified my declaration by sticking to the absolute truth. I hadn't seen the laptop before Jack unpacked it from Pete's boxes. I didn't put it in there and didn't recall seeing Pete use a device like that. I only had Jack's word it was ever in the box.

"My husband owned a white Apple Mac," I said, keeping my attention on the two uniformed officers and dismissing my plain clothed cousin. "It doesn't hold its charge anymore so I have to use it when it's plugged in. Would you like to look at it?"

The police officer on my left nodded and I strolled through to my bedroom and drew it out from its hiding place in the wardrobe. I never bothered stashing it in the safe. If a burglar helped himself to it, more fool him. He could keep the knackered one and I'd claim a new one on my insurance. Nobody stole it the last two times the place was tossed, so I figured it to be worthless, old technology. I pulled it off the shelf and stuffed my jacket back into the empty space, handing it out behind me to the police officer who'd followed me in. "I'll get you the charger," I offered. "You'll need it." I yanked the white plug from a socket on the wall. "This was Pete's personal computer. I didn't wipe any of his stuff after he died; I just started new folders under my name on the desktop. It's got my lesson plans on it so please don't wipe anything." I smiled and studied the young man's expression of embarrassment. "Can you tell me what's going on?"

"No, sorry. Just come down to the station with us and I'm sure the detective will explain everything."

"Okay." I grabbed a cardigan off a hanger in the wardrobe. "I've got work in the morning so can we get this over with?"

The buzzer for the front door rang four times while I locked up my home and ignored Jack as he fought for my attention. We left as a tight-knit group of four, taking the stairs instead of the lift and reaching the ground floor together. "Can I have my keys?" I paused on the last step, bailing Jack behind me and eyeballing him as he poked around in his pocket. He handed them over and one of the uniformed cops leaned forward and took them from my open palm. I kept my eyes fixed on Jack, knowing he saw the turbulent rage bubbling inside. "Don't enter my home again without permission."

"He entered without permission?" The officer nearest to me shot Jack a look and I nodded.

"Yes, he did. I threw him out yesterday. I hope you had a warrant. I'm sure you should've shown it to me before searching my flat."

The other policeman swallowed and his cheeks flushed pink. "We didn't..."

"Yeah, you did. Would you like me to list the things you moved in the process?" I kept my voice level and the men exchanged a thin thread of concern.

Jack pressed the button for the front doors just as my downstairs neighbour emerged from his apartment. Ahmed stared in disbelief to see me escorted off the premises by two uniformed officers. I waved to him and he gaped in response, too surprised to raise his hand. I stood on Jack's foot as he held the door open, avoiding eye contact with him and leaning as hard as I could on his shoe with my bare foot. His wince gave me a flicker of satisfaction.

Outside in the cool night air my heart sank as I came face to face with Teina Fox standing on the doorstep with his finger on the buzzer. The cops acknowledged him with an upwards tilt of their heads and let the door bang behind them. Teina looked at me and cocked his head, mouthing, "Are you okay?" as I passed.

I nodded and gave him a wan smile, feeling anything but okay. I felt humiliated, betrayed and cheated; but there was nothing new in that. I urged him with my eyes not to acknowledge me and Jack looked at him with curiosity as Teina's eyes watched me leave.

He slipped past Jack as though visiting someone and my wily cousin nudged my arm. "Does he live here?" he asked, curiosity budding in his eyes. "Or is he visiting someone?"

I ignored him, letting the older police officer seat me in the back of the police car, guiding me under the door arch with his hand on my head. The car sped along the road and I wrinkled my nose at the faint scent of vomit masked with disinfectant. Jack sat in the back seat next to me and he leaned across and tried to whisper, one eye on the cops in the front. "Just tell them the truth," he hissed, barely making a sound over the purr of the engine.

"What?" I replied, raising my voice so the men could hear. "Don't tell the truth? It's a bit late for lying, Jack. I don't know how involved you are in all this but I won't be covering for you."

I heard the driver swear and the car veered towards the curb. The passenger got out and moved around the vehicle, opening Jack's door and yanking him out by his sleeve. "Get in the front!" he snapped and Jack glared at me before turning his body and leaving the vehicle. I heard raised voices and covered my smirk with a shaking hand.

I entered the police station still barefoot and followed the officers through a charge room to a line of doors marked as interview rooms. A group of teenage male drunks lolled around the charge area, giving the sergeant hell and wolf whistling as I trod the corridor to their left. I ignored their vulgar heckling and hoped I didn't spend the night listening to their even bawdier singing.

Jack tried to follow us into the room but one of the cops put his arm out to bar his way. "Not you," he said, sounding conflicted. He jabbed a finger in Jack's face. "Go get the detective and you'd better start talking pretty fast to get out of this one."

I turned my face to the wall to disguise a sadistic grin of revenge, wondering if the camera bulge in the ceiling had already taped my entrance. I thought about my sweet vicar and the mental list of confessions grew by one more item. I wrote it all down on a clean white sheet in my head, adopting a calligraphy script I couldn't do in reality. To my fornication and acceptance of stolen money, I added lying by misdirection.

"Take a seat, miss." The older man smiled and pulled out a chair. "Can I get you a tea or coffee?"

I thought for a minute and opted for water, pulling out of a request for gin at the last second. A glib sense of humour would get me so far, but it might not be in a direction I liked.

"Am I allowed a phone call?" I pleaded with my eyes and the younger cop furrowed his brow.

"You're not under arrest, miss."

I waved my arm to encompass the small, grey painted room. "This doesn't feel very voluntary. I get home to find you in my lounge and you bring me here. I thought my rights included a phone call."

The door opened with a thwack and a tall male entered, dressed in matching jacket and trousers. He blended with the walls to an alarming degree and I stared at him with more interest than fear, wondering if Auckland police colour matched all their detectives with their workplaces. "Thanks for coming in, Mrs Saint," he said, slumping into the chair opposite and placing a file stacked with notes on the table in front of him.

"I've asked for my phone call," I said, chewing on my bottom lip and feeling the skin crack where I'd done it so much. "How long do I have to wait for that?"

The detective looked surprised. "Oh." He sat back in his seat and hung his arms down either side of him. The older police officer left the room and the younger one seated himself opposite, his shirt sleeve brushing the detective's jacket every few seconds as he fidgeted. "You're not under arrest," the detective stated. "You can make a call if you like, but I can't see the point. You were asked here to answer a few questions. Isn't that correct, officer?"

The young cop nodded and I shook my head. "That's not true. I got home to find two officers already in my apartment. They asked me about a laptop which my cousin had in my home the day before. I fell out with Jack on Saturday and didn't see him again before today. The officers asked me to come to the station and I didn't realise I had a choice to decline." I stuck my bare foot out of the side of the table. "I didn't get a chance to put shoes on."

The detective let out a snort like an angry bull and directed his glare at the young man to his right. "Outside!" he snapped and rose to his feet. He shuffled the papers back into the wallet and left the room, the young officer slithering behind him like a naughty child. The door closed, but I heard the shouting through the walls. I hoped he'd included my treacherous cousin in his tirade.

The detective re-entered the room alone and without his papers. He sat opposite me and stuck his hand out. "Detective Inspector Odering," he said, smiling with his eyes.

I shook his hand, my fingers cold and clammy with suppressing the raging fear in my breast. "Please may I have my phone call now?"

"Let's start again," Odering said, holding his hands up, palm outwards. "You're entitled to have a whānau representative." He used the Māori word for family and it made me think of my mother. I'd love my mother to sit next to me, but suspected he wouldn't be able to arrange that. He shrugged. "I apologise for the way you were brought here but assure you; I just have some questions for you."

"Is Jack listening to this?" I asked, glancing at the camera in the corner of the ceiling. "I'm not saying anything with Jack listening."

The detective got up and left the room again. When he returned and gave me a reassuring nod, I believed him.

Three hours later and my brain felt ready to explode. I'd told him everything I knew and some things I didn't realise were tucked in my memory. I liked him in an older man kind of way and he treated me more like a human being than his colleagues had. When my order of cold water didn't materialise, he fetched it himself.

"Tell me about the day your uncle slapped you," Odering said. "Why didn't you report it?"

I shrugged. "My cousin did, but nobody came to speak to me. I wanted to forget about it."

Odering glanced at his notes. "Officers went to your home twice, but you were out both times. They would've followed it up."

"It's over now." I sipped my water thinking of Teina. "I'm not going back to the club so I won't see him again."

"You can see my problem over all this, can't you?" Odering leaned back in his chair and put his hands behind his close cropped hair, linking his fingers in a tight stretch. The rumpled shirt betrayed one of those never ending days I often had at work as it untucked itself from his trousers. "Your husband approached us with this information and we launched an enquiry with New Zealand Football and fraud squad members. We know the fraud's happening, but not who's orchestrating it. Peter Saint was prepared to tell me everything and then unfortunately, he died. Was your husband ever violent towards you?"

"No." I thought of the one time and knew Odering saw it in my face. Pete liked rough sex and I kept my bedroom door locked after that.

"Did you never wonder if his death was suspicious?" I leaned forward in my seat and waited for Odering to take a slug of his cold coffee before answering. He pulled a face and nodded. I rewarded myself for the clever distraction.

"We checked everything. My first thought was that someone wanted to shut him up, but we found no evidence of that. It looked like he'd overdosed on valium and then his vehicle went out of control on a greasy bend in the rain and hit a tree. He shouldn't have got behind the wheel but the suicide note he left gave us reason to assume that was the point."

"He wasn't wearing a seat belt," I said, closing my eyes and reading the coroner's report in my head. "But he always put his seat belt on. He said this stupid rhyme when he did it and drove me mad." For the first time in a long time, I missed my husband. It wasn't a passionate relationship for either of us but after the horror of his bungled visit to the public toilets, at least I knew everything. We rubbed along just fine and found a level of companionship outside of his sexual exploits. I let his handsome face waft across my inner vision; dirty blonde hair and blue eyes which sparkled in the sunshine. Athletic and vain, Peter Saint was a natural head turner and knew it. His loss hit me like a knife wound to the chest and I doubled over in pain as real grief bubbled out. Not the blank numbness of those first weeks or the anger when his solicitor informed me of my impoverished state, but a jaw aching grief at the loss of a close friend. I'd spent the last six months reeling from his betrayals and lost sight of who he really was. As the tears came and I used up most of the box of tissues Odering found, I realised I'd loved him despite everything. I'd loved him and he never knew. Now someone had taken his life as though he never mattered to anyone and I'd never got the chance to tell him.

Chapter 33

"What's the password for the laptop, love?" Odering looked at me with fondness in his eyes, perhaps sorry for my hitching chest and puffy eyes. "The techs will get into it anyway and do a forensic recovery of anything deleted. But you could save us some time and you've already been helpful."

"What about the money?" I asked, reluctant to give any more without some concession. "I know nothing about any betting scam and my uncle paid off the rest of the loan and bought me the car in good faith." I jerked my head towards him. "If the money's stolen, I lose everything all over again."

He tutted and reached to stroke my hand, thinking better of it. It made me wonder if he'd lied about Jack not being able to see or hear my interview. "I'll talk to someone," he promised. "But let's see what happens first."

I wiped my nose with the last tissue. "What about Pete's sexuality?" I gave a disgusting sniff but didn't have the energy to feel ashamed. "He didn't want people to know."

"Why?" Odering asked and I dropped the tissue on the table and stared at him in surprise.

"Because he was a Saint! There are some rules we just don't break."

Odering's nod seemed slowed down for effect and he stood and offered me his hand. "I'll stay in touch, Mrs Saint," he said, clasping my fingers in his. "But that password would be great. Your search history will be recovered by the techs, so it's best you tell me now, seeing as you've admitted logging into it. You have my word that nothing will go any further than it needs to, but it's possible the person in the chat room is connected to the scam."

"I don't think so," I replied with a sigh, pulling my cardigan across my body and stretching the seams too tight. "But the password's a swear word. Pete said it a lot." I leaned forward and whispered the two words which summed up my husband's life, embarrassed about saying them out loud.

Odering wrinkled his nose. "Yep. Wouldn't have guessed that," he said, dragging a pen from his shirt pocket to write on his hand. It looked incongruous, the awful words written on the back of the hairy flesh. He stared at it and I read it upside down, remembering how easy the password came to me as I sat in my classroom with the laptop on my knee. The detective's writing resembled his appearance;

rushed and messy. I read the upside down capital 'F' and he moved his hand to reveal the second word. 'Up' 'Effed Up.' I couldn't repeat it again, not even in my own head. My mother detested swearing, especially the 'F' word but Aunty Margaret spent a lot of time using it. It showed in our respective usage as adults.

"Thanks, Ursula," he said with warmth, using my first name as though we'd become friends. My smile didn't reach my eyes and he jerked his head towards the door. "And thanks for signing that other thing. It will save us a lot of time."

"Please may I have my phone call now?"

I called Aunty Pam and she fetched me, fussing over me in the car and in her kitchen. "This is awful!" she said after I'd told her everything. Larry stared at me in disbelief, swallowing as though saliva entered his mouth on a conveyor belt. "Do you know who the other man in the chat room is?" she asked, lowering her voice to a hush.

"You mustn't repeat any of this," I begged. "The cops asked me not to."

"We won't, I promise," Pam gushed, her cheeks flushed from my chaotic confession. "Who is it?"

"I can't tell you." I'd decided I wouldn't. I'd gone over and over the conversation in my head and felt sure I knew who it was. It could only be one person and I needed to speak to him myself.

"They're really gonna exhume Pete's body?" she whispered and wrinkled her nose in disgust. "I'm so sorry. That's awful."

"He didn't kill himself," I stated, surer than I'd ever been. "Mark Lambie behaved as though he'd been drugged. They'll check Pete's body for other drugs and signs of injury too, which they might have missed first time around."

Larry looked sick at the thought of samples being taken from a decomposed body and I watched as his colour moved from pink to grey and back again.

"It's bad about Mark," Pam sighed. "Dora's not good at all."

I sipped my strong tea and looked at my aunt through narrowed eyes. "Did you know about Dad and May-Ling?"

She quailed and Larry looked away, their faces shrouded in guilt. "Sorry, love," she said, chewing her bottom lip. "I didn't know how to tell you."

"Yeah, well thanks for that. You could've spared me walking in on them." I shuddered at the memory.

"Not doing it?" Pam's eyes widened in horror. "I thought you were exaggerating. I assumed she was staying with Jordan for her visa."

Larry sniggered. "Geez, she's earning that then."

Pam kicked him under the table and the movement slopped hot tea over my fingers. I stood and reached for a cloth. "Why would Dora think May-Ling was Mark's mistress?"

"Because she was." Pam lowered her voice and glanced towards the lounge where Alysha's son played in front of the TV. "He bought her on the internet because Dora wasn't supposed to survive the last round of chemo. Then she rallied and he'd already got May-Ling ready to be the next Mrs Lambie. Jordan agreed to let her live at his place and act as his carer, which gave her a legitimate reason for being in the country." She frowned, her face disapproving. "You wouldn't do that, would you, Larry?"

"Do what?" Poor Larry looked shocked.

"Get someone ready to replace me if I got sick."

"No!" Her husband's expression was hurt mixed with fear. "Don't talk about dying, please?"

I patted Larry's hand, watching the horror in his face at the thought of Pam not being around to iron his underwear or fluff up his delicate ego. "It won't happen, Uncle Larry." I offered reassurance which wasn't mine to give, hearing the futility of the words even as I said them.

"Jordan got attached to her, anyway," Pam finished. "And she threatened to leave if Mark didn't marry her before her holiday visa ran out."

"So Dad put a ring on her finger?" I crinkled my nose, comparing the lazy Asian woman to my saintly mother. "That's gonna bite his bum." The memory surfaced of May-Ling's lithe bottom going up and down in my father's lap and I wondered who'd got the worse end of the deal. It wouldn't end well. "Could Mark have gone off in a strop because he lost May-Ling?" I asked, trying to fit the jolly man with that image and failing. We'd taken him home and he looked fine, apart from being drunk as a lord.

Larry shook his head but Pam answered. "Na. He was fine about it. I think he came to his senses and realised it wasn't fair on poor Dora."

"And now she's all alone," I mused. "She's lost out either way."

"A bit like you, sweetie," Aunty Pam said, caressing my hand. "What will you do now?"

I shrugged and thought of Teina's soft lips on mine. I ached for contact with him, realising once again that I'd failed to get a number for him. "No idea," I sighed. "Live my life, I guess."

"I still can't believe Pete was gay," Pam said, lowering her voice. "We always thought he was a womaniser, didn't we Larry?"

Larry nodded but didn't commit fully to the movement. I saw his awkwardness and felt bad for him. Most men reacted with distaste as though homosexuality threatened who they were in their own skin. I gave him a comforting smile and squeezed his fingers, confused when he dragged his hand away.

"Do you want to stay here tonight?" Pam asked, her expression of maternal kindness reminding me of Mum.

"Na. I've got work tomorrow." I punctuated my sentence with a yawn and stretched. My dress felt dirty after a day's wear and the black sand had left dirty streaks ingrained in the fabric. "Could I please borrow a laptop? The cops took mine and I want to do some research about soccer match fixing."

"Why?" Pam pulled a face. "The cops will work it out."

"I've been at every single local game since the age of four," I said, standing. "If something's going on, I'd like to think I've tried to find out exactly what before the cops do. All Saints means everything to this family; if someone's cheating them, I'd like to work out how." I didn't add that I'd like to know who, convinced I already knew the ringmaster.

"Larry, give her Alysha's old one. It's in the spare bedroom. The charger's in the top drawer."

Pam's husband trooped off to the bedroom and returned empty handed. "Can't find it," he said. "I'll drop you home, Ursula. Don't get a taxi."

Pam groaned. "Men! You don't look properly for anything, do you? I'll get it."

I raised my hand. "It's okay. I'll do it tomorrow at work. Probably best if I just go to sleep tonight. I feel exhausted."

Larry nodded and fetched his jacket from the hook behind the front door and kissed his wife on her cheek. "I won't be long," he said with a smile.

"You always say that," she sighed. "I'll be asleep by the time you crawl into bed."

Chapter 34

I'd been in Larry's car a million times over the years and settled back into the passenger seat. We didn't speak on the journey back to my apartment but there was nothing unusual about that. Larry shared my introverted nature and we got along well in companionable silence. "I'll come up," he said, glancing up at my darkened windows and I smiled with gratitude.

"Thanks. I'm a bit nervous about going home at the moment. If Jack's there, would you throw him out for me?"

"Yeah. Course," he replied with a reassuring grin.

Upstairs, my apartment looked just as the cops left it. I straightened the items they'd fingered in the lounge and stripped the spare bed of Jack's sheets, dumping them in a pile in the laundry. Larry wandered around checking and rechecking windows before meeting me by the front door.

"Thanks for everything, Uncle Larry." I stood on tiptoes to kiss his rough cheek.

His lips parted and his hooded eyes narrowed to slits, his face expression perplexed. "I thought you wanted to talk," he said, tilting his head.

"We have talked." I sent my brain spinning through the conversation at my aunt's place, confused. "I'm tired now."

Larry's face took on an uncharacteristic hardness. "You said you wanted to talk to me. Here I am."

I floundered, drowning in confusion as the atmosphere took on a strange and frightening tinge. I shook my head. "I'm good, Uncle Larry. Just knackered. We can talk tomorrow if you like." I put my hand on the front door handle and he squeezed my fingers hard, taking me by surprise.

"You can't leave it hanging over me. What do you intend to do?"

"What?" I shook my head, wishing to dislodge myself from the bizarre day and fall into bed.

"I didn't want it to be like this with you." Larry's voice lowered to a hush and fear prickled my insides as instinct got there ahead of me. I swallowed, not sure what he meant by the peculiar statement.

"Like what?" The fine hairs on the back of my neck created a crawling sensation and I wanted to put my hand up to touch it. "Be like what with me?"

"I thought we understood each other." Larry's gentle face morphed into hard, desperate lines and the patch of baldness on his crown glowed red as his blood pressure hiked. "I've been good to you."

"I know." I pulled my hand from beneath his and forced a wooden smile onto my face. "You have. Aunty Pam and you have been like parents to me. I couldn't manage without you."

"So why?" Larry took a step towards me and I pressed my back against the wall. "Why are you doing this?"

"Doing what? You're scaring me, Uncle Larry." My chest tightened in anxiety and his breath caused my fringe to shift as he closed in.

"Why would you let them exhume Pete? Why would you do that?"

"I don't have a choice." A badly timed swallow cut off the rest of my sentence. An air of madness surrounded us like sulfuric fog. "The cops would've done it anyway."

"Geez, Ursula!" Larry turned and ran a shaking hand over his face. He'd always seemed so small and meek but his broad back eclipsed my view of the door and the only available escape route. The sinking feeling in my gut told me I should fear a friend and it hurt with a physical ache. I pushed myself against the wall and closed my eyes to stem the terror.

"I need to find out how Pete died." My voice wavered, a remote communication from my trembling knees. "I don't want to live the rest of my life believing it was my fault."

"It was your bloody fault!" Larry bellowed. "It's all your fault. Things were fine until he married you; he took the money and scored the goals but the guilt got to him. Because of you! Karen raised you honest, Ursula! Too bloody honest!"

"We were fine after I knew the truth," I stammered. "I thought he was my friend. We would've been okay."

The futility of my words sickened me. Teina's face flashed before my inner vision and stripped bare the lie. He'd opened my world to a greater love than my crush on Jack Saint and my passion for him slammed the door behind me so I couldn't go backwards. I might have been content with Pete but a whole big world out there would've threatened it eventually, dousing me with the cold water of sexual fulfillment and snuffing out my cozy, fraternal marriage.

"The truth about what?" Larry demanded, his grey eyes as hard as grit. "About the gambling or his preferences?"

"About him being gay," I replied, appalled by the whine in my voice. "It would've been okay."

"Yeah, that's what I said." Larry dislodged the fine hairs attempting to cover his bald spot and turned to face me. They hung down beside his left ear like a curtain, drawing my attention away from his eyes. "Give her babies and she'll be fine."

I dragged my gaze back to his face, realisation dawning and a lump forming in my throat. "You're the man in the chat room. You're Plus One!" I hissed the words, the remaining colour draining from my face. "I thought it was Uncle Terry."

Defeat etched itself over Larry's face and he groaned out loud. "So I've jumped the gun again." He shook his head. "It seems to be my specialty."

"Why did you tell Pete not to do something stupid?" I begged, my voice a whisper. "You were the last person to speak to him before he died."

"He didn't see that message," Larry replied, leaning with his back against the front door. "He turned up at my office. Decided he couldn't do it anymore. New Zealand Football were onto us. The cup final was one step too far. We got greedy and the payout was awesome. Pete was going under financially and it stood to pay everything off for all of us."

"What happened to the money?" I asked. "Pete died a bankrupt."

Larry laughed, a cruel, bitter sound. "We weren't supposed to win, you stupid girl!" he yelled. "They paid us to lose!" Blue veins stood out on his neck.

My jaw dropped and I remembered my father's elation at Pete's goal in the dying minutes of the game. My husband had looked across at me and smiled, kissing his fingers and raising them to me. He'd dedicated the goal to me and destroyed everything. "Oh, Pete!" I put my hands over my eyes and accepted his final gift; honesty.

Larry lurched and slapped my hands away from my face. "I just needed to calm him down," he said, his eyes wild and channelling dangerous recklessness. "He wasn't meant to die. I only wanted him to chill and not go to the cops."

I slid sideways, moving towards the kitchen using the wall against my back to bolster my spine and my courage. "He'd already gone, Larry. He didn't tell you, did he?"

Larry shook his head and curled his upper lip back in a snarl. "How could he do that to me? After everything we'd been through." He swallowed and white spit speckled the corners of his mouth like a frothing, rabid dog. Another head shake dislodged more victims of his complicated comb over and soon he carried a ribbon of hair down one side of his head. His sad smile made him look helpless. "You never score in the first ten minutes." He looked at me as though I should understand and I nodded, faking it. "The first thirty seconds or the first three minutes; it's like a red rag to a bull." He swallowed and licked his lips. "But he couldn't help himself. It didn't matter what we agreed with the other team, he had to do it. I think he wanted us to be investigated. He wanted to be found out."

I nodded and backed away, reaching the corner and readying myself to run. The phone handset sat near the microwave and I measured my steps, counting them out in my head while facing Larry as he ranted. "What about the suicide note? It looked like Pete's writing."

Larry grimaced. "I stopped him doing it once before. I found him in time. He bought painkillers and drank straight whiskey. I saw him at the liquor store and followed him up to the cliff top at Mangawhai Heads." Larry ran a hand through his strings of hair and seated them back on his head like a haphazard web. "Stupid bugger. The suicide note got shoved in the glove box and I guess he forgot about it."

"The cops found it." I remembered the coroner's confusion about its almost secretive placement in the vehicle, but it only seemed to compound Pete's desperation as he drove off the road into the tree, mangling himself, the car and the glove box.

I put my hands over my eyes and felt my heart labour under the burden of knowledge. "What did you do to him?"

"Pete? I drugged his drink. He said he wasn't going back to work and we planned to talk tactics after his bloody stupid stuff up of the cup game. I thought he'd be with me for longer and give the valium time to wear off, but we fell out and he got in the car. I sent the message on my phone but he never saw it."

"What did you fall out over?"

Larry rolled his eyes. "The syndicate went crazy after what he did. He took out loans to pay them off, but I was already maxed out."

"You're not even on the club's executive," I breathed. "How could you organise all this?"

I swallowed, waiting for the names of people I loved and respected to be dragged through the mud. My body tensed and I balled my fists in anticipation.

"Lambie wanted out this year. He couldn't take the pressure. Terry stayed in but that's because Margaret forced him to and they don't have two cents to rub together. There's a few players who do as they're told for a few hundred bucks a time and we've got other teams on the payroll. It wasn't a problem when we stuck to the low key games but we got greedy." Larry chewed his lip in frustration. "It would've been fine if Pete stuck to the plan." His eyes flashed and he turned towards me, his irises grey pits of smoke. "He wanted to go straight because of you. Your honesty shamed him out."

"He told you that?"

Larry smoothed his hand over a bristly chin. "Yeah. Said he loved you. Did you even notice he'd stopped the nights out after the games? We all got together at Lambie's house for beers and a yarn instead."

I shook my head. Out was out, but he'd returned home earlier and not so drunk. We hadn't shared a bedroom, so it never mattered. "Where's Mark?" I held my breath as I asked the question, figuring Pete's death was accidental but drug induced and Mark appeared suddenly wasted and ill in a short amount of time. "You and Pam were at the wedding. Did you drug him?"

"I just needed to talk to him." Larry licked his lips. "But I didn't leave the wedding reception. I heard you'd taken him home, you and that cop, but the syndicate boys got to him before I could. He's in the Manukau Harbour somewhere. Shark food."

My brain ducked Mark Lambie's fate and amplified the word 'cop' and I shook my head. "Jack wasn't there."

"The other one, the referee. I knew the game was up then. The syndicate wanted a referee on side but we couldn't risk it, not with him on the circuit."

"Teina's a cop?" I choked on the sentence, betrayal and heartache flooding in to overtake the shock. My legs buckled and I struggled to stay upright, sickness flooding through my body like acid. I pushed on the wall as my mind turned back to my own plight.

"You know him?" Larry's eyes narrowed and his grin spread from ear to ear. "Awesome! There's money in it for him and I can tell you what to say."

"No!" I raised my voice into a strangled yell. "You killed my husband but you're still not finished? What's wrong with you?"

I lurched for the front door but hit the wall of Larry's body and found myself tumbling sideways. My cheek struck the tiny hall table and I grunted with the impact, lying dazed on the cold tiles. I tasted blood in my mouth where I bit my tongue.

"Sorry, sorry!" Larry raised his hands up to the sides of his head, his face ashen. "I can't do it, Ursula. I can't hurt you but the syndicate guys will. You need to help us." He bent and tried to gather me to him and I smelled the fear oozing from his pores. Pulling my arm, he got me to a sitting position and ran to the kitchen for a tea towel to stem the blood dripping from my lip and coating my chin. "The minute I make that call, you're dead," he said as I heard him yanking open drawers to find one. "They know I'm here," he called, his voice husky as he settled on a roll of paper towel. I heard the paper tearing as he balled up more than he needed. "I called them from the spare room when I couldn't find the damn laptop. Told them you knew everything."

The door buzzer sounded and I hauled myself upright, my head beating a bass note in a protracted throb. My addled brain screamed danger but temper superseded it. I wanted to see these big syndicate names. They took my husband, sullied the legacy of five generations of Saints and pitched me into poverty through greed. I wanted to look them in the eye and knew it would probably kill me.

My hand touched the receiver as Larry pounded across my kitchen and into the hall. "No!" he shouted as the handset fell, dangling from the curly cord and bumping against the wall. I reached for the door release switch next to it but he rugby tackled me and crushed me beneath his weight, winding me and knocking an ear-splitting scream from my lungs. A painful pop issued from somewhere in my back and the locking of the surrounding muscles informed me it was serious. Breathing in hurt like a firebrand in my chest and breathing out stopped being a viable option.

Larry got off me and reached for the handset, listening before replacing it. "Probably just kids," he gasped. "Nobody there."

I rolled onto my side and shrieked in pain. My torso plunged into a debilitating spasm of pins and needles and I sobbed with the agony of it.

"Get up!" Larry tugged on my arm and my words emerged without meaning as I begged him to leave me alone.

One second he stood there, pulling on my right arm and bending over me and the next he disappeared like a magic trick with an enormous bang which left splinters and dust in the atmosphere. My airborne arm crashed back into my side and I wailed, noticing a small puddle of blood beneath my face, sticking my left cheek to the floor. The inside of my mouth swelled so I couldn't speak and then a knee appeared in the blood with a shoe next to it. The black work shoe nestled against the navy blue knee and I heard his voice. "Ursula, speak to me." Clicking and chattering ensued as Teina called for an ambulance and I willed the pain to draw me into oblivion.

Chapter 35

I didn't lose consciousness because good things don't happen to people like me. It would've been preferable to the zombie like state I became pinned in as cops and ambulance staff crowded my tiny hall, stepping over me as though I was the bristly doormat. I screamed in agony as they laid me on a backboard and braced my neck, clamping my swollen, bleeding tongue forward so I didn't swallow it in my shock. I remember the ambulance ride and the technical x-ray machine as it hovered around my sitting body.

Three broken ribs had detached from my spine but would allegedly fix themselves, the doctor hoped. After two nights in hospital and a painful stitch in my tongue later; I sat on the bed awaiting my ride. Nurses bustled around the busy ward, changing sheets and wishing me gone so they could return my tiny space back into a sterile area again.

"There's a guy outside," Helen said, gathering my blood-soaked clothes into a carrier bag. "The nurse said he's been here the whole time."

"I don't care." My hair hung lifeless around my face and she didn't push her luck, privileged to be the only person I'd allowed near me in the last few days.

The ride home felt like agony despite the painkillers and I insisted Helen drive me to my apartment, refusing her kind offer of sanctuary. The normal jolting of the lift caused multiple groans to issue from my pursed lips and I stood in the hallway and stared at my reinstated front door.

"Do you have a key?" Helen asked and I shook my head, not having thought that far forward.

"Someone put the door back on," I said with a sigh, grimacing as the stairs' door clanged shut behind me. Edgy and nervous, every harsh sound brought panic to my brain which went into overload and tried to force my damaged body to hide, run away, anything to avoid further injury.

"It's okay." Helen placed a gentle hand on my arm. "It's your neighbour from downstairs."

I turned and saw Ahmed hovering behind me, his face shrouded in awkwardness. He pointed to the door and gave a watery smile. Helen patted my shaking wrist. "He rehung your door and helped clear up. It was his wife who called me. My phone number was in your fruit bowl."

I smiled at Ahmed and nodded my thanks, my tongue swollen and the ends of the stitch catching every time I tried to speak. "I'm grateful," I said and he nodded with understanding, holding out a new door key.

"Change lock," he said. "Smashed."

"Thank goodness it was!" Helen replied, taking over and slipping the key into the shiny, silver lock. "If that policeman hadn't decided to call round here, you could've been dead." She winced and bit her lip. "Sorry. I'm not known for my tact." She busied herself letting us into the flat and Ahmed stooped to collect the bag.

"Wife wash," he said, dangling the bag in front of his face and turning to leave.

"Thank you." My voice sounded feeble in the echoing hallway and I offered him a more genuine smile, marred by a swallow. "I can pay you for your time and the lock," I slurred and he shrugged.

"Man already did." He waved over his shoulder and the door clicked behind him. I listened to his footsteps skip down the stairs and the loose window in the hallway clanged against its frame. Curiosity budded in the back of my brain, wondering who the mysterious man was who slept in a hospital reception and paid for my damages. I shuddered as Jack's face drifted through the halls of my inner vision and I dismissed it, not wanting to think of his betrayal.

My apartment looked spotless; much cleaner than I left it. My eyes followed the marks of a mop on the tiled floors and gentle Syrian fingers had wiped and cleaned every surface. My dead phone sat next to the kettle and I remembered the sight of my hands putting Helen's new mobile number into the fruit bowl; my chosen go-to place to find lost things when all else failed. The scrap of paper sat next to a browning apple and a lurid, overripe banana and I felt a flash of gratitude to Mrs Ahmed. Of all the people she might have called, Helen would've been my first choice. The couple's kindness made me glad he'd nicked my parking space although shame still blossomed at my behaviour over it. It seemed like such a stupid issue against the backdrop of the past week.

Helen left at my insistence, popping back and using a spare key to furnish me with a bag of groceries. I spent a week by myself, growing used to her visits after work and her easy chatter about school and the children. One evening she brought cards made by my class and I waited until she'd left to sob over the sweet messages copied off the blackboard and their depictions of me in various states of injury and undress. Lawrie seemed to think hospital involved nakedness apart from a mummified head wrap. Laughing hurt my ribs, so I cried instead.

After two weeks of isolation, ignoring the door bell and keeping my phone off, boredom finally bit and I decided to return to work on Monday. Helen's eyes widened in horror as she sat on my sofa and drank tea. "The hospital said three weeks!" she chided. "It's too soon. Free flowing breaks can lead to other problems. What if one of the children wants to sit on your knee, or you get hurt by accident? You could puncture a lung!"

"I'll be living my life," I muttered, hearing the sullenness of my tone. "Instead of hiding here."

"That detective keeps ringing me," Helen confessed. "Every bloody day. He asked for the spare key yesterday and I said I didn't have one. He said he's been coming here daily, but you won't open the door."

"I don't want to know what happened." My breathing hitched and I winced in pain. "I don't care anymore."

Helen nodded, not mentioning the gossip I could see crowding in her face and showing her allegiance to our friendship by squashing it. I'd avoided all forms of news and social media, reading books and watching reruns of old serials on the ancient DVD player. Baths helped the pain and I'd weaned myself off the medication once it started making me throw up.

"Have you seen your father?" Helen asked, sipping her tea. I realised I'd made it too strong for her taste but my right arm still locked if my brain thought the action might jar my ribs. I didn't take the bag out quick enough. I watched her nose wrinkle like a rabbit and felt useless.

"No. I haven't seen anyone." My voice sounded hard. I knew they'd all tried, Dad, Aunty Pam, Alysha, Jack, Detective Inspector Odering. Senior Sergeant Teina Fox.

The detective managed to get past the downstairs door by flashing his warrant card at my Indian neighbour, but he only got as far as my front door. His incessant banging sent me into the bath with a book and my CD player turned up and I didn't hear him leave. He put a note outside on my doormat but I threw it away without reading it. I couldn't face anything he might have to say and didn't want to talk.

Helen picked me up on Monday morning and I admitted to feeling much better. Getting out of bed hadn't been such an ordeal and I'd even managed to get a bra on without passing out. The children greeted me with enthusiasm and kisses and the staff behaved with awkward cordiality.

"Someone's very quiet," I said to Helen as Lawrie snuggled on my knee with his thumb between pink lips. "Has he been like this the whole time?"

She shook her head. "No, we've had a few meltdowns, but I used the strategies we put together and everything seemed fine. He missed you, but we all did."

The child groaned when I tried to move him off my knee and I found myself pinned on the tiny chair for the whole of morning tea. Helen brought me a drink and the boy fell asleep, enabling her to carry him to the beanbags in the corner and cover him with a blanket. "I think he's sick," I commented as the children filed off the carpet to begin putting their new mathematics skills into practice. "Can you manage if I ask Julie to call his aunt? He needs to go to the doctor."

"I'm good here." Helen gave me a smile of contentment and moved around the classroom, breaking up scraps over pencils and setting the children to their task with a few, well-placed looks of fake irritation.

I found Julie at her desk and asked her to make the call, popping my head around Vanessa's door. "Ah, glad you're back," she said, barely looking up from her emails. Her face showed strain and I felt a flicker of sympathy. "Just make sure you take it easy this week," she said. "I know you didn't have to come back so soon."

I tensed, expecting her to venture into the questions surrounding my absence and the carefully worded medical certificate but she put her head down and went back to her emails. "About Lawrie," I said. Vanessa looked up as though surprised I was still standing there. "You were going to book him an assessment."

The principal slipped her glasses off, dropping them to the desk with a clunk. She squeezed the bridge of her nose in a painful finger vice. "There's no money," she said with a sigh. "His family will have to pay. I can ask around and see if anyone will do me a favour but the going rate is four hundred dollars."

"I think he's autistic." I balled my fists in frustration. "He only lets certain people touch him, doesn't like eye contact or changes in routine and he suffers from significant communication problems. Yet he's highly intelligent."

"Then he should be at another school," Vanessa concluded, reseating her glasses on her bony nose. "You know the game, Ursula. We've been here before. We're teachers, not social workers, police officers or doctors. His family will have to pay for the initial assessment and then the gates to the money might just slide open enough to get him some help. I've got too many other children on the list waiting to be seen; I can't shunt him ahead of them. It's not fair and it doesn't work like that. Some of these mothers come to see me weekly, shouting, crying and threatening. Lawrie's hasn't been in to see me and at the moment, the ones who shout the loudest get the attention."

"I'll pay for it," I said, swallowing at the memory of my cornflower blue car still sitting in the parking garage at home. I didn't know if I would be able to feed myself next week, let alone source a special needs assessor for a child with nobody to shout for him.

"That would be highly unprofessional." Vanessa's reprimand coincided with the lowering of her eyes back to her emails and I accepted the dismissal.

"No answer," Julie said as I turned to face her. She sat at her desk outside Vanessa's office. "She's probably still at work. I think she's got more than one job."

I nodded in thanks and walked back to the classroom, working hard to keep my torso still as I moved. My back ached from standing and the merits of my early return seemed foolhardy.

Lunchtime arrived and Lawrie surfaced, his cheeks pink and the rest of his face pained and grey. "Where does it hurt,

Lawrie?" I asked, squatting next to him as he slid from the bean bag to the carpet.

"Hurt, Lawrie," he repeated through lips which looked dry and cracked.

"Do you think it's bad enough for the ambo's," Helen asked, raising an eyebrow.

"I don't know," I replied, fixing a smile on my lips for the child's benefit. "Try his family again. Talk to the other children; I think he's got a cousin in Year 5. Ask her for an alternative number."

Helen nodded and I stroked the tiny boy's damp hair away from his forehead as he balled himself up, knees raised and his chin resting on them. "What am I going to do with you?" I whispered and he blinked.

"With you," he repeated.

Chapter 36

"Hey, Urs." The gentle tones sent a wave of disquiet through my soul as I cuddled the sleeping child to my breast and rocked him, aware of his soaring temperature.

"Go away!" I hissed, not wanting my work self and my messed up love life to mix in a swirling mess of greasy oil and dirty water. "I'm busy."

Teina approached me and I heard the chatter from his radio buzzing through the earpiece like wasps around an overripe apple. "I needed to see you," he said, his tone laden with guilt and regret. "I wanted to apologise. I waited in the hospital but you wouldn't see me."

I snorted and the child in my arms jumped and whimpered in his discomfort. I shifted the cold flannel on his burning forehead and stroked his cheek. "It's okay, Lawrie," I whispered. "Whaea will be here soon and she'll take you to the doctor." He groaned and put his small hand over his stomach. "I know it hurts, baby," I whispered. "It'll all be over soon."

"What's wrong with him?" Teina asked, stepping closer. He peered over my shoulder at the fitful child and his brown eyes narrowed.

"We thought it was a stomach upset," I confessed, glancing at the newspaper covering the mopped space where the child vomited a few minutes earlier. "But I think it's more serious; appendicitis maybe."

"Is someone coming for him?" Teina asked with concern in his voice.

"I hope so." I shrugged. "His aunty looks after him but she's got six of her own. She works on the North Shore and does her best."

Helen poked her face around the classroom door. "I'm still getting voicemail from that other number," she said, glancing at Lawrie. "I'm not sure what to do. What do you think?"

I stood, hoisting the tiny boy in my arms with a grunt of pain. For such a big personality Lawrie seemed so frail and I clutched him closer. "I'll take him to the hospital in a taxi. This doesn't feel right. Tell Vanessa I'm sorry and send my class in with the Year 2s."

"How will you pay for a taxi? Do you have cash?"

I shook my head but having made the decision, stuck to it. "I'll work it out somehow. They might take a card. Tell his aunty what's happened and maybe grab her other children at the end of the day and put them in the after-school club."

Helen shook her head. "They won't take them, Ursula. She still owes them for last time."

"Tell them I'll pay!" I snapped. "Make them understand; she can't be in two places at once."

Helen's head disappeared and I bobbed down to collect my handbag from the bottom drawer of my desk, upending it in my efforts not to make Lawrie's body heave out another pitiful wail. Teina's fingers touched mine as he righted it and shoved fallen objects back into its copious folds. "I'll drive you," he said, his brown eyes soft as he looked at the stricken child in my arms.

He went ahead of me through the corridors to the front gate and I followed, my eyes straying to the neat bum encased in police issue blue trousers. The uniform made him seem even more capable as he held doors open for me and waited as I ducked under his arm. Once he brushed my shoulder with his fingers and I sensed something spark within my gut at his touch. I hardened my resolve; he'd lied about his chosen career and I'd grown tired of being a victim of my own bad choices.

Teina's torso looked stockier with the stab-resistant vest encasing his muscles. The tools hanging around his waist and from the wide pockets seemed to accentuate the width of him, making me crave a hug from the powerful biceps. I hugged the floppy child to my chest and followed Teina through the front gate, baulking at the sight of the police car in the visitors' car park. "Sit in the back," he said, authority in his tone. He held the rear door open and leaned across me, belting me in and allowing Lawrie to perch on my knee.

"Something's wrong!" I leaned down and listened at the tiny, snatched breaths coming from the small mouth and panicked. Teina put a finger under Lawrie's jaw and nodded, measuring the heart beats in his head.

"He's got a slow pulse. I'll use the sirens and call ahead." He slammed the door and Lawrie moaned and flapped his hands.

"We should have called an ambulance," I said, my voice breaking. "This is my fault."

"They're backed up," Teina called over his shoulder. "An accident on the motorway sent eight of them there half an hour ago." He started the engine and cranked the gear stick into reverse. He put his left arm around the headrest of the passenger seat and looked over his shoulder as the powerful car moved backwards. My eyes raked his face for help as my bottom lip wobbled in misery and Teina gave me a look of pure kindness, his brown eyes soft and filled with compassion. "It'll be okay, babe," he said. He dropped his hand and squeezed my knee, offering companionship and consolation.

The vehicle thrummed beneath my bum as the Holden took off, wheels squealing on the turn onto the main road. I saw the blue and red lights flash their reflection in the windows of shops and parked cars as the police car travelled at speed, calling out its screeched warning. Other vehicles pulled out of the way and we cruised through, navigating red traffic lights and dangerous junctions. Teina used his radio to speak to the control room and the operator confirmed she'd warned the emergency room at Auckland General hospital of our imminent arrival.

The traffic warden raised his eyebrows as Teina shunted the car into a narrow parking space outside the emergency room doors. The man moved on to find other unwitting victims, not wanting to tangle with a cop. Oblivious, Teina killed the engine and dashed to the curbside to open my door. Lawrie woke and muttered my name as we hustled through the automatic doors and I forced a bright smile onto my face and kissed his forehead. "It's okay, Lawrie," I promised. "We just had a little ride in a police car, sweetheart. You'll be all better soon."

"Bet soon," he repeated, his voice slow and hushed. "Bet soon, Saint."

I felt my heart clench. A nurse met us half way across the waiting room and Teina's uniform gained us immediate entry to the inner sanctum and medical help. I described Lawrie's symptoms and explained my fear that this was something more. I pointed out the site of his pain and suggested appendicitis, willing the nurse to fetch someone more senior and act with greater urgency than she appeared to possess.

I held my breath as sharp needles pierced veins I couldn't see and Lawrie slipped into a deep unconsciousness. I fretted and worried and the nurse sent me outside the curtain as the doctor arrived. Teina leaned against the wall, his thumbs wedged into the bottom pockets of his vest as I'd seen other policemen do and he watched me through calm, brown eyes as I paced and gnawed on my thumbnail. "Why didn't I do something sooner?" I wrangled, blaming myself. Teina's fringe flipped into his eyes and I fought the urge to push it backwards on his head and savour the silky tendrils against my skin.

Waiting for him to say something seemed to make my anxiety worse and I jumped and grabbed my side as a male nurse touched my arm. The pain radiated through the broken bones and sent electrical pulses into my spine. "There's a kitchen around the corner," the nurse said, his voice soothing. I focussed on the kindness in his eyes as I blinked and tried to listen to his words amidst my clanging panic. "Get a coffee," he urged. "They'll be checking the wee man out for a while. You've got a few minutes."

I nodded and followed the direction of his pointing finger, surprised to hear Teina's shoes tapping the floor tiles behind me as he kept pace. Anger flared in my chest and I darted into the tiny kitchenette and tried to slam the door in his face.

"You're making me look like a bloody pedophile!" I hissed as he stopped it with his foot.

"How'd you work that out?" His eyes widened, matching the look of astonishment on his face.

I put my hands on my hips and postured, no longer able to work out how I came to the bizarre conclusion, rummaging in my vocabulary for possible solutions. "Well! Well!" I managed and Teina smirked and closed the door with his heel. I backed up until the counter pressed into my back and he stepped towards me until I could feel his breath on my cheek. I used the heel of my hand to halt his progress and the sharp angles of his vest felt rigid beneath my flesh. "I brought a comatose child onto an emergency ward and now I'm being followed around by a policeman!" I flushed with embarrassment from chest to neck. The heat spread into the underside of my jaw.

"Idiot!" he snuffed and put his large hands either side of my face. "You're a complete nut job, ya know that?"

"And you're clearly not a lawyer!" I left the barb in my voice and Teina tipped his head to one side, studying me with concentration and something I couldn't read.

"I work in law enforcement," he offered, his inner amusement making my hand itch to slap his smug face. "I never claimed to be a lawyer. I didn't lie to you."

"You wouldn't know the truth if it bit you!" I snorted, realising I'd spun my own fantasy around him. I glanced at the door behind him and felt a tug in my breast, connecting me to Lawrie and knowing through instinct he was having a meltdown. "I need to go." I gave the solid chest a shove and heard the radio cackle. Teina glanced down at it and then back at me.

"This isn't over," he whispered, running his thumb over my bottom lip. "We're gonna talk, whether you want to or not."

"Not!" I said and blanched as the kitchen door opened and a face pushed its way through. I swallowed and gave a watery smile to the tired, grey complexion being worn by a woman in her mid -thirties.

"Is there coffee?" she asked, bouncing a baby on her hip and I nodded and moved aside in the small space.

Teina dropped his hands to my neck and bent down to press his lips over mine. The radio chattered again on his chest and he pulled the curly cable from behind his back and shoved the earpiece in, his other hand lingering on my shoulder. Giving his call sign, he lowered his lips to the black receiver and spoke to the controller. "Yeah, I'm five minutes away; show me responding."

I watched the generous proportions of his body as he winked at the baby on the newcomer's hip and turned away from me. My heart pounded in my breast and the woman clunked polystyrene cups and dug a spoon into the coffee. "Lucky lady," she said, her expression wistful as she glanced at Teina's retreating back. "Half your luck."

The child let out a miserable wail and rubbed his eyes. I noticed then the deformed legs which wrapped around his mother's body and the way he keened with his head on one side. "I know, I know, baby," she crooned, rubbing his shoulder and kissing the tear streaked cheek. The woman looked exhausted but the love in her face overrode any other external factor; trumping her rumpled clothing and lank, unkempt hair. Everything she wanted nestled in her arms.

"Good luck," I whispered and touched her sleeve, sending sparks of compassion through my fingers and praying she understood.

"Thanks. You don't need any though." She grinned, her eyes glittering. "He's hot and obviously has it bad for you. Hold onto him or there's plenty will have 'im off ya."

I nodded and made my way around the nurses' station and found Lawrie's cubicle, working by sound alone. His hysteria projected through the curtains, the familiar wail deafening the closer I got. I burst through the fabric to find a nurse trying to settle the small boy with a back rub, her torso leant across him, obscuring him from my view. His whole body juddered and shook and I recognised an adult in trouble as the nurse appealed to me with her eyes. "I don't understand what he wants," she said, rising and letting go of the thrashing hand in her grasp. She turned, so her back screened Lawrie from her confession. "He's saying something over and over and I can't catch the words."

"It's okay." I passed her, approaching the bed with trepidation in my heart. "Lawrie." I said his name and stroked the hot cheek, feeling the atmosphere change as he recognised me and held his breath. "You're safe, buddy," I said, squatting next to the bed.

The child's chest hitched and tears squeezed from the corners of his eyes. "I yop mane," he cried, his voice rising. The nurse widened her eyes and I used my sleeve to brush the tears away from his cheeks.

"I know you have, Lawrie," I said, lowering my voice. "This lovely nurse knows you've got a pain, baby. She's trying to fix it. Will you give her a chance?"

"A yance," he repeated, his blue eyes wide with terror. Trying to put his arm around my neck, the action met with resistance as the cannula in his tiny vein pulled taut and caused him pain. Lawrie let out a wail and I stood, slipping onto the bed next to him and hoisting him into my lap. The tube of fluid and antibiotic relaxed and he crumpled against my shoulder like a floppy newborn. My ribs tugged at the healing break and took my breath away for a moment.

"All better soon," I whispered and held him, feeling the knotty bones through his hospital gown. I closed my eyes, leaned back against the pillows and settled, hearing the boy's sigh of relief as he snuffed a few times and then stilled.

The nurse smiled and nodded. I heard her leave and paced my breathing to Lawrie's, feeling the soporific effects of nurturing as we both drifted off to sleep. I woke as the orderly took the brake off the bed, ready to move Lawrie to pediatrics. The child slumbered on and I laid him on the pillows with care as the nurse smiled with appreciation. "His aunty's here now," she whispered. "She's waiting in the children's ward. It's appendicitis and he's next on the list for surgery."

"I should probably leave then," I said, reaching for my bag.

The nurse shrugged and they waited long enough for me to kiss Lawrie's forehead, before winding him away through the corridors to the children's ward.

Chapter 37

The world outside the hospital seemed dark and empty as I sat on a bench with nowhere to go. School ended two hours ago and the world had slipped into its usual routine without caring about the fate of one more small child in agony. I'd wrestled with Lawrie since the beginning of the school year, knowing something didn't add up but powerless to help him. He wasn't willful or disruptive as the notes from his kindy claimed, once they eventually turned up. I'd looked into his wide blue eyes and seen a private hell, made up of sentences he didn't understand but repeated as though he did. Lawrie Hopu was afraid and I regretted my inability to help him. He'd spent ten weeks in my class being shepherded from activity to activity by Helen or me, perhaps even seen the inward sighs we took to master control of our irritation with the system which failed him and felt the sting of our combined dejection. Guilt pricked at my soul and I felt the urge to run. Nowhere. Anywhere. I resented the heartlessness of this big city with its shiny buildings and no compassion.

The taxi dropped me near the cemetery and I risked my credit card in his portable machine for the sake of a ride across the harbour bridge. I wondered about my car, resting in the parking garage at the apartment and wondered how long before the police detective confiscated it. The excitement of ownership paled against the guilt of knowing how Terry paid for it. I wondered if it made me complicit, the energy to deal with the mental logistics defeating me in my weakened state.

"Hi, Mum." I scooped a dandelion from the grass next to her grave and laid it where I figured her head would be if she were still inside. The alternatives filled me with misery and I shook them away. "I've stuffed up big time," I confessed, leaning my back against the corner of her headstone and crossing my legs. "How do I come back from this? It's a worse mess than a gay husband leaving me with a lorry load of debt." I spotted a daisy in the glow from the setting sun and picked it, leaving the stem as long as I could. Another and another blinked at me with upturned faces and I snagged them all, piercing their green spokes and threading one through another. "I met this guy," I said, concentrating on my task. "He's everything I ever wanted; strong, silent, wise and good looking. You'd like him. I wish I'd met him ten years ago because my life might've been real different." I snuffed out a laugh of regret. "Na, I probably would've messed it up somehow and I'd be sitting here divorced instead of just widowed and single."

Jack's face wafted across my inner vision and I cringed. "You'll never guess what," I added, fixing the daisies together in a continuous line. "Jack loved me; seems he always did. He said Dad threatened him but I guess you knew about that." I pursed my lips, wondering if she had, or whether she'd been as clueless as me when he chose Lacey as his ball partner. I preferred to believe the latter.

"I wish you could see me now, Mum. I've lost so much weight in the last five years, Aunty Pam says I look like you when you were thirty. In ten more years I'll be forty and it's gonna be weird because you never went there ahead of me, did you? I'll be something you never were." It made my heart ache that she didn't get to see the last of my teen years, fading out before I'd finished growing my breasts or learned to let my dark curls do what they wanted instead of taming them beneath clips and ponytails. I imagined her wandering the halls of heaven, searching for a fat girl with curly bunches and the sob caught in my throat. "Don't look for me anymore, Mum," I begged. "I don't think I'll be coming. I had sex with a stranger an hour after meeting him and knew nothing about him. I don't know where he lives or what his hobbies are." Foolishness enveloped me. Nothing I'd said mattered against the thought of Teina's arms enfolding me and the feel of his lips on my cheek. I sniffed. "I'm nothing special, Mum. You thought I was but I'm the same as all the other girls in this world. I know you'd be ashamed of me. I kinda wish you were here so you could tell me off and show me how disappointed you are. I feel like I need to be punished by someone who cares. The cops will be doing it soon enough."

I completed my daisy chain and hung it on the headstone. With the waning of the sun, the tiny buds closed their faces against my cruelty and hid their yellow beneath the tight, white petals. "Dad's up shit creek without a paddle, Mum. He won't be in heaven either at this rate." I worried at my lower lip as I contemplated his many misdeeds and sighed, unable to confess to my mother about his indiscretion with May-Ling or his possible involvement in the gambling scam. She'd loved my foolish old man and part of me wanted to leave her with the illusion of his invincibility. He'd cross the finish line soon enough and by then she'd know the sum of his life by his destination.

I stroked the dry earth and felt the heat of the day leave the crumbly soil as evening descended around me. "I don't think I want to be a teacher anymore," I whispered. "The joy went out of it today when I realised I couldn't help this little boy with his behaviour and he deserves so much better. What's the point of being on the front line when you can't help anyone?" I shook my head and prayed Lawrie's pain would disappear and someone far better than me would dish out a fairer education in future. "I'll quit and then pay for him to see an educational psychologist," I promised, as much to myself as to my mother.

I glanced around me, surprised at the passage of time. "I should go." Like everything else in New Zealand, the day winked out like the switching off of a light. The tides worked the same way, snapping open and closed like a mouse trap. The sunny resting place lengthened its shadows and began to resemble a scene ruined by horror movies and I clambered to my feet, feeling the blood surge behind my knees with agonising slowness. My ribs and back ached and I contemplated Peter Saint's empty grave a few hundred metres away. I couldn't be bothered to walk there and shuddered at the thought of how he might look with his flesh gone and his white bones exposed. His strong soccer playing legs would be wasted and empty, no longer skilled and trained to perfection; scoring goals which old men still talked about over pint glasses filled with hope. "I did love him, Mum," I said with a sigh. "I pretend I didn't because it makes me feel less of a fool, but I did. My greatest failure in life is seeing how broken Pete was and being unable to fix him. I'm surrounded by my own failure. I need to go away." I contemplated the irony. If the cops linked my new car and paid off loan to the dodgy club finances, I might be going away somewhere anyway.

My heels dragged as I turned away from Mum's grave; the only reminder to the world that she ever existed. Apart from me, I realised with a small smile. My long curled hair, soft brown eyes and bigger than average breasts pointed to her influence. I carried her with me, looped through my DNA. I half turned as I delivered the real reason for my visit and hoped she'd understand. "I haven't been to church for a few weeks, Mum. I'm not sure they'd want me anymore, not just because of the sex but because..." I remembered a girl at the club who everyone shunned, staring at her as she walked by with her sin on the outside. I'd admired her courage twenty years ago and wondered if I had what I needed to carry it off. I pursed my lips and gazed at the sandstone with the inscription of Mum's name turning grey in the darkness; Karen Landsdown-Saint. She'd loved me and from now on, I promised myself I'd do better and try to love myself.

"I think I'm pregnant, Mum. I'm fairly sure I fell in love with the stranger the first time he kissed me. Trouble is, he's a referee and a cop. I didn't just blow one rule, Mum. I blew the worst two."

Chapter 38

Lawrence Drive felt eerie and quiet as I walked along it, acutely aware of my isolation. Turning away from the sign for Hillcrest Road, I remembered my marital home, just a stone's throw away. It tugged at me but I resisted, locking that life in a box and throwing away the key. Coles Beach Road cried out with the amplified slap of the sea against rocks and I dreamed of a different time, turning to face the motorway and an impossibly long tramp home.

Traffic from State Highway One pounded the overpass as I tracked along the B19 in a world of my own. When the sleek car pulled up alongside me I had a moment of panic at my stupidity, casting around for assistance. "Easy." Teina held out his hand, palm upwards to still my fear and offer reassurance and my first reaction was, as always, foolish.

"Why are you here?" I scoffed, looking around the deserted road.

He smiled with his eyes, the stubble pricking through his dark skin and covering the lower half of his face in shadow. "Your cousin, Alysha said this is where you'd be."

"Oh." I swallowed. Damn traitor. I struck her off my Christmas card list with an imaginary pen. "What do you want?"

Teina got out and leaned his bum against the rear wing, folding his arms. The engine rumbled in the darkness. His dark jeans cast shadows which outlined his physique and the white tee shirt glowed with an odd luminescence in the inadequate street lights. "Thought I'd cruise by and have that chat now," he said, sounding casual as he added a yawn into the mix. "But if you'd rather walk back to your place; I'll drive behind you with my four ways on to warn passing traffic. It's your call."

I stared down at my feet, seeing the brown soil stains on my cream sandals and grimacing. The urge to take my shoes off and run through the grass like a child percolated into my brain and I craved the exhilaration of youth and innocence. My ribs jarred, reminding me it wouldn't happen. "I only make bad calls," I sighed and heard Teina's shoes grate against the loose gravel.

"I don't," he said. "I'm happy with mine so far."

I sniggered at his confidence. "Spoken like a true referee."
I put my hand over my mouth and added, "A blind one," just
for effect.

"Get in the bloody car, Ms Saint," he said with authority
and I fixed him with a steely, determined gaze.

"I can't. My life is shit. Toxic shit. You can't be near me."

Teina's eyes narrowed and he shrugged. "That's why you
should get in, Ursula. For once, do as you're told. And I
make my own decisions about who I want to be near. Don't
you think they tried to warn me off before? I'm a traffic
cop, Ursula, not a detective. They heavied me and I ignored
them." He opened his arms out wide as though to make his
point. "I'm still here and they're not."

I gritted my teeth and paced across to the vehicle, allowing
Teina to open the passenger door and close it behind me. "I
don't see why that means I have to get in the car," I grumbled.
I lowered my tone in a poor impression of him. "Your life's
shit so get in the car."

He ignored me but although I wouldn't admit it, his
presence in the driver's seat added to the feeling of safety
and I breathed a sigh of relief as he set off and the central
locking activated itself. He didn't ask where I wanted to go
and the energy to question him evaded me. I closed my eyes
and prayed for Lawrie, hoping I'd get the chance to make
amends for my inadequacy.

Teina stopped in downtown Auckland and parked his car
in a spot near the Sky Tower. I wrinkled my nose, knowing

even when I prayed for a parking space I rarely got one. He reached for me with one hand whilst feeding coins into the meter with the other and I crumbled into his embrace like a landslide, feeling pathetic and fortunate. "You ready to talk?" he demanded, kissing my temple and tilting my chin with his index finger.

"I don't know." I gave a wary shrug and he smiled, drawing me into his side as he led me to a bar near the waterfront. I gave up fighting and it felt natural to hang on to the back pocket of his jeans with my arm stretched around him. His scent intoxicated me and craving comfort, I nestled closer, feeling safe and wanted. Teina ordered me an orange juice without discussion and settled into a lemonade as we perched on stools around a high table. His hand rested on my thigh, his warmth through my trousers giving me courage.

"Please will you give me a chance?" he asked, his eyes dark with anxiety and his pupils obscuring the brown irises. He reached for my hand under the table. "I don't make a habit of falling into bed with strangers and it was never casual for me. Stuff got in the way but my intentions have remained the same. I couldn't tell you what was going on with All Saints because I blundered in there by accident and the detectives warned me off. I knew you weren't involved, for what it's worth."

"But I am involved," I sighed, seeing his eyes widen even more. I let go of his hand to reach for my drink. "Terry paid money into my bank account and bought me a car with cash.

If he was part of the scam, then that money was acquired illegally."

Teina screwed up his face. "There's no record of it; I've seen the evidence. It's a big mess though. It would've been genius if they hadn't got greedy." He stopped and chewed his lip. "The captains of the top two teams were involved. You do know that, don't you?"

I closed my eyes and resisted the urge to run out into the street and keep going. Teina touched my hand. "What are you thinking?"

"Why does it matter?" I asked with a sigh.

"Because I care, woman!" I heard the hurt in his voice.

"I'm thinking it never ends. The gift that was Peter Saint just keeps on giving and it doesn't matter what I do; I can't crawl out from under it all."

"What do you mean, babe? He wasn't the only one cheating. They've caught four of the twelve teams in the premier league all fixing matches. It's bigger than you think. There was a massive fraud going on and the bookies are mad as hell. This bust might actually shut down the league for the rest of the season."

I nodded and swallowed, remembering the kindness of the coroner six months ago as he called me into a private room. Pete's homosexuality and the lie he lived under had blighted the remainder of my twenties and I made a mental decision to leave it out of my relationship with Teina. He didn't need to know. I felt relieved, realising the prospect of telling him

I'd been in a fake marriage had hung over me like an albatross. I looked at him from under my eyelashes and saw the natural grace in his bearing and the way he fiddled when nervous. He turned his glass in a continuous arc as his eyes darted around the bar, ever watchful. "What else is there?" he asked, fixing me in his perceptive brown eyed stare.

"He left me with a lot of debt," I confessed. "That's why Terry and Margaret helped me recently because after Pete died, I needed to sell the house, car and anything else I could to raise cash. I put them in a position where they felt guilty and Terry bought the car and cleared the loan."

Teina nodded. "The lead detective's been watching your bank account. They know you've got nothing."

"But what about the loan being paid off?" I said, descending back into panic. "It's all hanging over me and it's best you're not involved."

"You're in the clear." Teina chewed his lip. "I shouldn't tell you this but Terry and Margaret Saint didn't pay off your loan or buy that car. It's what you were meant to think. Your husband's goal in the dying minutes of that cup game wiped them all out; they had nothing."

"Then who?" I demanded and Teina blanched.

"I'll tell you, Ursula but if you repeat it; I'll be in more trouble than you can imagine. I'm not risking my career for you to go charging off half-cocked." The seriousness in his expression brought me up short and I nodded in acceptance of his terms. He threaded his fingers through mine under the table. "But first, I need to know where I stand with you."

Chapter 39

I could've lied just to get the information but I didn't need to. I wanted a relationship with the gorgeous cop and decided I no longer cared what it cost me, bargaining my allegiance for the second time in my life, but this time with a smile and a kiss.

"Well, you're a sight for sore eyes!" Dad grumbled as I pressed my lips to his forehead and smoothed stray hair back from his downy crown. He slapped my hand away and scowled. "I suppose you've heard about the team," he said; statement not question. "Bloody idiots! Five generations of Saints and you lot mess it up for everyone."

I opened my mouth in surprise and then closed it. If it seemed easier for my father to blame Pete and the other captains instead of levelling the blame at Terry, Larry and

Mark Lambie, so be it. I no longer cared. "Yeah, I heard," I said, keeping my tone light.

Dad screwed up his face and wheeled his chair towards the kitchen. "I suppose you want something to drink now you've bothered to show up?" He rattled in a cupboard at knee height and retrieved a mug, reaching up to flick on the kettle. I sat and watched, not shoving myself forward to take care of him as I used to.

"Where's May-Ling?" I asked, casting my eye over the apartment. It didn't look as though she'd abandoned her post yet. A pink thong dangled over the back of the sofa and I shuddered and looked away.

"Gone for a driving lesson," Dad replied and grinned. His top set of false teeth clacked down over the lower set, creating a visual disturbance in my brain. "And yes, I'm still gonna shag her."

I shuddered and closed my eyes, unable to drive out the mental imagery and still not sure whether to barf or laugh. "I've got a boyfriend actually," I said, dropping it into the conversation with casual assurance and no longer afraid of my father's cluster bombs of misery.

"Who?" He rolled the wheelchair to the end of the counter and stared at me, eyes narrowed. "Not some bloody yahoo from that school of yours, is it? Some ponce with a ponytail and a pole up his ass."

"No." I fixed a steady gaze on my father and saw what everyone else did; a mean spirited, selfish old man who'd ruled me like a king and threw my life away like a dandelion in the wind. For the first time in my life I felt grateful for my mother's premature death; spared his draining displays of tantrum and bile. "You know him. I'm dating Foxy."

Dad's eyes bulged and his jaw grew slack as he gaped like a fish. The colour worked its way back into his complexion, moving through shades of pink and purple and contrasting with the tufty white hair and pathetic comb-over strands. "This is a joke, right?" he demanded, getting ready to pitch forwards out of his chair in temper. I imagined him hurling himself around the tiles in a break-dance of fury and couldn't contain my snort of mirth.

"No, it's not a joke, Dad." I stood. "I intend to keep seeing him and you need to live with it."

"I won't!" he shouted and jabbed a sharp finger in my direction. "He's a shite referee and Saints don't marry refs!"

"He hasn't asked me to marry him," I said, cocking my head to one side as though just considering the prospect. "But if he ever does, I'll say yes so here's a heads up, Dad. You'll give me away and you'll do it with a grin on your face."

Jordan Saint's jaw flapped and he looked comical. Realising I wasn't playing his sick game anymore, he clutched his heart with a wizened hand and slumped in his seat. "My chest," he gasped. "I can't breathe."

I ground my teeth and kept my nerve, waiting it out instead of reacting for once. As the act continued I started to wonder and in the last seconds before I reached for my phone to dial an alarm, the front door rattled and May-Ling let herself in, looking pleased with herself. "He say I do test, ole man," she called, before noticing me. "Oh, hi." She halted in the small lobby with a look of distaste on her face and I kept my expression neutral.

Behind me, my father made a miraculous recovery, pushing himself upright and jabbing his finger in my direction. "She's no daughter of mine!" he screeched and May-Ling jumped in surprise. "She's dating a referee!" The veins stuck out on his neck and his wife turned her slanted eyes to him, then me and back again.

"He criminal?" she demanded and I shook my head.

"No."

"He citizen of New Zealand?" She mangled the name of my homeland with her cute accent.

"Yeah."

May-Ling turned to my father and slapped the top of his head as she breezed past and seized the stray mug he'd got out for me. "Stupit ole man," she scoffed. She peered into the mug and waved her spare hand. "She fine. Girl is grown-up lady. Let her live life."

I smiled and waved as I let myself out of the apartment, closing the door behind me with a gentle click. May-Ling could have my father's dwindling stores of cash; it no longer bothered me. As far as I could see, she'd earn every last cent of it between now and the end. I'd put money on the poor woman dying first. Dad had the genes to go on forever, like bacteria. He'd paid off Pete's loan and bought me a car and I felt satisfied with my lot. I wished I'd got the chance to kick him in the guts with the knowledge that not only did Teina Fox referee; he was also a cop.

I sniggered to myself in the lift and ran a hand over my aching guts. Period pain still sucked at thirty, only this time it bought relief. I wasn't ready for a baby and probably never would be. It didn't seem so important anymore and a new wholeness enveloped me, self-reliant and couched in a surety of who I was.

Teina waited by my car, his neat bum leaned against the cornflower blue paintwork. He held up the tiny fire extinguisher from my tool kit. "Need help putting your tail feathers out?" he asked and I laughed.

"Na. I think I've learned to be immune to his fire breathing. It's taken all the fun out of life."

Teina fixed his arms around my waist and kissed me, his lips soft and tender. "Are you ready, Ms Saint?" he asked, searching my face for signs of nerves.

"Ready as I'll ever be," I conceded, slipping my fingers beneath his tee shirt and enjoying the contact with his olive skin. "Am I allowed to date the teacher?"

"I'll make an exception." He grinned. "It depends how you plan to buy me off."

I slapped his chest. "Not funny!" I leaned my breasts against his pectorals and looked up into his eyes, putting on my best seduction face. "What would it take to get full marks?"

He snorted and kissed me again, his eyes losing their humour as he glanced up at my father's window, five floors above the car park. "Your dad's rubber necking down on us."

I tutted. "Amazing. He must've finished his heart attack quicker than planned. What's he doing?"

"Eyeballing me." Teina glanced up again and bit his lower lip. "And shaking his fist and, yeah, I probably won't replicate that hand gesture."

I lifted my lips to Teina's and gave my aged father a show of real passion, hoping it made him want to jump out of the window. Teina spoke with his lips resting against mine, his eyes laughing. "He's gone a weird colour. Do you want to go back up there?"

I shook my head and turned, waving to Dad. I pointed at my ring finger and watched his eyes pop like boiled eggs in their sockets as the full horror hit home. I shouted up to him, knowing he heard through the open window. "Forgot to mention it, Dad, I'm off to referee training now. With Teina."

Jordan Saint hammered on the window with his fists and I watched as May-Ling pressed her face against the glass and then shrugged without caring.

"You told him I'm a cop?" Teina asked and I shook my head and grinned. "No, I'm saving that one."

He laughed and opened the passenger door for me, pinching my bum as I shinned into the seat. Jangling the keys to my car, he rounded the bonnet and looked up at the window, through which my father yelled obscenities. He gave a small salute with his right hand and I watched Dad's eyes widen in disbelief. He recognised the New Zealand Police salute and pitched himself at the glass in fury.

"Oops! That's gotta hurt." Teina climbed into the driver's seat and started the engine, gunning my car out of the car park. Behind us, Jordan Saint raged about Saint rules in his insular Saint world, surrounded by bitterness and self-made Saint misery.

I sat the Level 1 test for New Zealand referees and passed with top marks, celebrating with a trip to church to confess my many sins. The sweet vicar didn't care, embracing me like an old friend and praying a blessing over me with shaking, elderly hands. "What have you been up to, Ursula Saint?" he asked me with a smile.

I stared at him for a moment and decided on the truth. "This and that, Vicar. This and that."

Please can you help me?

If you haven't left a review yet, I'd be really grateful if you could do that for me. Reviews are probably the most important thing you can do for a writer.

Love the book or hate it, it's your chance to say so and I'm interested in your opinion.

If you go to ktbowes.com, you can pick your retailer and follow the link to leave your review.

And thank you. I appreciate it.

Join Me

I have a reading group which you're very welcome to join.
You can do that by signing up on my website ktbowes.com
In return, you'll receive four free eBooks sent to your inbox
and an email from me once a month.
I'd love for you to join us.

Love from Kate x

About the Author

K T Bowes is a bestselling teen and women's author. Her novel, *A Trail of Lies*, was the winner of the genre award for Author's Cave in 2014.

Phoenix Du Rose was considered for the prestigious Ngaio Marsh awards for 2021 and *Her Quiet Legacy* in 2022.

K T Bowes is an Englishwoman in exile in New Zealand, swapping rugged cosmopolitan for mountain ranges and terrifying rivers. She loves Māori culture and has learned to weave flax using traditional methods. Her other passion is Rongoa Māori, which involves creating medicines from native plants. She is a student of Te Reo Māori.

You can find her hanging out on social media in the following places.

Check in and say hello. Maybe suggest she gets back to writing and stops watching cat videos.

FACEBOOK
https://www.facebook.com/NZauthorKTBowes/
INSTAGRAM
https://www.instagram.com/k_t_bowes

Also by this Author

The Hana Du Rose Mysteries Series:
Logan Du Rose
About Hana
Hana Du Rose
Du Rose Legacy
The New Du Rose Matriarch
One Heartbeat
The Du Rose Prophecy
Du Rose Sons
Du Rose Family Ties
Du Rose Vendetta
Du Rose Blaze
The Hana Du Rose Mysteries; Generation Z
Phoenix Du Rose
Wiremu Du Rose

The Calculated Risk Series:

The Actuary

The Actuary's Wife

The Actuary in Trouble

The Heart of The Actuary

Troubled series for teens:

Free from the Tracks

Sophia's Dilemma

A Trail of Lies

Gone Phishing

Escaping the Back Country NZ Series:

Pirongia's Secret

Deleilah

Standalone novels:

Artifact

Demons on Her Shoulder

All Saints

Her Quiet Legacy

Humorous Cozy Mystery Series from New Zealand

Dead Straight

Bad Hair Day

Side Parting